ALKI POINT

HENRY WALTON

Forrell Publishing

This book is a work of fiction. Any references to real people, events, establishments, organizations, or locales are intended only to give the fiction a sense of reality and are used fictitiously. All other names, characters, places, and events are the product of the author's imagination and any resemblance to actual persons living or dead or locales are entirely coincidental.

Cover art and book design by Henry Walton

Library of Congress Control Number: 2020907690

ISBN 978-0-578-67733-0

ALKI POINT

Chapter 1

Last Thoughts

Terry stared out at the deserted boat launch ramp where, only hours earlier, it had been a beehive of activity.

He thought, 'I wonder what the young woman's last thoughts were as she went under the frigid black surface, alone in the darkness of night, water rushing into her car, at first shocking her with its frigid cold, then bringing stabs of pain as it stole her warmth.'

He hoped the pain was short-lived and quickly replaced with a feeling of calm as the sea took her consciousness and let her slide into peace, the lights of the Seattle night skyline fading to black through the rippling surface of Elliott Bay overhead.

He shook his head and finished taking down the yellow police tape he had strung around the area hours before.

The crime scene detectives were gone, along with the black Ford Focus they retrieved from the water at the base of the ramp. That vehicle now sat, dripping, in the Police impound lot.

The medical examiner's staff had left with the woman's body. It now laid in cold storage at the morgue awaiting examination by the coroner.

Other than a few hangers-on, most of the press and mass of onlookers that crowded the parking lot earlier had all dispersed. The ramp itself empty. It was too stormy for anyone in their right mind to be out on Puget Sound today.

Terry shivered, threw the police tape into the trunk of his patrol car, and drove back to the station, troubled by the events of the morning.

Earlier

"I said left, left, not right."

Michael was losing patience with his father's lack of skill backing the boat trailer down the launch ramp. It didn't matter how many years they had been making their early morning fishing trips on Elliott Bay, his father had never got the hang of steering a trailer when backing up.

Their family boat was not large or cumbersome, just an old eighteen-foot outboard runabout they had bought several years back to go fishing and cruising around on Puget Sound. But every trip was the same. The trailer would swerve left, then right, then left again, zigzagging down the ramp threatening anything and anyone within twenty feet of its path.

For as long as the lanky fourteen-year-old could remember, he and his father had performed this early morning ritual, most often in the summer, but at least once a month year-round, always before sunrise, and always at this launch ramp. The Alki ramp had always been a popular launch point for the residents of West Seattle, with easy access, proximity, and direct entry into Elliott Bay.

As usual, they chose an early start to beat the rush of other anglers and to have the ramp all to themselves while Michael's father wrestled with backing up across the gravel parking area and down the inclined concrete. Other than an SUV that was pulling out of the lot when they arrived, there was not another vehicle or boat to be seen at the launch. Michael thought to himself that they should not be out in these conditions. It was stormy and the white caps on the water would make for a rough and possibly dangerous ride.

"Did you unfasten the tie straps?" his dad yelled over the wind from the cab of their black quad cab pickup.

Michael was walking behind the boat, guiding his father down the ramp, "Yes, yes, more to the left."

"Did you tie on a bow line?"

"Yes, now straighten it out"

"Did you put in the drain plugs?

"Of course."

He would never forget that again. The first time they had launched their boat, neither had known about the drain plugs located under the waterline at the stern and they had practically sunk while still tied to the dock.

"Hey, if you don't trust me why don't you come out and check everything yourself?"

"Because it's warm in the cab and I haven't finished my coffee."

John trusted his son to remember everything. It seemed he just checked more out of habit, and perhaps a little to cover his own ineptitude at backing the trailer. He couldn't wait until Michael turned sixteen and had his driver's license. Then he could relax and let his son back the trailer.

After taking a zigzag path across the lot and down the ramp, the boat trailer finally angled into the frigid water, its wheels went under the surface and the boat roughly floated off.

"Okay, hold it there. I'll line the boat out to the dock and tie it off"

Michael took the loose end of the bow line in his left hand and gave the boat a shove with his right. As it drifted out, rocking in the waves, the wind took it towards the right-side dock. Michael ran across the ramp and out onto the floating dock to intercept the runabout as it was blown toward him.

John put the truck into drive and slowly pulled up the ramp, every few feet sliding on the slick algae that coated the concrete surface below the high-tide line.

'Thank goodness for four-wheel drive' he thought.

Sunrise had been a little after five and the gray sky was beginning to lighten as John parked the truck and trailer and made his way back down to the dock. The wind was strengthening and the whitecaps on the bay looked more menacing.

Michael shouted over the wind, "Why are we even going out today? It's too rough."

His father waved him off, "We'll be fine. We'll just troll between here and the Duwamish river outlet. It won't be bad if we stay in close to shore."

Once on the boat, Michael's father went to the bow to cast off the front line as Michael turned the ignition key and brought the outboard motor to life. He would give it a couple of minutes to warm up before slipping the gear handle into reverse and spinning the steering wheel to back out from the dock.

When Michael was satisfied the motor was warm, he turned the wheel hard right, put the boat in reverse, and hoped the stern would swing out and pull away from the dock. "Okay, let the line go and I'll back out."

Michael's father let go of the dock and the motor pulled the boat back and away, as Michael turned the stern into the wind. Waves smashed into the flat stern of the boat and forced the two to hold onto the front windshield to prevent being tossed backward over the seats.

The boy was about to push the shift lever into forward and turn the bow into the wind when the craft bucked extremely hard and threw him and his father to the floor. At the same moment, a loud repeating metallic sound came from the back of the boat.

Instinctively Michael jumped up and threw the motor back into neutral, but it was too late. The impact had already snapped the shear pin on the propeller, and they were powerless to control the boat. The shear pin had done its job. When the propeller hit an object in the water, the pin, which normally locked the propeller to the spinning drive shaft, had sheared to let the propeller spin freely and protect the propeller and the motor from further damage. Now the man and son drifted at the mercy of the wind past the end of the dock and towards the waves smashing against the rocky shore.

As the boat drifted, Michael looked over the side to see what they had hit.

"Father, quick, we have to call for help." He pointed back toward the launch and pulled out his cell phone. As he did, a large wave rocked the boat and he dropped the phone overboard into the water.

His father looked in the direction Michael pointed and forgot about their own situation as he spotted the top of a car in the water. His own cell phone was still in their truck.

He yelled, "We need to jump and swim to shore before we hit the rocks. It will be too dangerous to get out when we're grounded. Follow me."

He jumped over the side of the boat and quickly swam the twenty-yard distance to shore where he climbed the rock embankment, looked back to make sure his son had made it to safety, and then ran to his car to call 911.

Michael followed close behind aware that shortly, their boat would be dashed onto the rocks and broken beyond repair. But that was not what consumed his thoughts as he exited the water and climbed up the shoreline rocks. He couldn't get the image of what he had just seen out of his mind.

The Call

It was a particularly windy, cold, and rainy March morning and Terry Carver was glad to be inside his patrol car where he was warm and comfortable. He cruised slowly along Alki Avenue, an arterial that wrapped around the peninsula of West Seattle, and gazed out through the car's rain spattered windows at the lights of downtown Seattle shimmering across the storm-tossed bay. The mottled-gray dawn light was just beginning to show through the dark storm clouds that hung low overhead.

As bleak as it was, Terry reminded himself of how much he liked both this time of day and this type of weather. There is not much activity for a patrol officer when it is early in the morning and miserable out.

He would drive his route around West Seattle, spend a little time at his favorite coffee shop, and possibly write one traffic citation during his entire shift. He smiled and said out loud, "This is the good life" as he made a turn that would take him up onto the plateau of West Seattle and to Velvet Green Coffee and Tea.

A little after six, and about halfway up the hill to the coffee house, Terry's pleasant mood was disrupted by a call from dispatch. A fishing boat with a man and his son aboard had struck an object at the local boat launch and their disabled boat had been dashed onto the rocks nearby. The boat's owner reported that his propeller had struck the top of a submerged car at the base of the ramp and he thought he might have seen someone still inside the vehicle.

Terry switched on his lights, made a quick U-turn, and floored the pedal, making it back down the hill and to the launch ramp in less than two minutes. He didn't really expect to find anything more than a cold, wet man and boy along with a wrecked boat. Most likely the two had struck a waterlogged tree and mistaken it for a car. They were probably in shock from the accident and cold water and their imaginations had taken over from there.

Of course, another possibility was that the report was simply a crank call. Terry hated false alarms, but he had to admit that, on a morning like this, he would prefer to find nothing at the ramp and remain in the comfort of his car. He steered the cruiser into the launch parking lot and over to the ramp.

At the top, where the concrete began to slope down to the water, he pulled the shifter into park and strained to spot the caller through the rapidly sweeping wiper blades. There was no one to be seen on the ramp or the floating docks to either side. And if there was a grounded boat, it was grounded out of sight.

After a few moments scanning the launch and surrounding water, he turned and looked out through the right-side passenger window across the public parking lot. There, on the far side sitting in the shadows, was a lone black pickup attached to an empty boat trailer.

Terry cursed under his breath, "Damn, who in their right mind goes out on Elliott Bay on a morning like this?"

He opened his car door and was immediately struck by the brisk north wind that clipped the tops off the white caps and pelted his face with salt spray. He involuntarily stiffened and pulled his collar up and turned toward the parked truck.

Two figures emerged from the truck and began to shout and run toward Terry before veering off toward the long narrow floating dock that ran parallel to the right side of the ramp. Their words were lost in the roar of the wind, but Terry could just make out the gist of the message to follow them.

He ran to catch up as the man and boy sprinted out onto the dock. Large waves battered the structure and it bucked violently as if trying to break its moorings. An experienced boater himself and normally quite adept at keeping his balance on rocking vessels, Terry found that he could barely maintain his footing on the heaving, water washed platform. Just short of the far end, the two figures stopped, and Terry caught up to them. Now he could see that one was a middle-aged man and the other a young boy.

The two men grabbed each other for support as the boy shouted and pointed to a spot in the water about twenty feet away.

Even though the wind cut through his clothing like an icy knife, Terry was not chilled from the wind or even from the sea spray. Instead, he now shivered from what he saw in the water.

Exposed

The tide was going out and the top of a black sedan was clearly exposed in the troughs of water that separated the two-foot storm waves. Either someone had ditched a stolen car by pushing it down the ramp or some unfortunate soul had driven into the bay.

Terry strained to see into the dark car interior between the waves. It would be too late to save anyone if they were still in the submerged vehicle but whatever he saw would determine his next steps. Either he would simply call for a tow truck to retrieve an abandoned vehicle or he would be calling in reinforcements to investigate a death.

The water between two waves dropped enough to expose the entire driver side window and Terry thought he could just make out a shape, but he wasn't certain. Another trough swept past the window and his heart sank. As much as he hoped against it, Terry could make out a figure sitting in the driver's seat. He keyed the microphone on his radio and reported a possible dead body found.

Soon, the empty ramp, docks, and parking lot would be filled with patrol cars, one or more Seattle Harbor Patrol vessels, and crime scene investigators, along with the press and curious onlookers.

He turned and shouted to the fishermen, "Follow me. You can warm up in my car and tell me exactly what happened."

The pair nodded, and all three struggled back across the rocking dock and up to the idling police car. Once inside the lighted the car, Terry could see the man and boy better. The man was probably in his late thirties and he guessed that his son was somewhere between thirteen and fifteen.

Terry also noticed that both were shivering uncontrollably. The best of rain gear couldn't protect them from the cold waters when they had jumped overboard.

Terry turned the heat up to high and retrieved two blankets from his trunk. Then he radioed for medical assistance. It would be no use asking the father and son questions now. Police investigators would talk with them once they were warmed and stabilized.

Terry pulled his personal phone from his pocket and dialed. There was no answer, so he left a brief message.

Brothers

Reed was in a deep sleep dreaming about hiking on his favorite trail on the Olympic Peninsula when his cell phone rang. The phone rested in a charger on the dresser across the room and made the sound of waterfalls. The ringtone was soothing, and he had no intention of answering the call until his wife kicked him, "Hey, your phone is ringing."

He rose up onto his elbow and scowled at her, "Seriously? You couldn't tell I was just ignoring it?"

Reed was not a morning person. In fact, the only thing he hated more than mornings in general was being woken by someone calling way too early in the morning. And that would be any time before nine. Angela kicked him again, "It might be important."

"More likely a robocall." He grumbled.

Reed pushed himself out of bed and walked over to the dresser. The ringing stopped just as he reached for the phone.

"Hey honey, since you are up, could you make me a cup of coffee." Angela's head peeked out from the covers and she smiled meekly at him before pulling them back up over her head. He was just about to toss his phone at her when he saw that it was a call from his brother, Terry. The voice message icon flashed, and he dialed for voicemail.

Terry's voice came on, "Hey brother. Sorry to get you up, but I am down at the Alki boat launch. There is a car in the bay with a body inside and I thought you might want to come down and take a look."

Reed perked up and looked over at his wife buried under the covers, "That was Terry. There is a submerged car at the West Seattle launch ramp with someone in it. I am going over to check it out."

Reed may have not liked mornings, but he was always interested in opportunities to watch the police in action, especially if it involved something unusual. He had listened to Terry's stories and would sometimes do his own investigating on the side to see if he could solve a crime before the police did.

Over the years, it became apparent that Reed had a talent for sleuthing. On one case he had uncovered key clues that were instrumental in helping the police unravel what had been a spider's web trail of leads. Officially, the police department did not like civilians poking around their cases but inside the department, no one saw any harm in Terry inviting his brother to crime scenes if he stayed out of the way. Most of them knew Reed from social gatherings and knew him to be quite intelligent and have the common sense not to do anything stupid.

Terry had repeatedly encouraged his brother to become a genuine detective, but Reed had no desire for a structured job. He preferred to be on his own, reporting to no one. Sleuthing was mostly a brain game for him.

Reed pulled on a faded pair of jeans and t-shirt and walked downstairs to the kitchen to boil water and grind some fresh coffee beans. While the water heated, he layered on a wool shirt and hooded sweatshirt that hung over the back of one of the kitchen chairs. Angela shuffled into the kitchen in a pair of green and blue plaid flannel pajamas and fuzzy slippers and sat down. "What do you think happened?"

Reed poured boiling water into the French press and looked over, "Not sure. Maybe somebody was drunk and accidentally drove out into the

Sound and couldn't get out of their seatbelt. That would be a hell of a way to go."

Angela answered, "I hope that's not what happened. That would be so sad."

"You would rather it was a murder or a suicide?" he asked.

"No. I would rather there was no car in the water with a body in it." She tilted her head to the side and shrugged.

"Of course. But there is."

He poured some coffee into her mug and walked over to the kitchen table.

"That is probably why Terry called. It could be a mystery. And you know I am the best at solving mysteries."

Terry set her coffee down and shrugged with mock confidence.

"Who knows. It might even be a grisly murder and I will be the only one that can solve it."

Angela shook her head, "You helped the police solve one case and now you think you are Sherlock Holmes. Mind your head doesn't get too large to fit through the door."

Reed ignored her comments and kissed Angela on the cheek before he retrieved a puffy down jacket off an octopus shaped coat hook next to the front door.

"I'll give you a call when I know what is going on and when I'll be home. Love you."

Angela waved, "Love you too baby."

Reed and Angela lived on a houseboat on Lake Union just north of downtown Seattle. The floating home was painted driftwood grey and they named it The Grey Kraken. The walk up the dock and across the street to his car was short and, from his parking spot, it was less than a mile drive to the interstate on-ramp. It would only take about fifteen minutes to make it to the Alki boat launch.

Reed enjoyed the view across the bay at this time of morning on a Sunday when the traffic was virtually non-existent. Today, Elliott Bay was a maelstrom of green and grey, speckled with white caps. The bay was devoid of boats except for one rust colored freighter sitting low at anchor, two green and white car ferries passing each other further out in the Sound, and a blue and white Seattle Police boat speeding toward the West Seattle peninsula, blue lights flashing on top of the pilot house. Reed could also see several blue and red clusters of lights flashing on the shore directly across the bay. He pressed the accelerator and sped up, wondering what Terry had found.

Reed was Terry's older brother by two years, but you would swear Terry was the older one based on appearance or behavior. Growing up, Terry was outgoing and athletic and had lettered in more than one team sport. Reed had always been laid back and preferred to read a good book, solve puzzles, or go on a hike in the nearby forests.

They grew up in the Seattle suburb of West Seattle within blocks of the Alki Point lighthouse. Their father had been a Seattle Police officer and their mother a stay-at-home mom. Both parents hoped their boys would follow in their father's footsteps and join the department. Terry did, but Reed preferred to go his own way and he started a chain of boutiques called The Silkworm Factory, with his wife, Angela. Their shops were quite successful, with Angela running store operations and Reed managing the finances. Even though Reed could never see himself in an official role in the police, he enjoyed puzzle solving and liked trying to solve cases as a hobby.

Witnesses

Less than a quarter mile down the beach from the public boat launch ramp, the West Seattle passenger ferry dock afforded a good view of the flurry of police activity at the public ramp. Onlookers started crowding the dock shortly after local news reported police activity at the launch and unconfirmed reports of a body in a submerged car. Umbrellas blew inside out, and hats blew off, but the spectators braved the storm out of morbid curiosity.

As the group watched a Harbor Police boat arrive at the launch, two patrol cars pulled into the ferry parking lot. One officer exited each car and they approached the onlookers together before they split up and approached the line of people from opposite ends.

The officers asked each person how long they had been in the area and if they had observed any unusual activity. All of them answered along the same lines. They had just arrived after hearing or seeing the news and had come to the dock out of concern or curiosity.

It did not take long for the patrolmen to complete their interviews and return to their cars. No one they talked with had been there earlier that morning or witnessed anything suspicious in the area.

One of officers drove straight back to the ramp while the other drove slowly up and down the street in both directions, jotting down the license numbers of the parked cars.

Shortly after the patrol cars left, two males standing at the rail nodded to each other and turned to walk to the parking lot. There, they paused to confirm that the police had left the area and climbed into a white SUV. The driver pulled out of the parking lot and turned in the opposite direction of the ramp.

The passenger, tall and slim with black hair looked across the at the driver and asked, "So, do you think they will buy it?"

The driver, a short stout man with an additional decade of life on him shook his head, "Hell no. This was just a diversion. But it should point them in the wrong direction and just maybe save your neck."

The passenger stared at the driver with a look of contempt, "My neck? You think I wanted this? It was your monumental fuck up that killed her. That was the last thing I wanted. I should turn you in myself."

The driver smirked, "Really? And just how do you think that would turn out? You're not innocent here, and if you get any smart ideas about coming clean, you will go down with me. I will make certain of that."

The two sat silent for the rest of the drive.

Depression

Terry told the shivering father and son to wait inside his car for the medics to arrive while he cordoned off the area with yellow police tape. As he made his way around the scene, the entire area came to life with lights and sirens. Additional patrol cars pulled into the parking lot followed by several unmarked department cars. Just offshore, the flashing blue lights of a Seattle Police Harbor Patrol boat bounced up and down as the vessel pulled up to the ramp area and started circling. It would be carrying divers suited up in their dry suits.

Within a few minutes a fire department emergency vehicle pulled into the parking lot and Terry directed them to his squad car. Right behind the aid car was Terry's friend and fellow officer Jack Ross. Jack parked his cruiser next to Terry's and joined Terry in stringing the police tape.

The vehicle on the ramp was no longer completely submerged, but no one swam out to examine it. It would be foolish for anyone to enter the cold waters without a dry suit at this time of year. To do so would invite hypothermia within minutes. Police divers would make an initial examination of the car and then attach a winch cable to the rear to pull it clear of the breakers.

By the time Reed arrived, he had to park his green Mini Cooper over a block away from the ramp due to the police cordon and the gathering crowd. He tucked the Mini between two large pick-up trucks and walked back to the police tape where he spotted Terry and Jack a short distance away.

"Terry." He shouted out over the wind.

Terry looked over and waved, "Reed. You got my message."

Reed responded, "Yes. Thanks for the call. I'll stay out of the way and go to the lookout over there."

He pointed to an observation area that bordered the launch and was outside of the fluttering tape. Terry gave a thumbs-up and answered, "I'll come over as soon as I am free."

Reed walked across a cement path to the overlook. The area sat a good fifteen feet above the water and afforded a clear view of the current activities. He could see two divers bobbing on the surface like shiny seals to either side of a partially submerged car.

One called out to the shore, "There is one body."

The other waved his arm in a circle over his head to signal a waiting red and white flatbed tow truck to back down the ramp and then play out its steel cable. The truck backed down to within fifteen feet of the water and a diver walked up to the rear of the vehicle and grabbed the hook that was attached to the tow cable. The tow truck driver threw a switch on the cable winch and the diver walked back down to the car as the steel line played out. When he reached the car, the diver reached under the rear bumper and attached the cable. Then he signaled to the tow truck driver to start the winch.

Reed listened to the high whine of the tow truck winch as it struggled to extract the sedan from the bitter grasp of the sea. The front wheels were locked, and the car resisted moving, as if in defiance to being forced from it resting place. The scene reminded him of an old movie clip of rain drenched whalers winching a black lifeless carcass up some water-splashed processing ramp.

Slowly, the car cleared the waves as streams of water cascaded from the door jams and spilled out onto the slick green algae that covered the concrete. From his vantage point, Reed could now make out that the driver side window of the vehicle was down, and a figure was slumped forward, head resting on the steering wheel.

The combined sound of the wind, waves and winch put him into a daze as he watched the surrealistic scene. A voice called out and jerked him back to reality, "Can you tell if it's a man or women?"

It was Terry walking towards him. Terry had been up in the parking lot helping with crowd control until Jack suggested he take a break. From where he had been working, all he could see was the swarm of reporters and local gawkers lining the police tape, their glistening umbrellas straining in the wind and providing little protection from the cold rain that pelted their faces and sent rivulets of water down their necks.

Once Terry was close enough for Reed to speak at a normal volume, he answered Terry's question. "It looks like a young man. He has a buzz cut."

About then, the sound of the winch stopped. The vehicle was far enough from the water to allow access to those other than the divers. Now, the investigative work would begin. This was a well-rehearsed choreography of examining the vehicle and body for any clues that may indicate if this were the scene of a suicide, homicide, or tragic accident. When the detectives were finished with their initial examination, they signaled to a waiting black SUV and two men from the coroner's office walked down the ramp towards the car. One of them carried a black bag and laid it next to the driver's side door.

Then, the first man knelt and wrapped his arms around the body's legs as the other leaned in and reached under each arm. The first man counted to three and they lifted the lifeless body out of the car and onto the open bag. As they did, the victim's entire head and face were exposed to Terry and Reed.

"What the hell?" Terry gasped

Reed cringed. "It's a girl."

Now they could clearly see the face of a young woman, head shaved on one side and long black hair with blue streaks streaming down the other.

Terry looked at Reed, "She doesn't even look old enough to be out of high school. Crap. Sorry I called you. I just thought…. I didn't expect a teenage suicide."

"I know. You thought there might be a good crime scene and I might like to see it for myself. Maybe you even hoped that there would be a dead

13

drug dealer inside, and it would open an interesting new case. You certainly weren't expecting a dead kid."

This was not the first young suicide victim Terry had witnessed but they always hit hard. He had his own teenage daughter in the local high school, and they hit too close to home.

He looked at Reed, "What can be so bad that it makes someone want to end their own life? That girl could have talked with someone and worked things out."

Reed looked back a Terry. He knew that Terry was tough when it came to seeing accidents and death but always struggled when he had been called to a suicide, "When you're depressed, you are certain that no one understands what you are going through. You don't see any light at the end of the tunnel and you just want to stop. Stop the noise. Stop the light. Stop everything. I know. I've been there."

Reed knew a little about depression. He had suffered with bouts of it his entire life and several years back started taking medication to control his mood swings. He was a vocal advocate for mental health awareness and treatment.

"I bet this girl came down here last night in the depth of depression, opened the window to let the water in and drove down the ramp to find serenity. Something she probably hadn't felt in years. I am not condoning this, but I understand it. She is at peace. It is her parents that have to deal with the pain and suffering now."

Reed glanced at his watch and saw that time was getting on. He knew that Terry's shift ended at 12:30 and he patted his brother on the shoulder, "Isn't your shift over soon? When you go home you need to get some sleep and then take Michelle and Kim out for dinner tonight. Celebrate life and your family. It will make you feel better."

Terry thought a moment and answered, "That's not a bad idea brother. Besides, this is my Friday. I am off for the next two days."

He paused, "Hey, since I don't work tomorrow, why don't we meet for breakfast in the market? It's been a while."

Reed wasn't fond of mornings but was happy to rouse early to have breakfast with his brother. Besides, maybe the girl hadn't committed suicide and there was a crime to solve after all. Terry would call his colleagues in the morning and get an update. Reed agreed to the breakfast, said goodbye, and walked back to his car.

Terry returned to his patrol car and called Michelle to make plans for the evening. It turned out that she was grocery shopping for dinner food when her phone rang, and she was thankful for the invitation to eat out. She had struck a blank on what to make for dinner and, had Terry not called, they would probably have ended up with frozen pizza. Terry drove his patrol car back to the station, switched over to his personal red Jeep Grand Cherokee and continued home.

Chapter 2

Family Time

Michelle and Kim were out when Terry arrived home and the house was silent except for the purring of his daughter's cat that now rubbed at his legs as he walked to the bedroom to change out of his uniform. He changed into a pair of khakis and a faded Seattle Seahawks t-shirt and retired to the basement television room. Emotionally drained and physically exhausted, he dropped lengthwise onto the couch and tried to catch some sleep but, try as he may to relax and clear his mind, it kept racing with thoughts of the girl's body at the ramp.

How would he feel if it had been his daughter in the car? How many times had she come to him for advice or comfort when he had felt too busy to talk? The times she would want to discuss something on her mind, and he would tell her to come back later or that her problems were not really that big and that she needed to grow up and deal with them on her own. How would he feel if he was not there when his own daughter needed him and, in her isolation, felt driven to end her life? After what seemed to Terry like hours, he fell into a troubled sleep.

An hour later, he woke up refreshed but still troubled. He looked forward to dinner with Michelle and Kim. Lately it seemed that they shared too little time together as a family. Kim was active in several school activities and was out most evenings with her friends.

He walked up from the basement to the living room and sat on the couch.

As he settled in, Michelle walked in the front door, "Hey honey, what came over you today? It's been ages since the three of us went out for a nice evening together." she asked almost before she had finished closing the door behind her.

Terry looked up, "Didn't you hear the news today?"

She set two canvass shopping bags on the dining room table, "No, I have been out and about all day and didn't have the radio on. Why?"

"There was a suicide at the West Seattle boat ramp. At least I think it was a suicide. Reed and I were there when they removed the body of a young woman from a car that had driven into the water. For some reason it hit me hard and I kept thinking of Kim and her friends.

Michelle looked shocked and asked, "Did you recognize her? Was it anyone we know?"

Terry answered, "No. Her driver's license shows she was a seventeen-year-old from Gig Harbor. Also, not likely to be one of Kim's friends. She had a shaved head and dyed hair. Not the type Kim would hang out with."

Michelle walked over and sat down next to him, "Why didn't you tell me this on the phone?"

"I didn't feel like going into it right then. Anyway, right now I just want to spend some time with Kim and you this evening. We don't do enough of that anymore."

Terry got up and walked out to the kitchen and pulled a bottle of Captain Morgan from the cupboard. "But first, I need a rum and coke."

"Make me one too. And then you can tell me more about today." Michelle had seen Terry get upset before when he had been called to a particularly bad accident or crime and she knew it calmed him down to talk it out. She turned on the gas fireplace to make the room more comforting and sat back on the couch to hear more about the drowning.

In the kitchen Terry took two tall glasses and added a few cubes of ice to each followed by a generous amount of rum topped off with an only slightly greater amount of coke. As he finished stirring the drinks, he heard his daughter Kim burst into the house, "Daddy, did you hear about the girl drowning at Alki? Were you there? Was she from West Seattle?"

The home's front door opened directly into the living room and Michelle jumped up to intercept Kim as she entered, "Kim, calm down. Yes, your father was there. But right now, he and I are going to relax and visit for a few minutes by ourselves. Then we will all go out to dinner. You can talk with him about it then. Now go clean up and get ready to go out."

Kim headed down the hallway to her room as Terry came back into the living room from the other direction and flopped onto the leather couch next to Michelle. He looked pensive as he swirled the drink in his glass, "I'm no detective, but something doesn't seem right about the drowning this morning."

The flames reflected off the hardwood floor and mesmerized him as Michelle rubbed his shoulders. He continued, "I've seen my share of suicides. Even though they are always tragic, they are typically straight forward. Jumpers, shooters, hangers, wrist cutters, and pill takers. It is rare for someone to drive into the water to kill themselves, though it definitely happens."

After a pause he continued, "There was no suicide note in the car."

Michelle stopped rubbing, "She may have left one at home. I'm sure if there is something suspicious the investigators will find it?"

"Of course." He said.

Michelle resumed rubbing his back and asked, "And if it wasn't suicide, what do you think it was? Maybe a drug overdose?"

Terry thought, "Maybe, but it would be a huge coincidence for someone to take drugs in their car while sitting at the top of a boat launch ramp with the car facing the water and still in gear, and then accidentally overdose, pass out, and drive down into the water."

Michelle smiled, "It does sound like a bit of a stretch when you put it that way."

She put her arm around her husband and the two sat in silence as rain pattered against the living room windows, the random pattern only occasionally broken by the hiss of a car passing the house, slick tires raising curtains of spray as they tracked through the streams of water coursing the street.

Kim walked into the room, more subdued than when she had come home earlier. She looked at her father and said "I heard you were at the launch ramp today. Can you talk about it?"

Terry pushed himself up and off the couch and walked over to his daughter to give her a bear hug. "We can talk over dinner. Grab your coat and we'll go right now."

Normal

He pulled on his own jacket and waited for the girls. Outside, the family climbed into the Jeep and headed through the rain to a neighborhood steakhouse about ten minutes away. The small restaurant was an older establishment that had probably seen its best days in the 60's when it was called a supper club, but it still served great beef and seafood with style and the prices were reasonable. The tables were covered with linen, the waiters and waitresses wore black pants and white shirts, and the lighting was set low to create an atmosphere of sophistication.

Terry thought the subdued lighting was also to cover up the threadbare carpet and aging furnishings. Seeing the true state of the establishment would probably put one off their dinner. Even though the restaurant continued some pretense of being an upscale venue, the current diners ran the gamut from those dressed up for a special evening out to those in jeans and tee shirts.

An older hostess with platinum blonde hair and too much make-up led the three to a cozy booth in the far corner of the room near a fireplace that was built into a river-rock stone wall. Terry guessed that she had probably held her position here since the restaurant opened and wondered if she missed the days when she would have seated women in their formals and caught the eye of young businessmen in their best suits. Despite her obvious advanced age, she still showed grace and a little flirtation as she led them across the room.

At the booth, Michelle and Kim slid across the worn brown vinyl bench seats opposite each other and Terry sat down next to Michelle. The table butted up to large leaded glass windows with a view over the shipping lanes on Puget Sound. A wavering glow from the fireplace filled the room and illuminated a broad assortment of maritime memorabilia that included fishing nets with colored glass floats, models of sailing vessels, and a brass deep-sea diver helmet. The space was warm and comfortable, and the view of the water and marine traffic always had a calming effect on Terry.

Shortly after the three were seated, a lanky young bus boy with his white shirt-tail half untucked walked over to the table and filled their water glasses while stealing a few sidelong glances at Kim. She was totally unaware of his attention or, at least, gave that impression. After another few minutes, a college age waiter came over to take drink and dinner orders. He also seemed a little too interested in Kim for Terry's liking, looking only at the teenage girl as he read the evening's dinner specials from his notebook.

Terry forced the boy's attention back to him by immediately ordering his usual Prime Rib with extra Horseradish, and then asking Michelle what she was having.

As soon as they had ordered, and the waiter left, Kim looked at her father and spoke up. "The news reports aren't saying who drowned in the car. Just that it was a girl. Was she from West Seattle? Was it anyone I know?"

Terry was always amazed at how young people can forgo all small talk or pretense and go straight to their current point of attention.

"Thank you, my day was fine. How was yours?"

Kim looked only slightly apologetic. "Sorry. I already know your day pretty much sucked. I just want to know if the girl is anyone I might know."

Terry considered how much he should share. By now the next of kin had most likely been notified so he felt safe telling Kim and Michelle the identity of the girl. The crime scene team had found a driver's license in the car that matched her face.

"I don't think it is anyone you would know. She was seventeen; same as you, but her driver's license has a Gig Harbor address. That's almost an hour's drive from here."

Terry did not expect the reaction he got from his daughter, "Did you say Gig Harbor? Dad, I think I might know who it was. What was her name?"

Terry was skeptical that his daughter would know the girl. Kim was levelheaded and would be classified as somewhat conservative, just the opposite of the drowning victim. What reason would either of them have had to run into the other, let alone know each other.

"Her name was Marissa Archer."

Kim slumped down into the seat. "My God."

Terry looked surprised, "You actually knew her?"

His daughter didn't hear him, "What happened? Did she commit suicide? No, that can't be. She seemed okay that way."

Terry could see the moisture building in Kim's eyes, flickering with the reflection of the small votive candle that rested in the center of the table.

"You always surprise me Kim. How do you even know this girl? She didn't exactly look like the type you would hang out with."

He looked over at his wife, "The girl in the car had blue hair and one side of her head was shaved. Not exactly normal if you ask me."

His daughter glared back, "Normal? What is that supposed to mean? Define normal. Am I normal just because I dress and make myself up according to your definition of normal? You don't know anything about Marissa, and you are judging her."

Terry remembered why he avoided talking with his seventeen-year-old daughter even though he wanted to be closer to her and be more involved in her life. It seemed that she constantly challenged whatever he would say no matter what the subject was. He tried to move the conversation along and asked Kim how she knew a girl that lived over forty miles away.

Kim answered "I didn't really know her that well. She was a friend of Keith Martin and he introduced me to her after school one time."

Kim paused and thought. "I saw her and Keith several times after school out by the track and practice field. They were always laughing and smiling."

Terry knew the location. Even when he had attended the high school there was a group of boys and girls that would stand out by the running track, several of them smoking, mostly cigarettes, but a sweeter blend of smoke would also carry over from the area.

It was there that you could find almost any contraband you desired and were inclined to try. He knew that this was still going on and he regularly patrolled the area in his police car. He would cruise past the high school and there would be the current group of teenagers huddled in a cluster until they spotted the marked car and quickly dispersed. Some things never change.

Terry asked, "If it turns out she didn't commit suicide, do you think she might have been doing drugs with that boy? Those kids that hang out by the track are no saints. If she overdosed by accident while she was with him, he could have staged the scene at Alki to throw suspicion away from him."

21

Based on what Kim had just said, an overdose scenario now seemed probable to Terry.

Kim answered "No. He doesn't seem like the type to be into drugs. He is just a little different. You know. He always has his hood pulled up and he wears earphones whenever he isn't in class. It's like he is trying to block out the noise. And he is introverted. He never talks very much. But when you talk with him, he is really smart and seems like a nice guy."

"So how is it that you talk with him if he is so different?"

"He's my lab partner in chemistry, first period. He might skip some of his other classes, but I know he loves chemistry. Weird, huh?"

Not too weird, Terry thought. He had been involved in some meth lab busts and an interest in chemistry would fit for someone running a lab. He began to feel more suspicious of Keith, despite his daughter's view of the boy.

"Yeah, that is a bit of a coincidence. Did he ever talk about Marissa to you?"

Kim perked up, "Yes, all the time. I think she may have been his only friend and he always talked about how special she was. The only problem was that her dad did not like him. He blamed Keith for changes she made to her appearance, like dying her hair and shaving one side. He also accused Keith of getting her into drugs."

Terry asked, "Why would her father think that?"

Kim answered, "I don't know. But Marissa's father told her to stop seeing him and banned Keith from their house. Since he couldn't go to her home to see here, she would sneak over to West Seattle and spend time with him behind her father's back."

"Maybe her father had good reason to be concerned." Terry wondered if the boy was as innocent as his daughter seemed to presume.

The waiter came with their meals and Michelle suggested they change to a lighter topic during dinner. She took Terry's hand in hers and said, "You know, my thirty-year high school reunion is coming up in July. And I do plan to go. With or without you" She smiled.

Terry always complained about going to the high school reunions but had to admit that he enjoyed the get-togethers despite himself. They had attended the ten year and twenty-year reunions with Reed and Angela and always spent the evenings laughing at how much or how little people had changed. The girls seemed to laugh most over the balding men and the two guys marveled at how some of the most attractive girls in high school had become dowdy and how many of the so-called Plain-Janes had become so attractive.

"I'm meeting Reed for breakfast tomorrow. I'll ask him if they want to go with us again this year."

Michelle smiled again, "No need. I already talked with Angela and they are going, whether Reed knows it or not."

The rest of dinner was spent talking about the reunion and other day-to-day business. Terry did not want to dwell on the accident anymore. Besides, it sounded like Keith would be a good place to go for answers. Terry would call an investigator on the case first thing in the morning and tell him about the boy.

Sweet Sixteen

Becky Rose lived in Coeur d'Alene, Idaho in a household that neighbors described as the model of family values, love and balance. She was an only child and her parents doted on her, enthusiastically supporting her interests in soccer and acting. She was exceptionally smart and mature for her age and school studies came easy to her, so she had no problem balancing schoolwork with a full schedule of afterschool activities that included regularly being cast in local community theater productions and the heavy rehearsal and performance schedule that ensued.

In addition to being intellectually advanced, Becky was an early developer physically. At age eleven, she began to show obvious curves that did not go ignored by the boys at school. Several teased her and some of the bolder boys tried to touch her breasts. Fortunately, her parents had instilled in her a strong sense of good self-image and her self-confidence enabled Becky to deflect the young boys' advances and ignore their comments. She focused on her interests and looked forward to the future.

This changed during her eighth-grade year. It started one evening after a theater rehearsal when Becky's father accidentally walked in on her just as she stepped out of the shower. Startled, the young girl screamed and yelled for him to leave immediately as she drew the towel across her chest and body, more embarrassed than angry. A look flashed across his face that she had never seen before, and he paused a moment before leaving without saying a word.

A few days later her father visited her bedroom late in the evening after her mother had fallen asleep. He told her how beautiful she was and asked her to stand naked before him. She hesitated and he repeated the request, saying it was okay and that he was her father and wouldn't do anything that was wrong. She reluctantly complied and pulled her nightshirt off over her head while he told her that she would be a famous actress one day with her beauty and talent and that she should be proud of her body. After a few minutes he left. This became a regular routine, sometimes occurring several times a month. He would wait until her mother was asleep, come to her room and sit on her bed as he watched her undress. He would praise her, tell her how much he loved her and then say goodnight and leave. She knew what they were doing was wrong, but she loved her father and justified the ritual by telling herself that he was doing no harm. After all, he never touched her.

That was until Sunday. It was Becky's sixteenth birthday and her parents had thrown her a big party at their house with several of her friends from school. The gathering was a raucous event with the girls singing songs from the current school musical, Mary Poppins, and talking in their best English accents. The last of her friends left at nine o'clock and Becky was in her PJs and under her covers by nine-thirty, ready for a good night's sleep. As she drifted off, she was could just make out her parents talking through the bedroom door and heard her father saying goodnight to her mother. She didn't know how much time passed before her father came into her room like he had many times over the past three years and touched her shoulder, rousing her out of her slumber. She knew what it meant and, despite overwhelming drowsiness, got out of bed, stepped out of her pajama shorts and pulled the t-shirt up over her head. But this time something was different. She could smell alcohol on his breath, and he looked at her in a new way. After she stood naked for a few moments he asked her to come over and sit by him on the bed. She pulled on her robe and sat next to her father.

He put his arm around her shoulders, "You know, soon every young man around is going to want to go to bed with you."

She blushed, "Dad."

"And you will want to have sex with them too. I bet you already do."

"Dad, stop. I'm not stupid. I don't need 'the talk'."

"No, I am sure you don't." He pulled her closer, "But you deserve to know what good sex can be like before some bumbling boy messes it up."

"What are you talking about?"

"You are sixteen and I think it's time. I am going to teach you tonight."

Her head swirled as he opened her robe. She didn't know what to feel. She was afraid, but she loved her father. This was all wrong. He had always been good to her. She went numb and her mind was a fog. Her father laid her down and took her virginity.

Afterwards, he told her how much loved her and then added that if she loved her mother, she would never to tell her or anyone else what happened. After he left the room Becky cried throughout the night. She was in pain and overcome with guilt and confusion. The next morning, she had a late-start day at school. After her parents left for work, she would stuff some clothes and a sleeping bag into a backpack and grab a small camping tent from the garage. Then she would go out to the highway and hitch a ride to Seattle where she could hide and decide what to do next.

Chapter 3

The Market

It was nine o'clock Monday morning and the Pike Place Market was waking up. The smell of fresh produce and cut flowers mingled with that of fresh caught fish as local farmers set out their harvest and fish mongers created elegant displays of seafood on mounds of white shaved ice. Soon, thousands of tourists speaking a variety of languages from around the world would pack shoulder to shoulder as they wandered through the open stalls and shops in a state of sensory overload.

Reed preferred the market early in the day before the throngs arrived. He enjoyed visiting with the artists, farmers, and fish mongers while they set up their stalls, and would often buy a colorful bundle of flowers for Angela along with fresh salmon or Dungeness crab for that day's dinner. The Grey Kraken was less than three miles from the market, and he could make the bike ride in fifteen minutes or even less if he pushed it.

This morning, he chained his bike to a pole outside of the original Starbucks and crossed the street to his favorite place for breakfast in the market. Inside the restaurant, he walked up a set of stairs to the second floor and sat down at a table by the large windows that provided panoramic views of the water and mountains.

From several window tables that ran the length of the room, diners could look out to the west over the waterfront piers to watch white and green ferry boats plying Puget Sound to and from the Seattle Ferry Terminal. Just across the bay sat the community of West Seattle, with its peninsula jutting out from the Duwamish flats.

Only a few minutes after taking a seat, Reed spotted Terry walking up the wooden stairway and called out, "Hey little brother. Good morning."

Terry walked over to the table, slid one chair out and threw his coat on it, then sat on the other chair opposite Reed.

"Well, aren't you chipper. I thought you hated mornings."

Reed responded, "It's not really that I hate them. I just prefer to lay in. Anyway, I am curious if you found anything more on the accident yesterday. Did you talk with your buddy McManus?"

A waitress walked over, and Reed didn't wait for her to reach the table. "We'll take two coffees right away please. I need my caffeine fix bad today."

Both men already knew what they would order for breakfast and would take care of that when she returned with their brews. The waitress returned with the coffee and took their identical orders for eggs over easy, bacon, and wheat toast. She put the orders on separate tabs, but Terry knew that Reed would pick up both bills. He always had, and Terry didn't even bother to try to pay any more.

Terry took a sip of coffee and set the mug down, "Actually I did give Robert a call and he gave me some info. Most of it you have probably already seen on the news. The girl's name was Marissa Archer. She was seventeen and from Gig Harbor. Her father is Ryan Archer, the superintendent of the Washington Women's Correction Center over there."

Reed nodded, "You're right. I caught all of that on the news. But there must be more. What about the autopsy?"

Terry answered, "The autopsy won't be completed until later today."

Reed, "So, we don't know anything more than what was reported?"

Terry, "Well not exactly. A cursory examination of the body was made yesterday by detectives."

Reed, "And?"

Terry, "Well, there was a fresh needle mark on her left arm that may indicate drug use. Also, she showed signs of bruising around her one of her eyes, so she may have been assaulted. And finally, there were several old scars from cuts on both of her arms. I don't know what this girl was into, but it wasn't good, and it might have something to do with her death."

Reed whistled, "Wow. From my thinking it was a suicide to becoming a potential assault and overdose. This could turn into an interesting case yet."

Terry stabbed at his eggs and slid them around the plate without looking up. "Kim knew the girl. Not directly, but the dead girl was dating a boy that Kim knows from school. His name is Keith Martin. Kim describes him as being a loner and little different."

He took a bite of egg and continued, "Apparently, the girl was meeting him in secret after her father told her to stop seeing him. Her father only met Keith once, but blamed him for Marissa's recent changes in behavior."

Reed took a sip of coffee and asked what seemed to be an obvious question "Has anyone talked with the boy yet?"

Terry replied, "The investigators will today. I told Robert what Kim told me, and he said Marissa's father had already pointed a suspicious finger at the boy."

Reed thought a moment, "Interesting. It's definitely suspicious that she died near where her boyfriend lives, but I think it is a little early to jump to conclusions."

He paused before continuing. "If Mr. Archer runs a state correctional facility, isn't it highly likely he has enemies that might want to hurt him or his family? I certainly hope the investigators are looking into that."

Another pause, "Or it was a drug deal gone bad."

Terry spoke, "Or she was kidnapped, and something went wrong."

Reed responded, "Exactly. There are several possibilities. I think we need a few more facts before jumping to conclusions about Marissa's boyfriend."

Terry picked up a piece of slightly over cooked and under buttered wheat toast and swirled it in the soft orange egg yolk that rested in the middle of his plate. "Still, you must admit that it is suspicious that she died in West Seattle, a significant drive from her home and, coincidentally, in the same neighborhood where the boy lives. My money is on the boy."

He continued, "Robert told me that Superintendent Ryan Archer has a PhD in psychology. He considers himself a strong judge of character and he told investigators that he believes the boy is a non-conformist and potential trouble. He is certain that Keith is somehow involved with his daughter's death. Robert should know more after they question the boy and complete the autopsy later today. Who knows, the father may be right, and this will be cleared up within a day or two."

Reed rolled a coffee stained white mug back and forth between his hands and took another sip of the strong mixture of French Roast, cream, and sugar. Something still bothered him.

"I wouldn't be so sure. Look, if the boy was involved in her death, and if he has a shred of common sense, he would not have dumped her body a couple of miles from his home. He would have taken it away from West Seattle to throw suspicion elsewhere. That is what I would do."

After the toast had soaked up a sufficient amount of the yellow goop, Terry put it in his mouth and shrugged his shoulders at Reed. "I agree. That is what an intelligent person would do. Maybe this boy is just stupid."

Reed could tell the death of a girl so close to Kim's age was weighing on Terry so he changed the subject, "Hey, I know it's short notice, but how would you and Michelle like to come over for dinner tomorrow? Angela wants to start planning for the school reunion in June. If the weather holds tomorrow, you and I can take the kayaks out on the lake while the girls drink wine and make their plans."

Terry didn't hesitate, "That sounds good. I'll clear it with Michelle but I'm sure she will be up for it."

"No need to call Michelle." Reed chuckled. "Angela suggested the dinner idea last night and doesn't think that I will remember to ask you this morning, so she will no doubt call Michelle today to ask on her own. We are thinking of making it early, around four o'clock, since you will be back on duty Wednesday. I really don't know how you handle the crazy shifts."

"It isn't so bad once you get used to it. My favorite is first watch when the city is waking up. Except for yesterday. Anyway, dinner tomorrow sounds great."

"Perfect." Reed pushed his plate away. "Are you okay if I to poke around the Alki thing on my own a bit? I promise to be discreet."

Terry smiled, "I was hoping you'd ask."

Reed stood up and threw a ten and a twenty on the table.

Terry slid his chair back and stood, "Thanks for breakfast. Again. One of these days you need to let me pick up the tab."

Reed laughed, "That will never happen. Consider these breakfasts as my contribution to the Local Policemen's' Charity Fund."

Terry punched him and the two headed down the narrow café stairway and out into the bustling market where they gave each other a hug before heading in opposite directions. Reed stayed at the market and meandered through the flower stalls in search of the perfect fresh bouquet to take back to Angela. Terry left the market and walked through Post Alley where he grabbed a latte on the way to his car parked on the steep grade of Pine Street.

School

At West Seattle High School, the hallways buzzed with talk of the drowning over the weekend. Constructed in 1917, the large two-story brick structure was typical of city schools built during the early 1900's and it still retained its classic brown brick exterior and multi-paned windows. Kim made her way down the wide main hall through the sea of students and occasionally waved to one of her friends, hoping no one would ask if she knew anything about the accident. It was common knowledge that her father was a policeman, so she expected some inquiries even though she had already texted her closest friends that she knew nothing more than what was reported on the news.

Kim's first period class was chemistry, and the room was comprised of two sections, the front half with standard desks and rear area with several lab tables. The lab tables were tall so students could stand while working on their experiments. Each had four stools arranged around the perimeter and incorporated its own sinks and gas connections for Bunsen burners. Bisecting each table was a narrow shelf that held an assortment of laboratory paraphernalia that the teacher had prepared earlier in the morning including beakers, thermometers, scales, and graduated cylinders. At the front of the room, containers of chemicals awaited today's lesson. The white board announced: The Effects of Solutes on the Freezing Point of Water.

Mr. Forest, the chemistry teacher, greeted each student as they came in the door. His slightly balding head with wisps of out-of-control white hair, plus his thin gold rimmed glasses and white lab coat gave Mr. Forest the appearance of a mad scientist, and the students loved it. His easy demeanor, quick wit, and wealth of fun science trivia made him one of the most popular instructors in the school. While other teachers seemed to go through the day in autopilot, Mr. Forest honestly cared about the students and showed an infectious enthusiasm for chemistry. Many of his students had gone on to pursue degrees in science based largely on their positive experience in his classes.

As Kim entered the chemistry room Mr. Forest approached her.

"Good morning Kim. Was your father working this weekend?"

Kim replied, "Good morning Mr. Forest. Yes, he was. And yes, he was at the boat launch and saw the car and girl."

Trying not to sound rude or dismissive Kim continued, "But he really didn't talk about it at home, so I don't know anything other than what was in the news."

Kim hoped her answer would defray any follow-up questioning and it did. Mr. Forest gave her a knowing nod and said he understood.

The last student entered the room and Mr. Forest closed the classroom door, "Everyone please take their seats so we can listen to morning announcements."

As Mr. Forest turned up the volume on a television mounted on the wall, the door opened again, and Keith walked in and took his regular seat next to Kim. He was wearing his usual green hoody sweatshirt with hood up over his head, large earphones covering his ears. He pulled the earphones down around his neck as he sat, and several students began to ask him about the accident. The drowning had been the lead story on the local Sunday evening news and this morning all the stations again led with the story, identifying the girl as Marissa Archer of Gig Harbor. Several students knew that Keith hung out with a girl named Marissa and that she was from Gig Harbor. The information had spread through the halls that morning like wildfire.

Mr. Forest called out, "Okay, okay, quiet down so we can hear the television."

Typically, the morning announcements were delivered by students and revolved around upcoming school events, special recognition for sports or scholastic feats and school lunch information. Half of the students listened while the others doodled in their notebooks or quietly visited among themselves. However, appearing on the monitor this morning was the somber face of the high school principal Dr. Steele, and everyone in the room turned their attention to the screen.

"Good morning. As many of you are aware, there was a fatal accident yesterday morning at the Alki boat launch ramp. Police reported that the drowning took the life of a young women. I know many of you are concerned that she was a classmate and are anxious to hear her identity. This morning the police released her name and she was not a student of West Seattle. She was a senior from Gig Harbor High School and her name was Marissa Archer."

Dr. Steele paused and nervously adjusted his tie. "I have been told that some of you knew Marissa. I know this must be difficult time for Marissa's friends and I understand that an accident of this kind can be difficult for many of us, whether we knew Marissa or not. Because of that, for the next several days we will have grievance counselors available to meet with you at any time during the school day in addition to special hours before and after school. Please don't hesitate to talk with a counselor if you are feeling anxious or depressed, or even if you simply want to talk. That is what they are here for. I am sure we all share our sympathy with Marissa's family and her friends. That is all for our announcements today. Thank you."

The television screen went blank and the room was eerily silent except for a low hissing noise coming from the speakers and the mournful sound of Keith at the back of the room, his head buried in folded arms on the desktop, his back heaving in unison with his muffled sobs.

Mr. Forest turned off the television and seemed puzzled at Keith's reaction.

Kim offered, "Marissa and Keith were close friends."

The teacher made his way through the rows of desks to the back where Keith sat. "Keith, I think you should go see the counselors. Don't worry about class today."

Then he looked over at Keith's lab partner, "Kim, would you please walk with Keith to the office. I don't want anyone bothering him on his way there."

"No problem Mr. Forest." Kim looked over at Keith's desk. Without a word he had already stood up and walked out of the room, head down, not looking at anyone or anything.

Skipping Out

Kim hurried to catch up with him in the hall. Her escort was not really needed as the halls were now mostly deserted while classes were in session. It occurred to her that Mr. Forest was probably more concerned that Keith would just walk out of the school instead of going to the counselor's office.

"Keith, I am sorry about Marissa. I don't know what to say."

Keith stopped and looked at her for the first time that morning, his eyes red from crying and lack of sleep. "You know something? You are the first person to act like they care about how I feel."

He leaned back against a locker, "You are one of the only people around this hole that talks to me like an equal, other than the kids out by the track."

Kim did not know how to respond.

He continued, "I get it. I am not comfortable talking with everyone and would rather just listen to my music. You understand that. Marissa understood that too. That is part of what made her so cool. She saw the good in everyone. At the same time, she hated hypocrisy and enjoyed poking at the establishment. That is why she started dressing like me and changed her hair. It really pissed her father off and I think that was part of the reason she did it. She was my only real friend. What am I going to do?"

Kim reached out and touched his arm, "Hey, if you want to talk, I am here."

"Thanks."

He looked toward the school offices and then back at Kim, "I have an idea. Let's get out of here, right now. I don't feel like sitting in an office talking to some counselor that doesn't know anything about me or what I am going through. And there is nothing they can say that would help anyway. I just want to go someplace quiet and talk with you."

Kim knew this was an extremely bad idea. If she agreed to leave with him, she would get in trouble for skipping school. But that was not the worst of it. She would be skipping out with the boyfriend of a girl that had just been found dead. Even if the police confirmed Marissa's death to be accidental, Kim knew enough about the police to know that, at this point, everything was being considered; including the possibility that any friends of Marissa might have had something to do with her death, and Keith would be on that list. In effect, he might be a person of interest and she would be helping him.

And what if the police came to the school to talk with Keith and he wasn't there? All logic told her to decline his invitation, walk him to the counselor's office, and go on about her business. Instead she pointed to a side door. "Okay, let's get out of here. I may regret this but the last thing you need today is to be here getting hounded about what happened. I'll smooth it over with my father later."

Her heart raced as they snuck out of the door and walked quickly to the student parking lot hoping no one would look out and spot them. When they reached her car, Keith thanked Kim. "Hey, I really appreciate what you're doing. Why don't we go to the Seattle Center? I'll treat you to a ride up the Space Needle and you can be back to school before lunch."

It was now eight forty-five. Kim knew she would already get in trouble for not taking Keith to the counselor, so she figured it couldn't be much worse to miss the entire morning. It was obvious to her that he needed support right now and, even if he wasn't the type of boy she would normally hang out with, he still needed someone to talk to. Besides, she felt in an odd way complemented that he would turn to her for help.

Kim drove a 2008 yellow Chevy Cobalt that she had paid for herself with money saved working part time as a receptionist at a local hair salon. The color of the car reflected her sunny personality and suited her appearance. At five feet three, blond haired and blue eyed, Kim was outgoing and always energetic. She was acutely aware of how odd the two must appear with Keith's scraggly black hair and weathered dark hoody in sharp contrast to her short blonde hair and bright spring dress.

As she thought more about her decision to leave with a boy she knew nothing about, she began to second guess the wisdom of agreeing to his request. After all, she didn't really know him other than their conversations in first period. Now, a girl he was seen with regularly was found dead a long way from her home and close to his. Maybe he was involved in whatever happened to her.

Kim pushed that last thought away as she drove along the waterfront toward the Seattle Center. She knew her father was meeting Reed for breakfast right about now and that their regular meeting place was in the

Market overlooking the waterfront. She prayed that her father would not look out of the restaurant windows and somehow spot her bright yellow car down below. Only after she arrived at the Seattle Center and pulled into a parking spot did she relax.

She turned the engine off, and Keith said his first words since they left the high school parking lot, "Thanks again. I know you don't know me that well, but I know enough about you to know you are someone I can trust."

She smiled, "I get it. Let's get out and walk."

Unbeknownst to the two teenagers, a non-descript black sedan had just parked a short distance away, its occupant taking keen interest in the tall scruffy boy in black jeans and hoody walking and talking with the petite brightly dressed girl.

After a minute the driver, a tall man in his late twenties wearing faded blue-jeans, black t-shirt, black jacket, and wrap-around sunglasses exited the vehicle and tailed the couple from a distance.

Kim and Keith crossed the street and passed under the monorail tracks that led into the Seattle Center grounds. The Cherry trees were in full bloom and the two walked side-by-side, a few feet apart, across a carpet of pink and white blossoms. They made their way up the slight incline to the Space Needle entrance unaware they were being followed. At the ticket window, Keith bought two tickets for the elevator ride to the observation deck. Then they walked a short distance to the elevator entrance and joined a family of tourists that talked excitedly about their plans for the day while they waited for the next lift. When the elevator arrived, a pert hostess invited everyone into the lift and asked if there were any out-of-towners in the group. The family of four answered in unison, "We're from Denver."

The hostess enthusiastically replied, "Wonderful! Welcome to Seattle. I'll give you a brief overview of the Space Needle and views as we ascend to the restaurant and observation levels."

She looked toward Keith and Kim, "And you three must be locals. Welcome to you too."

Kim and Keith looked around. They hadn't noticed the man wearing sunglasses enter the elevator and take up a position behind them.

The glassed-in elevator zipped up the outside of the tower's center support in less than sixty seconds, providing breathtaking views during its rapid ascent. The hostess concluded her talk as the elevator slowed to a stop and opened out to the restaurant level. The family exited to enjoy breakfast in the rotating restaurant leaving only the hostess, Kim, Keith, and the man.

When the elevator doors opened again, Kim and Keith walked over to a door leading to the outdoor observation deck that ringed the upper level of the Space Needle and provided a sweeping 360-degree view of the region. Up to this point their conversation had danced around the topic of Marissa, but now it appeared Keith was ready to broach the subject.

"It should never have happened. I thought we were working things out." He stuffed his hands into his pockets and leaned his head forward against the lookout glass.

Kim's mind raced. What did he mean? Did he just admit to killing Marissa? And what was she supposed to say now. She became nervous and moved slightly away.

Keith saw her move and turned quickly, "They are saying she might have committed suicide."

She stopped, "Didn't she?"

If he had killed Marissa, making it look like suicide would certainly be something a killer might have do.

"If she did, I might be responsible."

Kim was curious how he might be responsible for Marissa taking her own life but, before she could ask, he continued.

"But that is not what happened. I am sure of that. She would never do that."

Okay, Kim thought, he just threw out a good defense. Maybe he didn't kill her, but he might still have been involved. She didn't quite know how to phrase the next question that came into her head. She felt that she was here to console Keith, but she also wanted to figure out what may have happened over the weekend. She figured she had a little of her father and uncle's detective traits in her blood and threw caution to the wind.

"Keith, don't get mad at me for asking, but were you two doing drugs Saturday? Could she have overdosed or passed out after you were with her and driven into the water by accident?"

His face flushed red. "Absolutely not. I didn't even see her last weekend. Her parents were trying to stop us from seeing each other. I told you that before."

"Yes, but she has been pretty good at getting over here in the past, hasn't she?"

"She wasn't here." He repeated.

"Well, apparently she was." Kim blurted and immediately regretted it. "Sorry, that was a crappy thing to say."

Keith responded, "I don't know why Marissa was in West Seattle. You must believe me. I didn't have any idea that she was over here. And, by the way, I don't do drugs and I am pretty damn sure she didn't either."

Kim felt a pit in her stomach. This conversation was out of control and was not helping anyone. She turned and walked away. Keith turned and walked in the opposite direction and after ten minutes they met up again on the opposite side of the circular observation deck. By now both had settled down a bit and Keith continued. "I haven't seen Marissa in over a week, let alone last weekend. I texted her last week, but I didn't get any replies."

Kim said, "You said you two were working things out. What did you mean? Were you having a fight?"

She knew she was really stepping onto thin ice now.

The boy leaned his head back against the glass and said, "I can't talk about it."

He pulled his earphones and hoody back up over his head.

After several minutes of silence, Kim walked over to him, "Let's go back down and walk around the grounds for a while."

She turned toward the doors leading back inside the observation deck and he followed her to the elevator for the return trip to ground level.

They spent the balance of the morning walking the grounds and sitting by the round International Fountain, the mix of water spray and the scent of spring blossoms temporarily taking their minds off the accident. They didn't speak of Marissa any further.

On the far side of the fountain, the man from the elevator also enjoyed the setting as he sat on a bench and took notes on a small tablet resting on his lap.

Hitching

Becky made good time to Seattle only having to change rides once. A big rig driver named Paul gave her a lift from Coeur d'Alene to Ellensburg, Washington where he was stopping to pick up a load. The ride was mostly quiet, and the driver didn't ask any personal questions other than if she had accepted Jesus into her life. She said yes and showed him the cross that hung on her necklace. He seemed a nice man and she guessed that he picked her up knowing full well she might be a run-away and had intended to do a little missionary work. After she showed him the crucifix, he simply smiled and turned up the country station on his radio. The friendly truck driver let Becky off at a combined truck and auto filling station on the edge of Ellensburg where he wished her luck on her journey. He reminded her to let Jesus be her guide and smiled and waved as he pulled away.

She only had to wait about thirty minutes before her next ride showed up. It was a young woman named Julie, a recent graduate from Central Washington University in Ellensburg. Julie was in the process of moving back to the Seattle area and had stopped at the station to top up her gas tank before driving over Snoqualmie Pass to her parent's home in Bellevue. While Julie stood by the pump and waited for the nozzle to click off, she spotted Becky standing to the side of the parking lot holding a small cardboard sign with Seattle written on it in black felt pin. Julie typically wouldn't give a ride to a stranger, but the young girl holding the sign looked innocent enough and it would be nice to have company for the drive. When she finished paying for the gas, she walked over and invited Becky to join her. The young girl's face showed both gratitude and relief.

The girls drove the first several miles in silence until Julie asked Becky where she was from and why she was hitching a ride to Seattle. At first, Becky made up a story that she was from Spokane and was going to visit friends. She knew that Julie would see through the lie. She should have been in school and was obviously running away from something. Julie didn't challenge her or push for more information. She simply asked if Becky would like to listen to some music before she turned up the volume on the radio.

Fifteen minutes later, Becky decided that she needed to tell Julie what had happened to her the night before. Maybe the older girl could advise her on what to do next. She turned the radio volume down and looked over at Julie, "Sorry. I know that was rude, but I need to talk."

Julie could see that something was on the young girl's mind and said, "No problem. What do you want to talk about?"

Becky wasn't sure where to start. She had never had an older sister to go to for advice and now she was about to share something deeply personal and troubling with a stranger, but she couldn't keep it in, and she hoped the older girl could tell her what she should do now.

She started by telling about what a wonderful life she had growing up and how good her parents had been to her. She talked about their support for her goal of being an actress and how they had given her the self-confidence to chase her dreams. Then she shared how her father started having her undress for him several years ago and finished by telling what had occurred a few hours earlier and that she was running away. By the time she stopped talking both girls were crying, and Julie had to pull over to the freeway shoulder to regain her composure. She leaned over and held the shaking girl. "Oh honey, it will be okay." She knew her words must sound hollow and provided little consolation. Her own emotions were a mixture of sympathy and anger and she had no idea how to advise Becky or how she would have reacted had her own father ever done such a despicable thing to her. It was several minutes before she could regain her composure and speak again. "Is there someone in Seattle that you can stay with?"

Becky shook her head no.

Julie responded, "Then we need to find you a shelter when we get there."

Becky shook her head again. "No. When my parents realize I am gone my mother may think that I was abducted, but my father will know that I ran away. He is sharp and will guess that I went to Seattle. He will check the shelters and I can't risk that. You can just drop me off in town and I will make my way from there."

"Whatever you want, I will help however I can. But I am worried for you."

Becky looked over with teary eyes, "Hey, don't worry about me. I am a tough country girl and have camped out a lot. I'll just find a place to set up my tent and I'll be fine."

Julie thought on what Becky said about camping and responded, "You know, in Seattle you can find groups of tents with homeless people under practically every bridge or overpass, especially downtown. If you just want to set up your tent for a couple of days, you could probably do it fairly easily."

Becky's face brightened, "Okay. That sounds like a plan. We can look for a spot where there are just a few other tents and you can drop me off. I will figure out what to do from there. Thanks."

After that was decided, Julie changed the subject and the girls talked for the rest of the drive about theater and college. It turned out that Julie had also been in drama in high school and the two traded stories and laughed at each other's experiences. Becky did most of the talking and Julie let her, knowing it was probably the young girl's way of blocking out the events of the last day. The hour passed quickly, and they were still trading stories when they crossed the Lake Washington Bridge into Seattle. A short distance past the bridge, Julie took an exit that led to the International District.

She pulled in front of an area populated with an assortment of tents and tarps and stopped her car. "Are you sure you really want to do this?"

Becky looked a bit apprehensive.

Julie noticed and said, "You can still change your mind if you like. We can look for a regular shelter, or I can call my parents and tell them that I have a friend with me that needs a place to crash tonight. You can sleep on the couch."

Becky responded, "No. Thanks for the offer and maybe later but right now I just want to set up my tent and be by myself to lie down and think for a bit."

Julie reached out to a sticky-notes pad on her dashboard and pulled off a page before fumbling around the back-seat floor for a pen. She found a crayon and wrote her name and phone number on the pink square and handed it to Becky. "Good luck. If you need anything or want to talk again, give me a call. Really. I will help you if you need it."

Julie gave Becky another hug before the young girl opened the door and stepped out onto the sidewalk. After Becky retrieved her backpack and tent from the back seat, she shut the door, made a meek smile and waved goodbye to Julie. As Julie pulled away, Becky remembered that she only had ten dollars in her pocket and cursed herself for not thinking to ask Julie for spare change. She would get her tent set up, have a short rest, and then explore. Maybe she would even try her hand at panhandling. She had read that some panhandlers make fair money.

Mother's Trust

Kim decided to skip dance class on Monday and go straight home from school. She wondered if the counselors had called and told her parents about her unexcused absence that morning. When she arrived home, Michelle greeted her at the door. "Are you okay?"

Kim didn't immediately answer and instead searched her mother's eyes for a clue. Michelle could read her daughter's questioning look, "Yes, the school called this morning and I know you skipped out with Keith Martin. Your father was still out with Reed when they called so he doesn't know."

"Are you going to tell him?" Kim asked nervously.

Michelle put her arm around her daughter, "I don't think we need to worry him with that right now. Unless Keith told you something that is important to the case."

"No." Kim replied. "He just told me that he doesn't know what happened. He said that he didn't even know she was in Seattle on Saturday."

Kim took off her coat and sat down. Michelle could see that her daughter was under stress and said, "Hey, your dad is at the hardware store right now but should be back soon. Go change into something comfortable for dinner and we'll just keep this between us. Okay?"

Kim visibly relaxed, "Thanks mom."

Chapter 4

Sanctuary

Angela was in the kitchen Tuesday morning preparing for Terry and Michelle's visit that afternoon. It was early, and she was still in her green flannel pajamas as she stretched up on her toes to reach for a can of tomato paste on the top shelf of the pantry. At five feet four, this was a challenge. She knew that she could just grab a step stool from the closet, but it somehow seemed easier to grab the can en pointe than go for the stool.

One minute and two toe cramps later, she had the can of tomato paste in her hand and walked back across the hardwood floor to the butcher block preparation table. In the corner, a small television broadcast the morning news. The weather forecast called for early fog burning off by mid-morning with a sunny afternoon in the mid-40s.

Angela had decided that Spaghetti was the perfect meal for kicking back and relaxing with family that evening. They would start with a Caesar salad and homemade bread and then move on to Spaghetti with her own special meat sauce accompanied by a nice Cabernet Sauvignon from a local winery. She would top the meal off with Tiramisu and espressos. She began to prepare sauce from a family recipe, browning a couple of pounds of ground beef while she sliced several portabella mushrooms, a white onion and a handful of black olives. When the ground beef was sufficiently browned, she added the onion, olives, and mushrooms along with tomato paste, diced tomatoes, crushed garlic, and a potpourri of herbs and spices, and covered the mixture to simmer for the rest of the day.

As she wiped down the counter she looked out across the lake. The morning fog had lifted off the water and now the clouds hovered at treetop level creating the illusion of a large grey woolen blanket draped across the lake and held in place on the edges by the structures rimming the shoreline. The water was glass-smooth aside from the wakes of two large pleasure boats that cruised northward to the Ballard Locks on their way out to Puget Sound.

Satisfied that everything was in good shape for the dinner party, she retired to the bedroom and changed into her running gear. A morning run had been a regular part of her routine for years and she cherished the daily time alone with her thoughts as she ran the roads and paths around Lake Union. After stretching for a few minutes, Angela headed up the long floating dock to the shoreline and began her run. Today she would run the entire lake clockwise, setting off south towards Lake Union Park and then up the west side and over to Gasworks Park before continuing around the north end and back down the east side to their home. The six-mile run would take her a little over an hour. It didn't take more than a few hundred yards for Angela to find her rhythm and get into the zone. As she jogged, she thought of the fun they had over the years with Terry and Michelle and looked forward to an evening of friendship and laughter. She admitted to herself that she was also curious about the drowning at Alki and wondered if Terry would tell them anything that had not been in the news.

When she and Reed had lived in the Alki area, she would regularly jog from the Alki Point lighthouse along the beach and around to the boat launch ramp where she would turn around in the parking lot for the return run home. The run had always cleared her mind and she had never thought of it as dangerous, Now, it unsettled her to think that someone had died at the very same ramp. Reed had told her that the girl's death may not have been an accident and that made it even more disturbing.

Angela had always felt safe on her runs but now she thought about the possibility that someone had killed Marissa on her old jogging route and started to feel uncomfortable with her current run. Did someone murder that girl in West Seattle at random. Could they be looking for their next victim? Could she be a target as she ran alone around the lake?

She cringed and suddenly felt vulnerable and nauseous. At the next intersection she made a turn to abbreviate her run and return her to the sanctuary of her home.

Foul Play

Terry agreed to meet investigator Robert McManus on Beach Drive near the bathhouse at 0900 Tuesday morning. Even though it was Terry's day off, he was anxious to hear of any new details on the death of Marissa Archer. He was out of the house early and decided to drive past the boat ramp on his way to the meeting. It was not that he expected to spot something, he just wanted to see if driving by might trigger a memory of anything unusual that he may have seen on Sunday but hadn't recalled before.

He slowed as he passed the ramp on his way along Harbor Avenue, noting the sign that marked the entrance to the parking area. Few fishermen knew the proper name of the ramp and even fewer were aware that the ramp and adjacent viewpoint were named in honor of a Deputy Sheriff killed in the line of duty in the mid-1950's. In addition to being active in several community service groups, Deputy Don Armeni, like many in the community of West Seattle, had been an avid fisherman and in 1955 the ramp was given its current name, The Don Armeni Boat Ramp.

The drive by the ramp did not trigger any new memories and Terry continued along the shoreline drive to the public beach further along. Only a few beachcombers and joggers dotted the beach and jogging path today. It would be several more weeks before crowds of sun worshipers and tourists flooded the popular destination on a daily basis.

As he approached the Alki bathhouse, Terry spotted several open parking spaces and an unmarked police vehicle, a dark blue Ford Interceptor SUV, parked across from the local fish and chips shop. Terry pulled in and turned off his headlights. By the time he had pushed the shift lever into park and set the brake on his car, Investigator Robert McManus was already out of the Interceptor and walking back to greet him. Terry guessed that Robert was in his mid to late thirties. At six feet five, the athletically built McManus was an imposing figure. The investigator knew that his appearance could be used to his advantage and he consciously enhanced his intimidating look by wearing tailored suits that accentuated his muscular build. While the result was unnerving to suspects, Robert also enjoyed effect that his build and well-tailored outfits had on women. He would brag to Terry that he could use his size and looks to put fear into the soul of a suspect one minute and then charm the pants off a beautiful woman the next.

Terry and Robert knew each other well and would often get together both on and off the job. Their friendship started shortly after Robert joined the department. Robert heard that Terry owned a classic 1955 Harley-Davidson FLE Panhead police motorcycle and, being a bike enthusiast himself, looked Terry up to ask if he could see the bike. Robert owned a 1985 Harley and the two of them immediately struck up a relationship and had taken several rides together over the years.

"Good morning Terry. Why don't you come on up to my car? It's roomier."

Without waiting for Terry to answer, Robert turned and walked away. Terry knew Robert wasn't trying to be rude. He was simply all business when he was on the clock and in public. Once they were in the SUV Robert dropped the stern facade.

"Hey buddy." He smiled and patted Terry on the arm, "How's it going? And how is Michelle?"

Terry answered, "Michelle's great. I think the whole boat launch thing has her bit upset, what with the girl being Kim's age and all, but I have to admit, it is a bit too close to home for me too."

"And Kim?"

"I don't know. She stayed home from dance last night and she never does that. I think this is the first time someone she has known, even if it is only through a classmate, has died. I remember when a boy I knew at school was killed in a car crash during our senior year. A drunk driver crossed the center line on California Avenue and hit him head on. Suddenly, death became real and it was a shock. Unfortunately, bad shit happens. I think she will be okay. It is just one of life's tough lessons."

Robert put his car into gear and pulled away from the curb,

"Terry," He paused a moment. "I'd like to ask you for some help. You've lived here your whole life and know this community as well as anyone. Plus, you have a daughter at high school. I would like you to use your connections in the neighborhood to help us turn something up."

45

Terry became curious, "I thought this was a case of suicide or overdose. What I am looking for?"

"It might be more. We just don't know. We plan to release some of the autopsy information later today but are withholding portions for reasons that will be obvious when you read the report. It goes without saying; you can't share this with anyone."

Robert handed Terry an unmarked manila envelope containing several pages of typed notes. "This is just my summary of the full report, but it has all of the pertinent information."

Terry pulled the report out of the envelope and began reading. The body of a seventeen-year-old girl had been found in her submerged car. The examination for water in her lungs showed none indicating that she was probably dead before the car entered the water. The coroner put the time of death sometime around noon on Saturday, so the car with the body inside may have been left at the ramp several hours after her death. A fresh needle mark was found on the girl's left arm. Some slight bruising was evident around her right eye. Initial toxicology tests determined there was no alcohol in her system but detected traces of opioids. It would take a few more days to get the final toxicology report and know exactly what was in her system.

Terry looked over at Robert, "So it was a drug overdose after all."

McManus pointed at the notes on Terry's lap, "Keep reading. It gets more interesting."

Terry flipped another page. After the external examination, the coroner performed a dissection. Examination of the chest, abdominal and pelvic organs showed no abnormalities. The examination of the brain indicated that an object had entered the frontal lobe and severed an artery resulting in a fatal brain hemorrhage. No object was found in the brain and the coroner re-examined the head to find an entry point.

"She was shot?"

"Oh no. That would be too easy. Read on."

Robert turned off Beach Drive and wound up a hill, climbing above the low fog that clung to the beachfront and up into the bright morning sun that would burn off the lingering fog on the water by noon. The sunlight reflected off the white paper and Terry squinted as he continued reading. Further examination by the coroner detected a small entry point in the upper left corner of the victim's right eye socket where a sharp object had pierced her head. That entry point lined up with the damaged area of the brain.

"My god," Terry exclaimed. "She was stabbed in the eye?"

Robert looked over. "That's what it looks like. Maybe she and someone else were so high they had no idea what they were doing. Seems weird as shit to me but, then again, she had old cuts on her arms indicating she was probably into self-mutilation."

Terry, "Do you think she may have been high and jammed something into her own eye?"

"I don't know about that, but I do know that there was nothing found in the car that could have caused the wound. There was also no syringe in the car. She was with someone else when she died, and they dumped her body at the ramp. Maybe she stabbed herself. Maybe someone did it to her. I don't know, but there is someone out there who does."

Terry felt nauseous as he pictured the young woman being subjected to torture by someone stabbing a pick into her head. He had seen his share of homicides over the years but nothing like this. He was visibly shaken, and Robert gave him a few minutes to absorb the news and calm down.

Robert turned onto another arterial that led back down to the beach and Terry's parked car. Their meeting was almost over, but Robert had one more thing to cover with Terry and wanted to arrive at the parking spot in time to finish the conversation but with no additional time for extra talk or second thoughts on Terry's part.

He parked the car, turned to Terry and became even more serious. "We are not making public the part about stab to the brain. At this point only the killer, the coroner, the investigators on the case, and now you, know all the facts. As I said, I am asking for your help. You are free to share this with your brother, but tell him it goes no further. Maybe his convoluted mind can turn something up."

Terry still felt queasy but replied, "It just so happens, Michelle and I are going over to Reed and Angela's later today for dinner. I'll share this and turn him loose."

Terry started to open the door and Robert stopped him, "I have another favor to ask."

Terry pulled the door closed and Robert continued, "Did you know that your daughter skipped out of school yesterday morning and spent that time with Keith Martin, a good friend of the victim? And someone that just so happens to live just up the hill from where she died?"

Terry looked surprised, "No. She didn't say anything. Why?"

"When we talked with Marissa's father on Sunday, he pointed a suspicious finger at a West Seattle boy that Marissa has been hanging around with for the past few months. We visited Keith that evening, and he seemed genuinely distressed by Marissa's death, but we decided to put him under surveillance and track his movements just to be sure."

Robert paused and then continued, "Yesterday, one of our investigators observed Keith and Kim leaving the high school in Kim's car shortly after school started. He followed them to the Seattle Center where the two spent a couple of hours wandering around and talking. Around lunch time, Kim drove back to school with Keith. She returned to the school building and he walked home from her car."

He continued, "We decided to pick him up at his house and take him in for questioning, but the interview was fruitless. According to him, he didn't know Marissa was in West Seattle last weekend. We checked phone logs and we know he called her Saturday morning. When we confronted him, he said they talked briefly but maintained that they did not see each other."

"I don't trust him. I think he knows something he isn't sharing with the police. And I think he may have shared something with your daughter that can help us to either point the finger at him or prove his innocence."

Terry finally had an opportunity to speak, "So, you want me to ask her about their meeting? No problem, I can do that. But I am a little pissed off that she didn't share that with me already. I'll talk with her tonight."

Robert held his hand up, "No. I don't want you to confront her about it."

He hesitated before continuing and looked Terry in the eye, "Actually, I would like you to lay back and let them talk. It appears that Keith trusts your daughter and I hope he will ask her to talk with him again."

One last hesitation and then Robert asked, "With your permission, I would like to place a bug in her car. With luck, Kim and Keith will meet again, and we will be able to listen in and learn more."

Terry was shocked, "What are you saying Robert? The boy may be involved in the death of Marissa and you want me to put my daughter in danger's way to get information for you. Oh, and on top of that, bug my own daughter's car without telling her so investigators can spy on her activities. Sorry friend, but you are asking way too much."

"Terry, we have Keith under constant watch. There is always an armed investigator nearby. There is no way he can harm Kim. As far as the bug, we will not spy on your daughter. It will only be listened to when Keith is in the car with her. The car title is still in your name, so we don't need a warrant with your permission. The risk is nil and, if he confides in her, we may get the break we need."

"Jesus Robert. Think about what you are asking. You don't have a wife and children. I don't think you realize"

Robert cut him off, "I do realize, and I care about Kim too. Look, I am not asking you to do anything that would put her in danger. Just don't discourage her from seeing Keith should the topic come up and let things take their course. Who knows, maybe he won't even want to talk with her again."

Terry felt a pit in his stomach. "Promise you won't let anything happen to her."

"You know I would never let anything happen to Kim. Besides, there is a good chance that Keith didn't have anything to do with Marissa's death anyway. We just need to check everything out. Give me a call this evening after Kim has gone to bed and I will send someone over to plant the bug."

Robert reached over and shook Terry's hand, "Thanks again. It will be okay. You have my word."

Terry stepped out and shut the SUV door and Robert pulled away leaving him standing next to his car staring out over the water into a thick fog. He remembered when the old lighthouse sounded its foghorn on days like this. The tower's beacon still attempted to pierce the thick grey that masks boats and land from each other, but the horn had been stilled since 1984. Terry missed the foghorn. He had grown up only two

49

blocks from the lighthouse and always found the tone to be comforting. He wished it was sounding right now to give him some comfort.

Grips

As he drove home, Terry's mind wandered, and he almost ran up onto a three wheeled motorcycle that was cruising along the avenue at no more than twenty miles an hour. He was about to honk and give the rider a piece of his mind when he recognized the bike and rider. It was Grips. Grips was practically an institution around Alki and had been riding the beach route for over forty years.

Grips got his nickname from the red, white and blue tasseled grips that adorned every bike he owned over the years. The biker had been honorably discharged from the Navy during the Vietnam War after being injured in a carrier deck accident that mangled his left arm. Despite the accident, Grips was unapologetically patriotic and easy to spot on his red, white and blue painted Harley. He wore a weathered black leather jacket that was embroidered with a large American Flag on the back and he sported a stringy grey ponytail that waved in the wind from under a flat-black half-shell helmet. In the early years Grips rode choppers with long front forks and high handlebars but about ten years ago he switched to a three-wheeler.

Terry pulled out around the bike and waved as he passed. Grips waved back and flashed a big smile, recognizing Terry through the car's side window. Terry was thinking about the changes the old biker must have seen in the area over all the years he had cruised up and down the beach.

Everyone knew that Grips observed everything and never missed anything. Most evenings, he could be found in one of the local bars for an hour or two telling stories of the bizarre things he had seen over the past four decades. Most of them had to do with young couples having sex on the beach or in their cars, but Grips told the stories with such flair that he seemed less like a voyeur and more like someone who just liked to laugh at the absurdities of life.

Then it hit Terry like a thunderbolt. Perhaps Grips had seen something Sunday morning at the boat launch. It was a long shot that the old man would be out so early in the morning but, what the hell, it was worth a try. He knew that Grips didn't watch much television, preferring to spend the late evenings sitting in the darkened living room of his beachside bungalow following the shipping traffic through an old pair of high-powered binoculars. It was possible that he might not have heard about the accident at the launch ramp yet. Terry pulled over several blocks ahead of Grips and got out of his car.

A few minutes later the biker approached, and Terry waved him over to the curb. Grips smiled and steered his three-wheeler up to within a foot of Terry before stopping and shutting the engine down.

"Hey young punk. What's up?"

"Not much old fart. What's up with you?"

Grips laughed, "Same ol, same ol. Just livin the life."

Grips walked up to Terry and gave him a strong handshake. "When you going to bring your ride down and cruise with me?"

Terry had cruised around the beach several times with Grips, typically in the middle of summer, and the two made quite a sight riding together.

"Give me a few more weeks old man, when it's warmer and the sightseeing is better. Then I'll bring my shiny baby down."

Terry smiled and continued, "Right now, I am hoping you can help me."

Grips cocked his head, "You need help from an old stoner like me. What has Seattle's finest come down to?"

Terry drew closer to Grips and lowered his voice, "Grips, this is some serious stuff. Did you hear about the girl that was found dead at the boat launch?"

Grips replied, "A girl was found dead at the launch? No. When did that happen?"

Terry answered, "Sunday morning. Found in her car submerged at the base of the ramp."

Grips shook his head back and forth, "What the hell is this world coming to? What happened?"

"That is what we're trying to find out. I was hoping maybe you had been cruising by the launch that morning. I know your eagle eyes never miss anything and if you had been over that way you might remember something."

Grips shrugged, "Sorry man. I've been out cruisin the Olympic Peninsula since last Saturday. Just got back into town last night. Haven't even had time to catch up on the news. Shit, a young girl died at the ramp. Man, that just isn't right. I wish I could help."

Terry spoke back up, "Maybe you still can. There is a good chance there was foul play in her death. Whoever was involved might be a local or, if not, may have talked to a local."

"You hang out a lot and hear all the scuttlebutt. Keep your ears out for anything that might be pertinent. That would be a help. And keep your eyes out for any unusual activities in the area. Maybe the person or people that did this will come back and give themselves away."

Grips smiled again, "Yes sir. Anything I can do. This country is going to hell in a hand basket. It would be my pleasure to catch any bastards that are taking it there."

Terry thanked Grips and shook his hand again.

Grips fired up the trike and shouted over the rumble, "Got to go now. Need to do some shopping to restock my medicine cabinet." He smiled a toothy grin and held his hand up to his lips like he was smoking some weed, then waved as he pulled back out onto the avenue.

School Talk

At the high school on Tuesday, talk of the incident at Alki continued to dominate the halls. The morning news broadcasts had again led with the story and the police where now saying that the girl had not drowned but instead had been dead before entering the water and there were suggestions of foul-play. They were now considering the case a possible homicide.

When Kim entered her chemistry classroom Mr. Forest greeted her with a somewhat disapproving look.

"I hope you have a good excuse for not making it to the counselor's office with Keith yesterday."

Kim shrugged "I think I had a good reason, but I am sure no one else will agree so it doesn't really matter does it."

Mr. Forest shook his head. "Be careful Kim. You are a good kid. This is not like you."

Kim walked back to her place and was immediately set upon by her classmates. "What did Keith say? Was he with Marissa on Saturday? Does he know how she died?"

The whole day continued along the same line and Kim longed for the end of the day and the peace of her home and bedroom. Keith never showed up at school that day and Kim began to worry about him. It was clear that he would be a potential suspect in Marissa's death and even though she didn't think he was capable harming anyone, it still gave her pause. Her parents were spending the evening with Reed and Angela and she looked forward to having the house to herself and her thoughts.

Flashbacks

Becky woke up early Tuesday. She had spent the night tossing in her sleeping bag but not because it was uncomfortable. In fact, she was used to camping out and felt quite cozy and safe in her down filled cocoon. The night had been restless because of the continuous flashbacks to Sunday night. Her father had always been there for her. Whenever she was hurt or upset, she could go to him and he knew exactly what to say to make her feel better. He had been her rock, her foundation. Now, after Sunday night, he was as good as dead to her. In fact, it was worse than that. If he had died in an accident or for medical reasons, she would have lost her father but had only good memories of him. But now, all the good times were overshadowed by the memory of his actions. She could still smell his bourbon-tainted breath and feel his groping hands and the pain of forcible entry that night while he had muffled her screams with her pillow so her mother would not hear.

Before Sunday, Becky had fantasized about her first time. It would be a special evening and she and her lover would gently touch each other from head to toe, kissing every inch of the other's body until they finally made love. Now, the thought of being touched made her sick and she did not know if she could ever stand to be intimate with anyone.

Then, another thought, darker, more sinister, pushed into her head. How could her mother not have known about her father's behavior after all this time? How could she have been only a few feet down the hall and never woken to question where her husband was? Did she hear Becky's muffled cries on Sunday and do nothing?

Becky became physically sick and pushed her head outside of the tent to throw up. When she had nothing left to throw up, she continued to dry heave, and sobbed uncontrollably. For the first time in her life, Becky could not imagine a future worth living and she considered taking her own life.

Reunion

Angela looked like a different person from the one in black Isotherm tights and top running around the lake earlier. She now wore a comfortable pair of rolled-up olive chinos and a faded grey REI Co-Op t-shirt under an open green and tan plaid flannel shirt that matched her hazel green eyes. With her auburn hair and fair freckled skin, there was no denying her Irish heritage. While Reed was selecting a bottle of Cabernet from the wine rack, Angela busied herself setting the table. This was a casual meal, so preparations had been simple. Before dinner, she and Michelle would enjoy some wine in the living room and make plans for the high school reunion while their husbands took the kayaks out on the lake. Then they all would gather at the dining table for dinner.

At four o'clock sharp the brass doorbell in the front hallway announced the arrival of Terry and Michelle to the tune of the Westminster chimes. Angela answered the door and the aroma of garlic and spices encircled the two guests as they entered the Grey Kraken.

"Let me guess." Terry grinned, "Spaghetti with your famous meat sauce."

Angela gave Terry a big hug. "Wow Officer Carver, you should be an investigator."

"I don't think so." Michelle hugged Angela, "He couldn't even find his car keys when we headed out. And your spaghetti is our favorite. All the way over he kept on about how he hoped you made it today."

Terry added, "I just don't understand how spaghetti is the signature dish of a fine cook of Irish descent."

"Actually, I am an Irish, Scottish mix."

"And that makes her a Celtic mutt." Reed popped around the corner from the other room.

"And you can hush up!" She replied and turned back to Terry "Anyway, let's remember that over the years I have made you many a fine British meal and you have never been too appreciative. There was my Sheppard's Pie. You said it had too many potatoes. My corned beef and cabbage. You said it could have done without the cabbage. My steak and kidney pie. You just suggested I simply not serve that again. And the haggis. You wouldn't even taste it. But you always love my spaghetti. So that is what you get."

"And I am thankful for that." Terry laughed as he looked around and asked, "Where are the kids?"

Angela pointed upstairs, "They're being unsociable right now, but I am sure they will be down later."

Reed and Angela had two large blue British Shorthair cats, the breed that inspired the illustrations of the Cheshire cat in Lewis Carroll's Alice's Adventures in Wonderland. They were named Rainier and Baker and could be found most often sitting on the windowsills keenly watching the boats passing by. They were content to ignore the group for now, but most assuredly would be down later to get some attention.

Angela opened the first bottle of wine and poured two glasses for the ladies while Terry made himself at home by taking a bottle opener out of a drawer and popping open two beers from a local microbrew.

He handed one to Reed and toasted, "To old friends and relatives."

"Not old." Angela chimed. "To longtime friends and relatives."

"Okay, to longtime friends and relatives." he corrected.

Reed smirked and said in a stage whisper, "I think the 30th reunion is getting to the old lady."

"Don't even start." Angela sneered.

Terry looked at Reed, "I think it's time to hit the kayaks,"

Reed agreed and they took their bottles out to the deck where they unstrapped two kayaks from a rack that hung on the side of the floating house and set them into the water. After a couple more sips of beer, they settled into the rocking boats and pushed off from the deck. The water was smooth, and it only took a few minutes to glide to the other side of the lake where the two could look to the south and see the top of Mt. Rainier behind the downtown skyline. The snowcapped peak was beginning to turn a tinge of pink as the evening sun began its decent behind the distant Olympic mountain range. It made Reed think of the times he had enjoyed the last ski runs of the day on the upper slopes of the Cascades when they were bathed in the red alpenglow of day's end. He thought that was as close as he could imagine to being in heaven.

Terry paddled over to Reed and snapped him out of his daze, "Hey Reed, I need to share some new information on the Alki incident with you before Michelle and I leave. I'll race you back and we can talk on the deck for a few minutes before dinner."

Reed started paddling as soon as he heard the word race and pulled away quickly before Terry could react, yelling back over his shoulder, "You're on. Last one there buys."

The light was starting to fade as the two pulled up to the Grey Kraken and tied off the kayaks. Hearing the men arrive, Angela pulled two beers from the refrigerator and met them out on the deck. "Here you go boys. You can relax a few minutes while Michelle and I finish preparing dinner.

Reed pulled two Adirondack chairs away from the wall and sat down. "Okay, I am all ears."

Terry took a long pull on his beer, "I spoke with Robert McManus this morning. They have more results from the autopsy and this thing is getting very messy."

Reed responded, "Messier than cuts, drugs and assault."

"Yes." Terry took an even longer pull. "Here is what they have. It is so unusual; they won't release it all to the public."

Terry told Reed about the findings including the needle mark and scars from cut marks on Marissa's arms. He told him about the bruising around the eyes and traces of opioids in her blood. Reed knew about the marks and bruising, but the opioids were new.

"So, Marissa injected herself with heroin or some other drug and overdosed after all?"

"She may have had an injection of heroin, but that isn't what killed her."

Terry went on to tell Reed about the brain damage. Reed whistled, "Can this get any more convoluted?"

"Hell, you wouldn't think so, but you never know. One more thing. The investigators checked the call list from Marissa's boyfriend's phone, and he talked with her Saturday morning. He may have been the last person to talk to her and could be involved."

Reed, "Well that would tie things up nicely."

"It would, but there is not enough evidence to arrest him right now. Also, he was spotted talking with Kim and now Robert wants to have stakeouts on Keith and Kim to see if he shares anything of importance with her while I am supposed to stand on the sideline and not interfere. I am counting on you brother."

Reed whistled, "You have my word." Then he thought to himself, 'I hate pressure. This case is not going to be so much fun after all'

Reed and Terry walked into the house to join the girls.

"Can you believe it has been thirty years?" Angela said to Michelle as she broke bundles of stiff raw noodles into a pot of boiling water.

Michelle responded, "Yes and no. I mean, it seems like just yesterday that we were hanging out at the beach and cruising around in guys' cars, but then I think about all that has happened over the years and it seems like forever. I think it will be fun to see everyone at the reunion."

Breaking in on the conversation, Terry gave his input. "You know, it's no secret I don't exactly look forward to these things, but once every ten years is just about what I can handle."

Reed added, "I'm with you. I was not into socializing in high school and I don't have a strong desire to do so now. But, then again, it is kind of fun to just to sit back and see how everyone has turned out."

Reed and Terry returned to the living room while the women stayed in the kitchen and talked about their memories of how much better the area had seemed thirty years ago.

"My God, I have become my mother." Angela shouted as she remembered when her mother had gone to her own 30th reunion and bored her stiff reminiscing about the good old days. How old she had thought her mom was at the time and now she was the same age, saying the same things. Angela still felt young inside and realized for the first time that her mom probably had too, and she thought how unfortunate it is that we don't see our parents as they see themselves when we are growing up.

When the spaghetti noodles were ready, Angela drained them in a colander and divided the steaming pasta onto four plates. Then she ladled a generous amount of thick spaghetti sauce onto each and placed them on the table. Everyone sat down and hardly a word was spoken as the group enjoyed the spaghetti and fresh baked bread.

After dinner, the couples retired to the great room where the Space Needle and twinkling city lights were on full display through the tall floor to ceiling windows. Angela lit the fire and the girls sat on overstuffed pillows and paged through some of their old yearbooks. Across the room, Reed sat down on a couch while Terry made himself at home and went back to the refrigerator to retrieve a beer for Reed and a soda for himself.

"You girls want anything while I'm here?"

"Be a dear and bring us a couple glasses of Bailey's." Angela responded, already knowing that Michelle would go for the smooth desert drink.

After the girls had been served, Terry joined Reed on the couch to talk more about the case. Neither was concerned about the girls overhearing. They were too wrapped up in the yearbooks, laughing deliriously every few seconds.

"I can't believe you actually dated that guy." Michelle was laughing. Reed called across, "You must be talking about Bob. He was such a nerd. I never understood what Angela saw in him.

This triggered the two women to laugh so hard that Angela snorted loudly as Michelle fell over backward off the large corduroy pillow. "You idiot, we are looking at a picture of you. You really looked like a capital D O R K, dork."

"Hey, that was a good look for the times." Reed decided maybe it was better not to join the girls' conversation just now and he turned his attention back to Terry.

When the two women had recovered their composure, Angela pulled out an old copy of their school newspaper, the Chinook, from between the pages of one of the yearbooks. "I remember working on this like it was yesterday." She held it up for Michelle.

"I remember that issue. It was the annual alumni issue and you wrote an article on all of the famous people that had graduated from West Seattle High." Michelle took the paper and opened it to the article that Angela had written. It was accompanied by photos of several famous West Seattle alumni, most local but some nationally recognized.

"I had forgotten how many well-known people attended our school. My favorite was Ivar Hagland. What would Seattle be without Ivar's Fish and Chips?"

Angela said "Francis Farmer is still my favorite. When I was doing the article on famous alumni, I did some background research on her. The more I learned about her career and life, the more I became obsessed with her."

Angela glanced at the article and continued. "When she was a junior at West Seattle High in 1931, she made headlines by winning a creative writing contest. Her essay, entitled 'God Dies', received national press attention for its controversial theme and message. After graduating from high school, she studied acting at the University of Washington and later she went on to become a successful actress in Hollywood."

"Wasn't there something about her being insane too?" Michelle asked

"I didn't put it in the school paper article, but she had a reputation for being emotionally unstable and over the years was institutionalized several times. She wasn't insane, whatever that means anyway, she was just an emotional young woman with ideas that didn't suit the times. Her own mother had her committed. There were stories that she eventually received a lobotomy at the Washington State Hospital in Steilacoom but those have been debunked, though she was most likely submitted to other treatments such as electroshock. She continued acting after leaving psychiatric care, though her career never recovered. It was all rather sad."

Reed heard that last portion of the girls' conversation and spoke up. "Hey, does anyone want a bottle of beer or anything?"

"What triggered that?" Angela and Michelle both looked at him quizzically. They were still enjoying their Bailey's, their glasses only about half empty.

Then Angela saw the sparkle in his eyes and knew something was up.

"Well, to paraphrase Tom Waits, I'd rather have a bottle in front of me than a frontal lobotomy."

"You are one sick puppy Mr. Carver." Terry groaned. "I think it's about time for us to head out. I need some rest before I go on shift."

Michelle and Angela finished their drinks and they all got up and walked to the front door where Reed retrieved Terry's and Michelle's jackets.

Michelle and Angela gave each other a big hug before they all stepped outside. As Michelle and Terry walked up the dock Michelle called back to Angela. "Don't forget to give me a call later this week so we can set a time for you guys to come over. Thanks again for the great evening."

Back in the houseboat Reed flopped onto the couch and Rainier and Baker both climbed onto his chest purring loudly. Angela sat back onto the pillow by the fireplace and stacked the yearbooks next to her, "I couldn't really hear but it sounded like Terry shared some information on the Alki case. Did he say anything interesting?"

Reed knew anything he told Angela would absolutely go no further and shared what Terry had told him. When he had finished, she asked, "What do you make of it? Do you think the girl's boyfriend was involved?"

He shrugged, "I don't know. Kim told Terry that Keith and Marissa were close friends and that Keith is devastated by her death. But then, he could just be a good actor. If you had killed your girlfriend, wouldn't you try to act shocked to throw people off? I am not convinced that he doesn't have something to do with this."

Chapter 5

Trust

Keith returned to school on Wednesday and Kim questioned his absence the prior day. He explained that he just hadn't been ready to face people yet and had spent the day at home. He still looked disheveled and Kim had mixed emotions about his innocence now with the news that the police suspected foul play.

Unlike Monday and Tuesday, the other students were not so aggressive with their questions, preferring instead to whisper in suspicious undertones about Kim and Keith. Kim felt like she was becoming guilty by association.

At the end of the class period Keith said, "Kim, I need to talk to you during lunch. You're the only person I can trust."

Kim hesitated and Keith repeated the request in a more desperate tone. A loud buzz from speakers spaced down the hall walls told them that they were late for second period. The two only shared one common class so Kim had to make a snap decision before they headed in opposite directions.

"Okay, I'll meet you at lunch. But no skipping school again. I don't need the trouble. Okay?"

"Okay. See you then." The halls were almost empty as Kim ran in one direction and Keith slowly moved in the other.

At her desk Kim could not concentrate on today's lecture. As the history teacher droned on in the background about manifest destiny, the male instructor's low monotone voice was displaced with a louder inner voice asking relentless questions about Marissa's death and Keith's potential involvement. Was he innocent as she wanted to believe? And why had he suddenly befriended her? Could he just be using her because of her father? But that didn't make sense either. If you were guilty of something, why would you get involved with the daughter of a policeman?

Kim fidgeted at her desk. She knew people were already talking about her and Keith and the rumors of her being his friend. 'Great!' She thought. 'Now my reputation will be shot to hell.'

On the other hand, she had never really liked being stereotyped as a super straight student. That and being the daughter of a policeman had scratched her from the invitation list of more than one party. Maybe a little mystery about her would liven up her life a bit.

At lunch break Kim made her way to the grassy courtyard outside of the lunchroom. The area was dotted with picnic tables and students enjoying the spring sun. The temperature was a little on the cool side and the air still held a residual moisture from the morning fog that had burned off earlier.

Most of the tables were occupied by groups of students dressed in a bright collage of sweatshirts and light spring jackets. Kim walked over to the one table that held a single lone figure dressed all in black. As she approached Keith, she could feel the stares of other students burning in her back. Even Keith's circle of friends appeared to have deserted him.

"Thanks for coming." He said as she approached the table.

Kim sat down on the wooden bench opposite Keith and studied his face for a minute. "I don't know why you need to talk with me. What about your other friends?"

"Nobody wants to talk to me right now, including the group I thought were my friends. You may be the only person that doesn't suspect me. Plus, I think I can trust you."

Kim turned to observe the other kids in the courtyard staring at the two of them and wondered what she had gotten herself into. What started out as a simple act of trying to console someone had now attached her to a person suspected in a death and, by association, seemed to also make her suspect in her classmates' minds.

As Kim and Keith sat during the lunch break it became evident to her that Keith didn't really have anything to say. He kept repeating how badly he felt about Marissa and that he had nothing to do with it and begged Kim to believe him. As he talked, he kept his hand on a black leather backpack on the bench next to him as though it held something valuable.

Keith kept glancing down at the pack as though he was trying to decide something. Kim considered the possibility the he was truly crazy and might have a gun. He might even be planning to fire into the students gathered in the courtyard.

Keith saw the fear on Kim's face. "Don't worry. I just want to give you something to protect, but not here. Not in front of everyone. Meet me after school. Okay?"

Kim agreed, once again questioning the wisdom of her actions to herself.

Panhandling

Becky spent the better part of Tuesday walking around downtown Seattle and talking with other young people that were either panhandling or just hanging out. At first, she felt awkward and out of place but soon learned they were like her, simply people that came from bad situations and ended up on the streets. They told her where to find a local mission that served free hot meals and where the local shelters were located. She would avail herself of the free meals but was still not comfortable going into a shelter. They also told her about the best streets and tourist locations to panhandle and she decided to spend her Wednesday wandering around the Pike Place Market and trying her luck at asking for spare change. It might be awkward and humiliating at first, but she would tap into her acting skills and pretend she was someone else.

At the end of her first day of panhandling, Becky was surprised that she had collected a reasonable amount of money. Aside from two awkward instances when men offered her money for sex, the day had gone better than she expected, and she knew she would be able to survive for a few days living this way.

She also knew that, at some point soon, she would need to contact one of her relatives and ask for help. She had an aunt in Portland that had a level head and had always been there for her when she needed advice. Becky could trust her not to go straight to the police or her parents, but she was not quite ready to call yet. She still needed more time to herself to sort things out and decided that she would call on Saturday.

If she needed help or someone to talk with before then she could call the girl that gave her the lift from Ellensburg. She reached into her jeans and fished out the crayon note with Julie's phone number. Satisfied she had not lost it, she pushed the folded paper square back, deep into the front pocket.

Planning
Several miles away.

"Do you think we are in the clear."

"I'm not so sure. The police talked to me and I told them what you and I agreed to. The lead investigator is Robert McManus. He seems sharp and makes me nervous."

The older man remained calm. "Well, you just stick to the plan and we will both get past this. Plus, I have an idea to lead them further off track. After Friday, we'll be in the clear."

"What idea? What are you up to now?"

"Don't worry. I'll tell you tomorrow. Saturday we will be off the radar and can carry on like before."

Blades
After school, Keith was waiting at Kim's car. Kim did not know it, but Keith had skipped school after lunch and had only returned in time to meet her in the school parking lot.

Even without that knowledge, she was uncomfortable and said, "I don't think I should be driving you around anymore. Let's just talk here."

She opened the driver side door and hit the unlock button for the passenger door.

Keith got into the car and sat motionless with the black backpack in his lap, arms wrapped around it tightly. "I need to you to take some things."

He unzipped the top of the pack and continued, "They belonged to Marissa. If the police find them at my house they won't understand."

Across the parking lot an undercover officer watched the car through binoculars as he listened to their bugged conversation through his earpiece. Keith pulled out a small brown lunch bag from the pack and the investigator noted how clear the sound was. The latest bugs were exceptionally sensitive, and he could identify the sound of rustling paper followed by Kim's voice, "Before I take anything, you have to tell me what's in the bag and what you want me to do with it."

Keith answered, "Just hide it. Or dump it somewhere no one will find it. It just can't be found with me. Nobody will ever suspect you."

He set the bag on the console and opened the top.

Kim tilted the crumpled bag and looked in. "What is this? My god Keith." At the bottom of the bag was an assortment of razor blades tinged with dried blood, a scalpel, and a dissection pick that she recognized from biology class, also with dried blood on the tip. Kim stared at Keith, her breaths coming fast and a wave of sickness washing over her, and he reached across to grab her arm.

She dropped the bag, spilling the contents, and grabbed the handle of her door swinging it open madly. It made a loud crunching noise as it slammed into the car in the next spot and she leapt out and ran. The parking lot was mostly empty now, but she still bumped roughly into several parked cars as she dodged her way to where, she wasn't sure. She just needed to get away. Gaining on her, Keith kept calling for her to stop and listen.

The undercover investigator heard the interchange and was already out of his car and moving on a path to intercept the boy as the two teenagers ran towards the exit of the parking lot. Suddenly Kim stopped and turned toward Keith. The investigator stopped a distance away, hand on his gun inside his jacket, deciding to watch and see how the situation played out. He was an expert shot and, if the boy made any sort of harmful move toward the girl, he could take him out.

Not quite sure what compelled her to stop running, Kim waited as Keith came up panting.

Between gasps for air he said "It's not what it looks like. I never hurt Marissa. I was trying to help her."

She shouted, "What, by being into S & M?" She looked around to see if anyone else was in the lot and could hear them. Only a man in a black jacket was walking near the parking lot exit, too old to be a student and too scruffy to be a teacher. He was probably just somebody from the neighborhood taking a shortcut across the school parking lot.

"No! That's exactly what the police will think if they find these. That's why I need your help."

Kim took a moment to catch her breath. She really wanted to believe that Keith would never hurt Marissa and decided to listen to his explanation. She would just keep her guard up and make sure she was in a position to run if he made any threatening moves.

"Well, you haven't attacked me yet and you probably won't right here in the middle of the parking lot so, go ahead, explain just what that bag is and what you and Marissa were into."

The investigator watched as the boy and girl stopped running and stood in an open space apparently talking calmly. He cursed that they were not in the car where he could hear their conversation, but he decided not to interfere. He knew the backup plan was to get Kim to tell her father anything that Keith shared with her. He returned to his car and continued to watch from a distance. He could still intervene if the boy made any threatening moves.

Keith started to explain the bag to Kim, "Marissa was into cutting. The stuff in the bag was hers. She always wore long sleeves, so nobody knew about it but me and her best friend in Gig Harbor. I was trying to help her. She promised to quit cutting on herself and gave me these to prove it."

Kim knew some other girls at school that had cut on themselves. She didn't pretend to understand it but knew it happened. "Why didn't you just show these to the police and tell them about Marissa's habit. Maybe she was cutting herself and had an accident. Maybe she cut too deep and passed out and drove into the water. This might be helpful to the police."

"I'm not showing this to the police. Marissa died in West Seattle less than three miles from my house. Even if she did have an accident, no one will believe that I was not involved." Keith looked at Kim pleadingly. "I really need you to take these and make them disappear."

Kim closed her eyes and thought this must be what Alice felt like falling down the rabbit hole. There was no turning back now. She took a deep breath, "Okay. I'll take the blades. Now I really need to get out of here and think." She opened her eyes and looked at Keith, "I don't think we should talk for a while. Goodbye."

She turned and walked back to her car leaving him standing alone in the middle of the school parking lot. He stood in the same spot until Kim pulled out of her parking spot and exited the lot. Then he walked toward the exit, passing a late model sedan occupied by a man in a black jacket reading a newspaper. He recognized the man from the Space Needle elevator and could hear his own racing heart pounding in his ears. He hoped that the man had not seen him hand the paper bag to Kim.

Halfway up the block from the parking lot, Keith looked back. The man was not following him. He tried to tell himself that he was just being paranoid, but his heart was still racing, and his head was starting to ache. He pulled his earphones on and his hood up over his head and walked slowly the rest of the way to his house.

Worries

Wednesday was uneventful and Terry was more relaxed when he ended his shift. At home, he took a comfortable afternoon nap before watching the local news while Michelle prepared dinner.

Kim had still not come home from school and he asked Michelle, "Are we eating alone tonight?"

She answered, "Kim called while you were sleeping. She is grabbing a bite with her friends after dance class."

It was not uncommon for Kim to stay out for a meal with her friends after dance and Terry enjoyed the time alone with Michelle.

During a comfort-food dinner of pot roast, potatoes, and green beans Michelle was tempted to tell Terry about her conversation with Kim and that their daughter had talked with Keith on Monday. She decided against it and to keep her word to her daughter and say nothing to her husband. Besides, there was no need to upset him.

Across the table, Terry was wrestling with whether to tell Michelle about the details of his conversation with McManus and how Kim was going to be used to get information from Keith, but he decided against it. He thought it better that she not know and be burdened under the weight of the worries that now pressed down on him.

Both ate dinner in silence and lost in their thoughts, secretly worrying for their daughter.

Not far away Kim sat by herself in a booth at a local pizza place. She hadn't gone out with friends as she had said. She didn't like lying to her parents, but she just couldn't go home and face them right now. What she was doing for Keith was either very noble or insanely suicidal and she couldn't decide which. Maybe Uncle Reed could help her out. He had always been there for her when she needed someone to talk to.

Chapter 6

Hooky

Kim pulled her puffy blue goose down comforter up over her head and buried herself further into bed as her phone alarm sounded to tell her it was 6:30 and time to get up for school. She hadn't slept at all the previous night and felt both tired and sick. There was no way she could handle school today. After about ten minutes of trying to wish the day away, she sat up and straightened her pajama top before standing. She wondered if she was the only person that woke up every day to find their pajama tops turned sideways with the front buttons all the way around and under an arm.

Her father was on duty this morning and her mom was in the kitchen alone setting out cereal for Kim.

"Good morning sunshine." Michelle said as Kim walked in, dragging her feet.

"You look like you didn't get any sleep last night. Are you okay?"

Michelle was concerned. Her daughter looked pale and had dark circles under her eyes. She knew that Kim had talked with the boyfriend of the girl that died and that the whole situation was affecting her emotionally. If Terry had shared his meeting with Robert McManus with Michelle, her concerns would have been compounded ten times over.

Kim answered. "You're right. I kept thinking about Keith and couldn't get to sleep."

Michelle set down a glass of orange juice, "Well, if he didn't do anything, he has nothing to worry about."

Michelle didn't mean to sound so cliché, but it was all she could think of to say. As she watched Kim pick at her cereal, she decided to do something she hadn't done in ages.

"Honey, I think you need a hooky day. Why don't I call in to get you excused and well just go downtown and shop for the day? Get rid of the stress. How does that sound?"

Kim looked up. "Wow. That sounds great. I really don't think I can face school today."

"Then it's done. We haven't had a mother-daughter day in years. This will be fun."

Kim had one other thing she had planned to do today and now this would make it easier.

"Mom, before we go shopping, would it be okay if I went out by myself for a couple of hours? I just want to drive around and clear my mind."

Michelle wondered if that was really all Kim wanted to do, but she had always trusted her daughter and had never regretted it. Now was not the time to change.

"Okay, but be back by noon at the latest."

Kim smiled, "Thanks mom. I love you."

Then she gave her mom a big hug and went to change into her clothes before going out.

Kaykay

Reed only woke slightly when Angela got out of bed at six to dress and go to one of their boutiques to help set up a new merchandise display. Baker and Rainier lay on the pillows to either side of his head purring and lulling him back to sleep. When his phone rang at seven, he didn't know Angie had gone out and he hoped she would answer it for him. After several rings it stopped, and he drifted off until a few minutes later when it began ringing again. Reed reached over Baker and lifted the phone off the nightstand to see who the caller was. It would have to be someone extremely special to let them interrupt his morning bliss.

As soon as he saw the name, he snapped awake and tapped the answer button, "Hey Kaykay. What's up?"

Reed had given Kim the nickname Kaykay when she was a toddler and even though she was now grown up, she was still his Kaykay."

"Hey Uncle Reed, I am really sorry to call and wake you, but this is important. Can I come over for a little bit this morning? I need to talk with you about something."

He was quite sure he knew what she wanted to talk about but asked, "Sure, can you tell me what it's about?"

She hesitated and replied, "I'll tell you when I get there. I am already on my way and should be there in about twenty minutes. Oh, and please don't tell my parents. Okay?"

Reed replied, "You know the deal. What you tell me and Angela stays in confidence. Sort of like doctor patient privilege, we just call it uncle niece privilege. See you in a little bit."

After he hung up, Reed wondered what Kim might know. Maybe Keith had confided something to her that she felt the need to share with someone she trusted. If he had, and that information was disclosed to Reed, could he keep it secret? He knew about the plan to use Kim to get information from Keith in hopes that she would then share it with her father, but what if she didn't go to her father and, instead, shared it with him. He decided not to dwell on the point until his visit with Kim and hearing what she had to say. Hopefully, she just needed a friendly ear to talk to.

Reed gave each of the cats a friendly scratch behind the ears and got out of bed. He pulled on a worn pair of grey sweatpants and oversized Huskies sweatshirt and called out to Angela. When she didn't answer, he decided that she must out for her run and made his way downstairs to grind up some French Roast beans and brew a strong pot of coffee. Next to the French press was a note from Angela.

'Good morning lover. I am at the Fremont shop helping Maggie for a bit. I told you last night, but you were so wrapped up in your research, I don't think you heard me. I will be home by noon. Luv, Angie.'

She was right. He didn't recall her saying a thing.

The Bag

A brief time later Kim arrived at the landing and found an open parking spot. She was relieved to see the reserved parking place that normally held Angela's car was empty. It wasn't that she didn't want to see Angela, but she felt more comfortable talking with only Reed today. She fingered the brown bag on the front seat trying to decide whether

71

to take it or not. Then, grabbing the bag, she decided to put all her faith and trust in Reed. She got out of the car and clutched the bag to her chest as she walked down the dock to the Grey Kraken and rang the brass bell next to the front door.

The door opened, and Reed stood there with his arms open and a big smile on his face, "Kaykay, come here and give me a hug. It's been ages."

She could see the bags under his eyes and knew that she had probably robbed him of some much-needed sleep. As he gave her a bear hug, she apologized for disturbing his morning, "Uncle Reed, I am so sorry for getting you up, but I really, really need to talk to you."

Reed looked at the brown paper bag Kim held to her chest, "Did you bring me a gift?"

Kim glanced behind her and around the dock area with the look of someone who thinks they are being followed.

"Can we go inside? I'll be more comfortable in there."

Reed waved her in, "Of course. We'll sit in the kitchen. Would you like a cup of coffee or tea? Or hot chocolate?"

She relaxed a bit, "Hot chocolate sounds great. But I really can't stay for too long. Mom and I are having a mother-daughter day today and I said I would be back in two hours. She thinks I am just out for a drive right now to clear my head."

Reed responded, "No problem. Why don't you tell me what you would like to talk about while I warm some milk for your cocoa?"

Kim started with a question, "Has dad asked you to help find out what happened to the girl that died at the boat launch ramp?"

Reed figured there was no point in lying, "Yes he did. In fact, I was just starting to look into it last night."

"I hoped he would. You are so good; I know you will find out what happened."

Reed answered, "I hope so."

She asked another question, "Does he think her boyfriend Keith was involved?"

Reed knew he needed to be careful with how he answered this question and how much he should share with Kim, "I think he suspects everyone at this point. You know I really can't tell you much more right now and that is for your own good. I can only tell you that somebody was with Marissa when she died, but there is no strong lead on who that was. Do you know something that might help?"

Kim began to talk about her conversations with Keith. As Reed listened, he opened a tin container and scooped two portions of his home recipe cocoa mix into the cast iron saucepan of hot milk. He stirred the mixture until it was smooth and poured the steaming beverage into a white ceramic mug that was decorated with a blue octopus painted on the side. Finally, he topped the hot chocolate off with a scoop of whipped cream and set the cup in front of Kim. He sat down across the table and sipped at his coffee while he listened to, and observed, the young women he had known since the day she was born. She was a smart girl and had a good head on her shoulders. He knew he could trust her judgment and listened carefully as she described Keith and his friendship with Marissa. Reed began to believe that the young man was probably not involved in Marissa's death.

Feeling better and more relaxed than a little earlier, Reed broke into Kim's dialogue. He could tell she was under stress and he needed to lighten the conversation.

"How is the hot chocolate? It is my favorite recipe. Cocoa powder, a touch of sugar, and a pinch of chili pepper topped off with real whipped cream. You are lucky there was some whipped cream in the fridge. Angela and I had fresh berries from the market yesterday and whipped up a bowl to top them off. There was just enough left over for your cocoa."

Kim wiped a cream mustache off her upper lip, "Yum. It is absolutely perfect."

She was thankful for the break. She didn't know how her uncle would react to what she was about to share. Kim set the mug down and leaned over to pick the paper bag up off the floor.

She set the bag on the table and looked into Reeds eyes. "There is more. But please, before you jump to conclusions, let me explain."

Her trembling hands opened the bag. Remembering how she had reacted when she first saw its contents, she wanted to prepare Reed before revealing what was inside.

"Keith told me that Marissa had mental health issues. She suffered from bouts of depression that would debilitate her. Her father and schoolmates wrote off her mood swings as just being difficult and self-centered. Keith was one of the only people she trusted to talk with and open up about her struggles. One of the things she shared was that she was into cutting on herself, something she had successfully hidden from everyone else. When he found out about the cutting, he tried to understand."

She paused, "Uncle Reed, I believe him. I know other girls at school that have done the same thing. He said that he and Marissa made a pact to work together to help her stop. She gave him these to prove that she was trying to quit."

As she said this, Kim dumped the bag's contents onto the table. The sight made him catch his breath. The assortment of bloody blades and scalpels spread across the kitchen table was bad enough, but it was the wooden handled pick that caught his attention.

"Crap." He whispered.

"What?" Kim asked, not able to make out the whisper.

"Nothing. I, I guess I just don't understand anyone doing this to themselves."

Kim responded "I'm not sure the kids that do it understand either. It is part of depression and, unfortunately, it is pretty widespread."

Reed couldn't wrap his mind around it. School had always had its pressures, but he didn't remember anything like this when he was that age. Not kids cutting themselves. If it did happen, he was never aware of it.

But what bothered him even more than the array of tools the girl had supposedly used for self-mutilation was the small pick. Not only did it seem oddly out of place, it matched the autopsy report that a sharp pick-like object had penetrated Marissa's brain.

His mind was swirling with questions when Kim spoke up, "If Keith was found with these the police would assume that he had something to do with Marissa's death, so he asked me to hide them. But if I am found with them, the police will think I was trying to help a potential suspect."

"You ARE trying to help a suspect. And now you have brought me into the circle. What are you thinking?" Reed asked and was immediately sorry for having said it.

"Uncle Reed, I am sorry, but Keith didn't have anything to do with Marissa's death. You can help prove he is innocent."

Reed sat and thought. By all rights, he should turn this over to the police immediately. It could be important evidence in a murder investigation. At the very least he should share it with Kim's father. But Kim had spent time with Keith and trusted the boy. Reed knew there was a possibility that the boy was using Kim, but he also believed in intuition and was leaning toward trusting Kim's, at least for now."

He looked across the table, "Alright Kaykay. I'll hold onto these for now while I try to verify Keith's story. But here's the deal. Whatever I find, I will have to take it to the police, even if it implicates Keith."

"Fair enough, but it won't." She paused, "Is Aunt Angela helping you on this?

"I will probably ask for her help. Why?"

"I was just hoping you would. She sees things other don't. Just, please don't tell my father about our conversation. And ask Angela not to share any of this with my mom either."

Kim got up and gave Reed a hug.

"I better go now. Thanks again Uncle Reed. I love you."

"You be careful Kaykay. I know you have good common sense, but you need to be extra careful right now. I don't want you getting hurt."

Reed followed Kim up the dock to her car and watched as she drove away, hoping he had done the right thing in taking the bag. He would not share Kim's visit with Terry. He was not ready to break his trust with Kim, at least not yet. Not until he completed more research.

Kim left feeling that she had done the right thing and believing more in Keith and his innocence.

Intuition

It was a little after twelve when Angela arrived home from the shop. Reed was in the kitchen preparing a grilled chicken salad when he heard the front door open. "Is that you hon?"

Angela answered, "Sure is. I smell food. What are you cooking up for us?"

"Us? Well I was throwing together a chicken salad for ME, but I can throw a few more chicken strips into the pan and brown them up, no problem. How's the shop?"

"It looks great. We added a new line of dresses and Maggie set up an awesome window display. She asked for my help, but she didn't need it.

She is fantastic. I am so glad we hired her. How was your morning? Have you been up long?"

"Actually, I *have* been up long. Since about seven o'clock to be exact. Probably right after you left. Kaykay stopped by for a visit."

"Kim? What was she doing over this way?"

"I'll tell you all about it over lunch. Why don't you open a bottle of Chardonnay? It will go well with this killer salad I am making, plus I think you may need a little wine when you hear Kim's story."

Reed had already torn several spinach leaves into a large bowl and tossed in some mushrooms and black olives. Now he placed the hot chicken strips over the spinach, ground a little fresh black pepper over the bowl, poured on a generous amount of Caesar salad dressing, and then topped the whole thing with a fine layer of fresh grated Parmesan cheese.

"Voile, lunch is served."

He set the bowl on the kitchen table where Angela had just set the place mats and wine glasses.

"Okay, don't keep me waiting. What was Kim doing here? Isn't it a school day?"

"Michelle called the school and gave her the day off so they could spend the afternoon together. Kim came over here without Michelle knowing so she could share some information about the Alki incident. I promised that you and I would keep her conversation between us. I think for the time being, it's best that Terry and Michelle do not know anything about what Kim said and showed me this morning. When and if I feel it is appropriate, I will share it with Terry."

Michelle set down her wine glass.

"Now you really have me curious. So, what did Kim say?"

Reed recounted Kim's story and described the bag with its macabre contents. Angela pushed her plate away and took another sip of wine.

"I think any appetite that I had a few moments ago just left me. I had no idea that Kim was so wrapped up in this."

Reed had not had a chance to tell Angela about his conversation with Terry the prior evening.

"It gets even more complicated. Terry told me some information that has not been made public."

He pushed back from the table and picked up their glasses.

"Let's go out to the other room where it's more comfortable. This is going to take some time."

Reed and Angela left the kitchen area and stepped down into the sunken family room overlooking the lake. After Angela had made herself comfortable in the old overstuffed leather sofa, Reed paced back and forth in front of the picture window as he began laying out everything he knew, starting with the time of the girl's death the day before she was found and working through the details of her injuries. He told how the police had observed Kim spending time with Keith and how Robert had asked Terry to let her see the boy in hopes that he would share something in confidence with her and that her conscience would, in turn, lead her to share that with her father. And finally, he recounted again the conversation he had just had with Kim and described the bag of blades and pick she had entrusted to him.

Angela got out of the couch and walked over to Reed to wrap her arms around him.

"Wow, that's a lot to absorb. Are you going to tell Terry or the investigators about the bag?"

Reed was hugging Angela back as he answered.

"Not yet. The articles in the bag might trigger the police to jump to conclusions and arrest Keith. Odd as it may sound; I am not so sure he did it. I would rather keep this to us and snoop around for a couple of days without the authorities stirring things up. Also, I would like your help with this one love. I could use your intuition to help sniff out where this leads to. Kaykay even suggested you help. I didn't realize others recognized your special powers." He made haunting sound with his voice and Angela hit his shoulder as she threatened to put a curse on him.

In fact, Angela regularly helped Reed with his research. Reed called her intuitive but several of their friends believed she was downright psychic. She enjoyed reading Tarot cards and had successfully forecast several major events in the lives of their friends. She also had a perfect record in predicting the sexes of their friend's babies' months before they were born and that seemed to impress her friends the most. Angela attributed her mystical side to her Irish/Scottish ancestry. Her parents had often recounted stories of several generations of relatives on both sides of her family that displayed uncanny abilities. Reed just called

Angela his personal sorceress. Whatever the explanation, Angela could read people and situations and get to the truth like no one else he knew.

"Sure, I'll help. But I am a little curious that you believe Keith's explanation to Kim so easily. And if not Keith, then who did kill the girl."

"Let's just say I am going with my own intuition at this point. I think it is almost too convenient to suspect the boy. I want to see if it is possible to eliminate him as a suspect and, at the same time, come up with some other potential candidates. If not, then maybe he actually is the person responsible."

Chapter 7

Memorial

Friday morning Reed was up early for Marissa Archer's memorial service in Gig Harbor. The service was scheduled for eleven o'clock and he figured he could make the drive in a little under two hours with morning traffic, so he wanted to be out of the door by nine. He had a restless night and had been up since seven, an unheard-of time for Reed. He and Angela took advantage of his early rising and enjoyed a hearty breakfast of bacon and eggs together.

The two hadn't spoken much about the case since the day before and Reed was still not in the mood for talking. It seemed that the more he thought about Marissa, the more Terry's melancholy was rubbing off on him. He hoped he could turn up some information today that might provide some clues he could follow up on. Angela could sense where Reed's head was and didn't break into his thoughts. They would talk more when he was ready. Gazing out at the lake in silence they both finished their coffees before Reed stood up and walked to the bedroom to dress for the day.

He decided to wear a comfortable pair of black denim pants and a charcoal grey shirt and black sport coat. People didn't wear suits to services anymore and he wanted to look respectful and a touch casual at the same time. When Reed had helped Terry before, he found that he had a natural talent for gaining people's trust and getting them to talk, whoever they may be. Whether it was members of a bike gang or a group of religious missionaries, it didn't matter, he would dress to blend in, adjust his language, and find common ground for conversation. Then he would probe for the information he wanted.

When he was finished dressing, Reed walked back downstairs and gave Angela a hug before walking out the door without saying a word. He was already shifting from the Reed she knew to the one that would try to connect with the kids at the funeral.

Reed noted that it was a grey day with a light drizzle that had persisted throughout the morning. Conventional thinking would say that it ought to be sunny for a service that should be a celebration of Marissa's life, but Reed felt the grey and mist more appropriate. They seemed to reflect the cloud of uncertainty around her death and the sadness of a life cut short.

As he entered onto the I-5 freeway, the light morning drizzle was turning into a medium shower and, by the time he was passing Boeing Field twenty minutes later, the showers had turned into a full-on downpour. The Mini's windshield wipers worked furiously to keep up with the combination of heavy rainfall and the wheel spray kicked up by large semi-truck-trailer rigs he passed as he made his way toward Tacoma.

By the time he reached the turn-off for Gig Harbor, his shoulders ached from fighting the constant hydroplaning of his tires that seemed to conspire to pull the Mini into adjacent lanes and underneath the trucks that towered over him. He didn't relax until turning off the freeway to his destination.

The memorial service for Marissa was to take place in a funeral home on the edge of town. As Reed approached the harbor, he turned up the volume on his phone to let it guide him the rest of the way. He drove through the central part of town and out the other side before making a series of quick left turns. He was beginning to think he had made a wrong turn and was lost when he looked to his left and spotted the funeral home, an austere looking one-story white building sitting on a slight rise a hundred feet back from the street. A curved drive led up the left side of the well-groomed front lawn to the front entrance where a covered drive-through, supported by two large white pillars, protected visitors from the inclement weather. From there, the drive continued to the right, crossing the building to an adjacent parking lot with another entrance to the street.

The area in front of the home featured a large two-tiered Victorian fountain that sported three angels blowing bugles from the top. Reed found the fountain to be a little too kitsch, but he admired the putting green quality of the turf that surrounded the fountain and was, in turn, framed by a rich assortment of Rhododendrons and Azaleas now in full bloom.

When Reed arrived, it was only 10:40, but he was not surprised to find the funeral home parking lot already full. He suspected that many of the local high school students and their parents would be at the service. Gig Harbor may have grown over the years, but it was still a relatively small town. Events such as the death of a young person tended to bring the community together. After finding a parking place about a block away, Reed exited his car and walked back toward the home.

The gods are crying, he thought to himself as the deluge continued and made a loud drumming noise on his black umbrella. Once under the protection of the entryway, he closed his umbrella and sized up a gathering of people catching a quick smoke outside before going into the home. He recognized one from pictures in the paper. It was Ryan Archer, Marissa's father. The man looked tired and haggard and it was obvious the loss of his daughter was taking a toll on him.

The superintendent lit up another cigarette and a young man approached extending his hand in greeting. Marissa's father clearly recognized the boy and gave him a hug. Reed knew that Marissa had been an only child, so the young man must be a cousin or other relative. The boy had the build of an athlete, well over six feet tall and bulked up. After the two talked outside for a few minutes, they turned and walked up the steps and into the funeral home. Reed decided it was also an appropriate time to make his way inside.

To each side of the front entryway stood a man in a dark suit quietly greeting the visitors as they entered and directing them to the proper room for the service. Reed guessed that they were employees of the funeral home, but it was obvious they knew several of the guests. When Reed entered, the man closest to him gave a cordial greeting but also gave him a look of suspicion. The man did not recognize Reed and was probably leery that he was a reporter.

After a week of being inundated with the media hounding every person they could find for tidbits on Marissa and her family, on this day of all, the community simply wanted to be left alone to mourn their loss and Reed understood. He gave the doorman a nod and thanked him, saying nothing more as he accepted the memorial service program.

Inside the door people mingled in little groups, the high school students grouping together with their peers while the parents collected in twos and fours and talked quietly. Many were already taking seats in the main room, regrouping back with their respective families. At 11:00, one of the greeters from the front entrance came inside as the other one closed the tall gold trimmed white doors. Then they both invited everyone to please take their seats, so the service could begin.

Reed entered the memorial room and took a seat at the back, taking in the sound of the organ and low murmur of conversation. When the organ stopped playing, it seemed that all conversation also ceased as if the lack of music was a cue to stop talking. For what seemed like an interminable period, the only sound in the sanctuary was the dull rumble of rain on the cedar shake roof mixed with occasional sniffs and the shuffling of feet on the tile floor.

The music began again quietly, and Marissa's parents entered the sanctuary and took their seats at the front. Several aunts, uncles, and cousins had already taken their own seats in the front row where Marissa's parents now sat holding hands. Reed noticed that the athletic young man was not among them. Instead, he sat about halfway back with a group of students. He must just be a good friend of the family, Reed thought.

Shortly after the service started, one more person entered the room quietly and unnoticed and sat down in the rear next to Reed. When the service ended, the young man slipped out the same way he came in, quietly and unnoticed. Reed instantly knew why. It was Keith Martin.

The service ended with one of Marissa's cousin's singing Amazing Grace as the family walked down the aisle and out to the reception area. Then the ushers released each pew in order as they worked their way to the back of the room.

Accusations

Reed was the last to leave the main room and enter the sea of people in the crowded foyer exchanging greetings and sharing memories of Marissa. As he made his way through the crowd to the funeral home entrance, he could hear a disturbance outside and sped up to see what the commotion was about.

Once outside the doors he heard someone yelling "Get out of here or I'll beat the crap out of you. You're going to hell for what you did." It was the large athletic boy yelling at someone down the street. Reed looked in the direction of the boy's attention and saw Keith, in a long black leather coat, running off down the sidewalk.

"You know he probably killed Marissa. And now he has the balls to come to her memorial?"

"He never did strike me as too smart."

Two teenage girls were standing next to Reed and he couldn't help but overhear their comments. Both a little on the chubby side, one was wearing blue jeans and a blue denim jacket and the other a white skirt and short red wool coat.

"Excuse me, but I heard what you just said. Are you from West Seattle?"

"No. Why would you think that?" the one in denim asked incredulously.

"Well, it sounds like you know Keith, and he is from West Seattle not Gig Harbor."

"Who are you? Are you a cop or something?"

"No" answered Reed. "I write a blog on crime. Marissa's death is tragic, and I am just trying to learn more about her. I'm sorry. I didn't mean to intrude."

He had no idea how that cover came into his head, but it seemed to lower the girls' guard, and both started talking.

The girl in red went first. "A lot of people here know who Keith is. When he started seeing Marissa, he would hang out in town a lot."

The one in blue chimed in. "Then Keith and Steven got into some crazy ass fights after school when Steven caught Keith waiting outside for Marissa, only it was totally one sided with Steven pounding on Keith. Can you believe Marissa would break up with Steven to go with a loser like that?"

Red jumped in. "Steven told Marissa's father about Keith and that he was a stoner and Mr. Archer forbid her from seeing Keith. Mr. Archer always liked Steven and I think he thought Steven and Marissa would stay together. You know. Like forever?"

Blue. "Yeah, what is there not to like. He is good looking, smart, and is going to the U next year on a football scholarship."

Red. "Mr. Archer just wanted what was best for Marissa. And it's not like she was the greatest catch or anything? She was a little mental you know. One day on top of the world and the next, all Miss doom and gloom. She didn't know how lucky she was to have someone like Steven interested in her."

Blue. "Do you think you know who killed her? Do you think it was Keith? That's what everyone here is saying."

It took Reed a second to recover from the one-sided staccato conversation that had just taken place before he answered the two fidgeting girls, "Why do you think he would? People don't usually kill someone they care about and go out of their way to be with. Is there anyone here in town that might have wanted to hurt Marissa?"

The girls shrugged their shoulders in unison. From Reed's response they determined that they weren't going to get any additional information from him and decided the conversation was over.

Blue spoke up. "Well, um, it's been nice talking, but we gotta go. See ya."

They both turned and walked off toward the parking lot, their retreating figures reflecting off the wet asphalt drive as they picked their way around several shallow puddles that dotted the way.

Reed opened his umbrella and turned to walk in the opposite direction toward the last place he had seen Keith when the boy ran away. Maybe this would be a good time to hear Keith's side of the story if he could find him.

The voices at the funeral home faded as Reed walked down the driveway and fell into a contemplative state while he listened to his feet make a methodic slap-slap-slap sound on the blacktop. He noted that the pitch of the sound changed as he stepped from the smooth blacktop onto the course concrete sidewalk. After a few more steps he noticed that there was a second set of footsteps just slightly out of sync with his, coming from not too far behind.

"He didn't do it." A voice came from just behind him.

Startled, Reed spun around to see a young girl only a few steps back. "Excuse me? What did you say?"

"I said he didn't do it."

Reed found himself looking at a young girl dressed in black boots, short black skirt, and black hooded sweatshirt. Medium height and build, the girl's long copper red hair was interspersed with streaks of pink. He guessed she was a local middle school student or possibly a first-year student at the high school.

"I heard you talking with Buffy and Princess. They don't know what they're talking about."

"Talking with whom?" Reed asked.

The girl shrugged. "Oh, that's not their real names. I just call them that 'cause they're a couple spoiled little brats that think they know everything. You were just talking with them at the funeral home. I think you should know that Keith did not kill Marissa."

"And you are?"

"I'm Grace. I was a good friend of Marissa's. She was two years older than me and we only had a couple of classes together, but when we met, we became best friends."

Reed thought for a second and made a snap decision not to continue looking for Keith for now.

"Are there any good coffee shops around here?"

"Odd question, but yes, there is a small one that I like to hang out in not too far from here."

"Well, here's another odd question. Would you like to join me for a coffee? I would like to learn more about Marissa and her friends. And I want to get inside out of the rain."

Grace smiled. "Are you a reporter?"

Reed answered, "No. Actually I am just someone who likes to solve puzzles. My brother works for the Seattle Police and sometimes I help look for clues the police may miss."

"Really?" She smiled, "Have you ever solved a case?"

"Actually, yes. The evidence was there but those directly involved with the investigation were simply too close to see it. Sort of like 'not seeing the forest for the trees' as they say. Anyway, right now I am trying to help find out what really happened with Marissa."

"Okay. I would love to join you for coffee. Besides, nobody else has talked to the people that were closest to Marissa. Her father is telling everyone that Keith hurt her. There is no way that is true. I know, and I bet I can tell you some things that nobody else is talking about. We can go to Crème Café. It's in an old gas station on the main street at the top of the hill. You can't miss it."

Reed's spirits lifted. "That's great. Can I give you a ride?"

"No thanks. I have my own car. I know. I look too young, but I just turned sixteen."

She pointed toward the funeral home parking lot. "I parked just up there. See you at the café."

Grace turned and made her way up toward the funeral home as Reed walked the opposite direction, across the street and back to his car. He wondered what the girl knew, if anything, and hoped their meeting would be worthwhile.

Invitation

Kim returned to school Friday and her friends were curious about her absence the day before. They told her that Keith had been there all day, so they knew she wasn't with him. She explained her day off with her mother and the conversations always ended there. It seemed that nobody wanted to make small talk with her anymore, since the incident last weekend. She was beginning to question what friendships really were and how her friends stacked up when it came to being there for support.

During chemistry class, she asked Keith what he thought about coming over to her house after school and meeting her parents. To say he was shocked was an understatement. He wondered if it was some sort of trap and asked what was behind the invitation.

Kim felt awkward and didn't know what to say next.

"I kind of told my mom that I think you and I could be friends under different circumstances and that what is happening to you now is just some genuinely bad shit and crappy coincidences. Well, I didn't actually say bad shit and crappy coincidences to my mom, but that was basically the message."

"And?"

"And she said she would like to meet you and you could come over and stay for dinner after school today if you like."

Keith was not totally comfortable with the idea yet and asked, "What does your father think?"

Kim answered, "He'll be okay. He's a good guy and I'm sure he doesn't think you have anything to do with what happened at Alki. Anyway, mom said, if he makes a fuss, we can leave."

Keith was still uneasy, "Give me time to think about it. I might have other plans tonight. I will let you know at lunch."

Crème Cafe

Marissa's father and her ex-boyfriend were standing on the funeral home steps as Grace walked through the covered drive thru.

"Hey Grace. Who was that you were just talking to?" Steven asked as she drew even with the two. "Mr. Archer and I were just saying that neither of us recognizes him."

Marissa's father added, "I hope you aren't giving bad information to reporters or anything."

Grace didn't exactly know what it was, but something in his voice felt threatening and made a chill go down her spine.

"He is just someone that cares about Marissa and what happened to her. Anyway, what are you afraid I might say?"

Mr. Archer forced a smile and answered, "Look, I have had enough of people invading our privacy. That man probably didn't even know Marissa and now he has the nerve to come to her memorial. If he is a reporter, he is just out to make headlines with some theory about what happened. You don't need to be talking with people like that and giving them ideas. You understand little girl?"

The confrontation rattled Grace. She had never liked Marissa's father or Steve and the feelings were clearly mutual. Steven was a bully and Mr. Archer had a reputation for being strong headed and used to getting his own way. She tried to put on a look of impassivity and responded to Mr. Archer. "Whatever."

Then she turned and continued along the driveway, her heart pounding wildly in her chest.

A block away, Reed reached his parked Mini.

"You need a bath" he said out loud noting the muddy brown residue that covered car. Reed was almost fanatical about keeping his car clean. "You're getting a wash first thing tomorrow."

Leaning across the large puddle that occupied the space between the curb and car, Reed supported himself with his right hand on the roof and leaned down to open the car door with his left. The puddle appeared to be shallow, but Reed's left foot was still soaked up to the ankle from stepping into it earlier and he was not about to repeat that misstep and track mud into the car. He awkwardly dropped down into the Mini, barely missing hitting his head on the door sill as he swung in. He started the car and pulled away from the curb hitting a shallow pothole that sent a muddy spray up and over the passenger side of the car.

"Okay, now you're getting a wash as soon as we get back today."

His left shoe made a squishing sound when he pressed the clutch pedal and shifted. As he drove to the coffee house, he continued to mutter about the pothole and how it better not have knocked his wheels out of alignment. When he reached the main street, he turned right and looked for the coffee house. After driving for a few miles and passing a sign that read, 'Thank you for visiting Gig Harbor', Reed decided that he must have turned the wrong way and made a U-turn back into town. About two blocks past where he had initially turned onto the street, he spotted what appeared to be a 1950's era gas station painted white with green trim. A blue neon sign in the front window blinked - Crème Cafe. Next to the neon sign hung a rainbow flag. In front of the glass-paneled garage bay door, several vacant tables sat empty, their large umbrellas down and dripping, folds slapping in the wind. The garage door appeared as though it could be raised during warmer weather to open the entire cafe out to the street but now it was closed, protecting those inside from the blustery weather.

The parking lot was empty except for two cars, and Reed pulled into a space directly in front of the entrance. As he opened his car door he was immediately struck by the smell of roasting coffee.

'Ah, now that is the smell of heaven.' he thought. 'A well-made espresso or depth charge is pleasure enough but, combined with the smell of fresh roasting coffee beans.... that just can't be beat.'

Inside the door Reed took a moment to soak up the aroma coming from the roaster next to the window in the front corner of the shop not too far from the door. The brass trimmed burgundy machine made a swishing sound as it rotated and heated its contents of green coffee beans, roasting them to a deep caramel color. The heat from the roaster radiated into the cafe and warmed Reed's damp face and hands as he removed his jacket and shook it off before hanging it on a rack by the door.

The Crème Cafe was not large, and he spotted Grace in the back corner of the former garage bay next to a large bookcase stuffed with board games and used paperbacks. He walked over and saw that she was setting a backgammon board onto a wire spool table that sat between two worn red velvet wingback chairs. "Do you play?" she asked.

"As a matter of fact, my wife and I play backgammon several times a week. May I treat you to a coffee? We can play a game while we talk."

"Sure, I'll have a latte with a shot of vanilla. Thanks."

Reed walked back to the front of the shop and ordered a vanilla latte for Grace and a dark roast coffee with espresso shot for him. Reed gauged the man at the counter to be in his mid-thirties. He sported an earring and full-sleeve tattoos with nautical themes. On the left pocket of his flannel shirt he wore an engraved brass name tag that read, Dylan Hewitt, Barista.

While the man retrieved two mugs from a shelf on the wall Reed tried to make casual conversation, "This is a nice shop. Cool atmosphere and good music. I bet if it were in Seattle it would be packed."

"What do you want with Grace?" the man inquired, not showing a hint of a smile and ignoring Reed's complement.

Reed didn't immediately answer, taken aback by the man's abrupt response.

The barista continued, "I'm just curious. You see, this is my shop and Grace is a regular. Crème Cafe is a safe haven. Here, kids, and adults for that matter, can escape harassment they may get outside. It is a sanctuary of sorts for those that stand apart from the so-called mainstream. I don't want that compromised."

Reed began to answer but the barista stopped him. "And don't tell that me you're a friend or family because, when Grace came in a few minutes ago, she told me she was meeting with someone she had just met for the first time today at Marissa's memorial service."

Reed understood. "Yes, Grace and I met just a little bit ago after the memorial service. But she approached me and wanted to talk, not the other way around."

The goateed man still looked suspicious. He poured some milk into a stainless pitcher and talked over the sound of hissing steam. "Are you a reporter or with the police?"

Reed answered, "You could say I'm a private investigator. I'm helping to investigate Marissa's death. I'm not here to harass anyone or make trouble. Grace offered to help, and I accepted."

Dylan finished the drinks and handed them to Reed. "Marissa and Grace were close. I don't know how Grace will cope with losing her. I don't want to see her hurt."

Reed said, "I understand."

Before he turned to go back to the table, Reed asked, "Since you knew Marissa, is there anything you might know that might help me find her killer?"

Dylan shrugged, "Not really. When Marissa wasn't working, she was in here with Keith and Grace almost every afternoon. The three of them would sit in the back and play backgammon for hours on end. That stopped when Marissa's dad told her to stop seeing Keith. It drove him crazy to have his daughter seeing someone like Keith."

Reed, "So they were all good friends, but could Keith have possibly hurt her by accident? You probably overheard some of their conversations in here. Were they into any type of drugs or anything else that could have resulted in Marissa's death?"

Dylan shook his head, "No. They may each have secrets or bear scars that keep them to themselves, but they are good kids. I don't think any one of them would do anything to put the others in danger. If anything, they were saving each other."

Reed thought a moment on what Dylan said and then thanked him and returned to the table with the two hot mugs. He hoped the fresh brewed coffee and espresso shot would sharpen his mind so he could clearly process what he heard from Grace.

He sat down and looked closer at the young girl. He could see that she was nervous and not as self-assured as she had seemed earlier, and he thought she might be having second thoughts about meeting with a total stranger.

"Thanks again for meeting with me. I know you have no idea who I am, and I really appreciate this."

Grace nodded, "Not a problem. You look like an honest person. Marissa was my best friend and I want to find out what happened to her."

Reed paused before continuing. "Back at the funeral home you said Keith didn't do it even though that is what the others are saying. Do you know something that the others don't know?"

Grace didn't answer for a minute. Then she said, "Maybe, but it's not easy to explain. Why don't we start the game and I'll tell you what I think while we play?"

They each made three moves on the backgammon board while Grace gathered her thoughts.

"Sometimes I get feelings about stuff. My parents always said I had a strong sense of intuition. And now, I sense that my parents are still here and watching after me. Sometimes I think they are talking to me."

Reed looked puzzled and asked where her parents were.

Grace responded, "Oh, I guess you wouldn't know. My mother and father were killed in a car crash a little over a year ago. Now I live with foster parents. The Landsbergs. They are really nice, but I still miss my parents."

Reed said, "I'm so sorry. I had no idea."

Grace forced a meek smile, "How would you? Anyway, I am a survivor. And I am strong. Right?"

She flexed her right arm.

Reed smiled back. "Yes, you are. And you remember that."

Grace returned to the subject of her strong intuition telling Reed that she could predict events and was learning to read Tarot cards.

"Now you really think I'm crazy. Don't you?"

Reed answered, "I don't think you are crazy at all. As a matter of fact, my wife, Angela, is also intuitive. It's almost spooky. I could never get away with anything around our place. She would sense it and I would be in the doghouse."

Grace laughed.

Reed continued, "But seriously, I believe in intuition and I believe you should go with your instincts and let them guide you."

He threw his dice and repositioned two pieces on the board. "Maybe you can start by telling me about Marissa and Keith? And then what your senses are telling you about what happened to her."

Grace rolled a double four and captured one of Reed's pieces.

"Well first, Marissa and I met Keith at the same time. We were at a concert in Seattle and Keith was standing next to us in front of the stage. Marissa and Keith started talking and after the concert, the three of us went to a Starbucks nearby and talked until it closed. We were there for hours, but it seemed like only minutes. It was like we had been friends for years."

Reed rolled and brought his piece back in. "So, you were all friends, but she broke up with Steven for Keith. Right?"

"Sort of. Before meeting Keith, Marissa had been dating Steven for about a year and it was just one big miss-match. If you saw Marissa back then, you would think that she always wanted to be center stage. She tried to hang with the in-crowd and wanted to be everyone's friend. She could be loud and appeared to be very self-confident. Dating Steven just seemed like the right match if you didn't know her."

Reed asked, "So she wasn't part of the so-called in-group?"

Grace answered, "She tried to act like one of them, but she actually was more insecure than you could imagine. She needed someone that would listen to her and support her through her down times. Steven was not that person. After seeing Keith a few times, she decided to break up with Steven and be true to herself."

Reed dropped a brown sugar cube into his depth charge and stirred the syrupy mixture. "How did that go over with Steve?"

"Not so good. I was there when she broke up with him and he really lost it. He had met Keith once when he was over here, and Steve couldn't stand his type. All Steve saw was a guy that dressed weird and talked soft. He couldn't believe Marissa could prefer Keith and probably thought it would make him look like a loser if Marissa dropped him for Keith. He said he'd kill Marissa if she left him for that loser."

"He said what? Have you told anyone that?"

"No. Anyway he was drunk when he said it and it was just one of those things you say when you are Steven and you are pissed off. He's got a hot temper and started some fistfights with Keith a couple of times after that when Keith had come over to meet Marissa, but I don't think Steven would ever actually hurt Marissa. He just wanted her to come back to him."

After she said this, Grace remembered the threatening tone in Steven's voice earlier at the funeral home and another chill went down her spine.

It was Reed's turn to throw the dice and he slowly rocked the dice cup back and forth while he thought about Grace's comments. It seemed possible that one of Marissa's own friends, and not a stranger, may have killed her. Possibly Steven out of anger over their breakup, or Keith as a result of a drug mishap. If it was Keith, the innocent looking girl could be playing Reed to throw him off the track. He threw the dice and thought about his next move.

"So, tell me what your intuition tells you about who may have hurt Marissa. Do you think it was someone she knew, or a stranger?"

She thought a moment, "I don't know. If you had asked me yesterday, I would say it had to be a stranger, but after the funeral today, I ran into Steve and Mr. Archer."

Grace fell silent.

Reed asked, "And?"

Grace proceeded to tell Reed about the confrontation after the memorial service. It seemed to Reed that Mr. Archer's comments could easily be justified by the circumstances. It was the day of his daughter's memorial service and he simply wanted to find her killer and bring him to justice. Had Reed been in Mr. Archer's shoes, he may have reacted in the same way.

Reed was curious about the seemingly close relationship Mr. Archer had with Steven.

"Were Steven and Mr. Archer close?"

"You could say that. I think Mr. Archer thought a boy like Steven would be perfect for his daughter. You know, the whole star student and athlete thing. He didn't like her hanging around with people like me and Keith. I was never banned from visiting their house, but it was clear that I made her father uncomfortable and was not welcome around him."

"What about her mother?"

"Oh, she was always nice to me but seemed kind of quiet and always looked sad. No wonder, Mr. Archer was totally preoccupied with his job and hardly ever home."

She rolled a double six and punched at the air temporarily breaking the somber tone. "Yes!"

93

After moving her pieces and sending two more of Reed's discs to the bar, Grace continued.

"Marissa said that she got her mood swings from her mom. She said her mom had been on antidepressants in the past, but Mr. Archer made her stop."

Reed rolled his dice and brought one of his pieces back out onto the backgammon board.

"Did they know about Marissa's emotional problems?"

"For sure. A couple of weeks ago, when I was over visiting, they got into an argument about it. Right in front of us. Mrs. Archer had just discovered that Marissa had been cutting on her arms and told Mr. Archer that they should send Marissa for counseling. She thought that Marissa might need antidepressants. Mr. Archer said he had no time for that nonsense and that Keith was probably responsible for it anyway. He even said that Mrs. Archer was a perfect example of how useless counseling and medications are. I felt terrible."

"Who else knew Marissa was cutting?"

"As far as I know only me and Keith. Marissa always did a good job of keeping her arms covered. Keith was trying to help her stop."

Grace self-consciously rubbed her forearm.

Reed looked at the young girl as she slumped in her chair, staring blankly at the backgammon table. "And Marissa told you because she knew you are a cutter too."

Grace looked up and nodded her head, tears forming in the corners of her eyes.

"She was one of the only people that understood me, and we supported each other. Keith was trying to help her stop and she wanted me to stop too."

She picked up a napkin and dabbed it to her eyes. "Nobody understands cutting unless they've been there. Sometimes it just seems like nothing is real and cutting is the only thing that you can feel. It hurt, but at least it was something. Until now. Now I hurt because Marissa is gone, and I don't know how I will get through without her."

Reed didn't pretend to understand cutting and self-mutilation. Right now, he only wished he could reach out and take Grace's pain away. Instead of the scary looking young woman he met at the funeral home only a few hours before, now he just saw a lonely little girl searching for herself.

He decided they had discussed Marissa enough.

"Let's not talk about Marissa anymore. I am a little hungry and think I'll have a scone and another coffee. Would you like anything?"

Grace stammered quietly "I... I guess another latte would be nice."

After a few minutes, Reed returned with the drinks and scone. Grace looked even smaller and had melted into the overstuffed chair. Her knees were pulled up to her chest and tucked under her sweatshirt. Her arms wrapped around her legs.

As he set the food down, Reed asked, "You okay?"

Grace quietly answered, "Yes, I guess. It is just really hitting me again. I really hope you can help."

"I promise; I will do my best."

The two spent the next half hour playing backgammon and not talking about the case. Grace told him about her parents and how much she missed them. She also talked about her foster parents and how nice they were to her. She was happy that they let her be herself and trusted her to make the right decisions. They had even let her start driving as soon as she was legal age. Her car had been her mother's.

As they were finishing their second game, a small clock on the bookcase chimed three o'clock and Reed took the cue as an opportunity to end their visit, saying he needed to start the drive home. He wasn't really in a hurry to get home as much as he wanted to have some time to himself to think about what he had seen and heard that day.

Grace started to pack up the backgammon board and he said, "I enjoyed meeting you. If you want to talk some more, you can give me a call."

He thought about the loneliness Grace must be feeling and added, "In fact, if you like, you can come over and visit. My wife and I live on a houseboat on Lake Union and we like sharing the view with guests. Here is my card. Call anytime."

Grace picked up a napkin and wrote on it, "And here is mine. I hope we get a chance to talk again."

Grace thanked him again for the latte and they each headed to their cars. Reed decided to take the scenic way home and left Gig Harbor in the opposite direction than he had arrived. He drove north to

Southworth where he caught the ferry boat to West Seattle. He would drop in on Terry on his way home and give him updates from his day in Gig Harbor.

Capitol Hill

Becky had been panhandling around the waterfront and Pioneer Square tourist districts and was getting the hang of asking for spare change. If she had to, she could probably survive on the streets for an extended time, but she was ready to go to her aunt's in Portland and enjoy the comfort of a soft bed. Plus, her aunt would help her know what to do next. The Greyhound bus station was only three blocks from her temporary tent home and, first thing Friday morning, she walked into the station and bought a one-way ticket for a Saturday afternoon departure, scheduled to arrive in Portland shortly after five. She would not call her aunt until she arrived. She trusted her aunt but didn't want to go into details about last Sunday over the phone and she didn't want her aunt to possibly call her parents before knowing what had happened.

In the bus station restroom, Becky looked in the mirror and sniffed at her armpits. "Ugh girl. You need to get cleaned up before you get on that bus."

She fished out her phone and called Julie

Julie had programmed Becky's number into her phone and saw the young girl's name when the phone rang. She answered, "Hi Becky. Are you okay?"

Becky answered that she was fine and told Julie that she was leaving to see her aunt in Portland the following day. Then she asked if she could come to Julie's home Saturday morning. She wanted to visit with her again before she left town and wanted to take a shower before taking a bus to Portland if that would be okay. Julie said that would be fine and that she would come down and pick her up that evening if she liked. Becky could spend the night and meet Julie's parents.

The offer was tempting but Becky didn't want to have to explain her circumstances to any adults other than her aunt right now. She thanked Julie for the offer and said she would rather meet her in the morning. She added that she planned on panhandling in the Capitol Hill district on her last evening in town. She heard that the strip along Broadway was crowded with clubs and restaurants and, according to other kids on the street, good money could be made there on the weekends. If she got enough money, she would buy a fresh shirt in the morning to wear after her shower. Julie was uneasy about the young girl's safety but didn't push her to stay at her house that night. After all, the teenager seemed to have fended well so far. They agreed to meet at a coffee shop in Pioneer Square the next morning.

Conflicting Information

The ferry pulled into the dock a little before five and Reed was one of the first across the ramp. From the dock it was just a short distance up the hill to Terry and Michelle's house and he pulled into their driveway within five minutes of the boat docking. The driveway and surrounding grass were still wet from the day's earlier torrent and drops of water peppered his head as he walked under the branches of a large apple tree that bordered the path to the front door. Just before reaching the porch he looked up and saw Michelle standing in the open doorway waiting to greet him with a broad smile and a hug.

"Hey stranger. Didn't we just see each other a couple of days ago?"

"Yeah, twice in one week. I'm not sure I can handle that much of you. Hopefully, Terry reached you and told you I was coming." Reed stepped into the house.

"About an hour ago. Good thing I was home. I've been out at clients' most of the day."

Michelle had a small interior decorating business that she ran out of their home and her schedule varied from day to day.

"Terry should be home soon. Would you like a beer while you wait?"

Terry nodded and Michelle retrieved a cold beer from the fridge, "So, you're helping Terry with the Alki case. Have you found anything interesting?"

"Not much. I learned some new things today, but I am not sure what they mean."

Just then the front door opened, and Terry walked in.

Reed didn't bother to stand up, "Hey brother. Come on in and join us."

Terry looked at him, "Make yourself useful and grab me a beer."

Then Terry left to change clothes while Reed stepped out into the kitchen. As Terry walked down the hall, he stepped into the kitchen through the other entrance and whispered to Reed. "Don't mention the bug in Kim's car. Okay? I still haven't told Michelle about it."

That suited Reed fine. He didn't want to go anywhere near the topic of Kim and Keith anyway. Plus, he was still hiding from Terry the fact that he had met with Kim earlier and was withholding evidence. It seemed to him that he was the keeper of secrets and he wasn't extremely comfortable with the role.

As soon as Reed returned to the living room and sat down, Michelle looked at him suspiciously.

"I heard you two whispering. What was that about?"

"Oh, nothing. Terry was just telling me about a new IPA beer he's found from a local microbrewery?"

She didn't believe him but knew she wouldn't get any more information, even if she pushed it.

When Terry came back in, he sat down on the couch next to Michelle, picked up his glass from the coffee table, took a gulp, and then rested it on her knee while balancing it with his hand. "Reed and I want to chat about the Alki case for a bit. You are welcome to stay if you want."

Michelle was curious about the case, especially since Kim knew the victim's boyfriend, so she accepted the offer.

"Sure. I'd like to hear what you two sleuths have dug up."

She looked at Reed as she patted Terry on the knee. "This guy hasn't said a thing about it since Tuesday. First, he was obsessed with how and why that young girl might have died and now he says nothing. All I know is what they say on the news."

Michelle couldn't begin to appreciate how little she actually knew, and that Terry and Reed were both protecting her from information that would probably send her into a nervous frenzy.

Terry shifted and settled into the couch.

"There hasn't been anything to tell honey. Hopefully, Reed found something at Marissa's memorial service." He looked over at Reed for help.

Reed leaned forward, resting both elbows on his knees and rolling his bottle back and forth between his palms. He started out by recounting the incident between Steven and Keith. "It appears that Steven Schmidt and Ryan Archer are publicly blaming Keith for Marissa's death. After Steven accused Keith of murdering Marissa in front of the chapel, I spoke with a couple of girls about the confrontation. They said it was the general sentiment of the community that Keith was responsible for Marissa's death."

Terry interrupted. "Do they have any basis for their accusation?"

Reed answered, "Not that I can tell."

Reed went on to explain the close relationship between Steven Schmidt and Marissa's father and how Mr. Archer had approved of Steven dating Marissa and further, how he disliked Keith and blamed him in part for her behavior and emotional problems.

Terry asked. "Who told you that?"

Reed continued, "I met a friend of Marissa's after the memorial service. She was anxious to tell me that Keith had nothing to do with Marissa's death. We went for coffee and she gave me her insights on the whole group including Steven, Keith, Marissa, and Marissa's family. The girl's name is Grace. She was apparently very close to Marissa."

Terry had not heard the girl's name and was surprised that the investigators may not have talked with, or even known about Grace. If she was a close friend of Marissa's, you would think that her father would have mentioned her to the police or even asked the girl directly if she knew anything.

Reed continued. "Grace told me that Keith would do anything for Marissa and was the understanding shoulder that she hadn't gotten at home or from Steven."

He took another sip from his beer. "Remember those cuts on Marissa's arms? Grace confessed that both she and Marissa were into self-mutilation. Marissa wasn't being abused by Keith. Quite the opposite, he was trying to help her stop cutting. Those arm wounds were self-inflicted."

Reed almost slipped and mentioned the bag of paraphernalia that Keith had given Kaykay and that he was now hiding illegally.

Terry thought about the autopsy results. Only the police and Reed knew about Marissa's time and cause of death. If Grace had let any of that slip to Reed, it would implicate her or indicate that she might be protecting Keith.

"Did she say how she thinks her friend died?"

Reed knew what he was getting at and answered. "She doesn't seem to have any ideas about who may have been involved and she didn't give any hint of knowing what caused Marissa's death or the time of death. She just said she didn't think it would have been Keith."

Reed thought a moment and added. "She did say that she had a strange encounter with Steven and Mr. Archer at the funeral home today after we talked. They warned her not to talk with anyone and steer them away from Keith as the suspect. She also said that Steven had threatened Marissa once. That got me thinking about Steven as a suspect."

Reed sat back and set his beer on the oak end-table.

Terry thought a moment about Reed's information and then started telling what he had found out from McManus.

"Well, I don't have much for you, but this is what I know from Robert so far."

He collected his thoughts.

"You said that Grace mentioned Marissa having emotional problems. Well, the investigating team turned up similar information. School records show that she was regularly referred for counseling and the school recommended she get outside psychiatric help. Her father had declined to send her for therapy, saying he preferred to handle those things within the family. Apparently, he has strong opinions about the pharmaceutical industry and claims that most therapists are simply pawns of the drug industry, rushing to prescribe medication before trying alternative means to help their patients. He cites that some of the criminals in his care had committed their felonies after being treated with antidepressants."

Reed interrupted, "Did they also find out that his wife was taking antidepressants?"

Terry looked surprised, "That seems a little hypocritical and contradictory."

"Or it may be part of the reason he has an issue with them. Grace mentioned that Mr. Archer refused counseling for Marissa, sighting her mother as an example of the waste of drugs and therapy."

Up to that point Michelle had been sitting quietly next to Terry taking it all in, but the last comment caused her to stand up angrily.

"Excuse me for interrupting but Mr. Archer sounds like an ignorant ass. If his wife was going to therapy and still had issues, maybe he should take a good hard look in the mirror for the real problem. How can people be so heartless?"

Reed and Terry both jumped from Michelle's sudden outburst. Reed tentatively asked, "Excuse me, but who just jacked you up?"

Michelle calmed a bit, leaned against the fireplace mantle, and stuffed her hands in her pockets.

"Sorry. I just get pissed off when I hear stories like this. These two women needed help and this jerk thinks it's all about drug company conspiracies. What was he doing to help his wife or daughter?"

She walked back to the couch, sitting down and wrapping her arm around Terry's neck.

"Sorry again, I'll keep my mouth shut." She leaned her head on his shoulder.

Terry reached over and held her other hand. Michelle had lost their first baby seven months into her pregnancy when a distracted driver failed to notice a stop sign and t-boned Michelle's car on the driver's side. In addition to losing their baby, Michelle suffered a back injury and had to deal with both physical pain and emotional trauma. Her resulting depression was debilitating for both her and Terry and the two of them went through counseling together. Michelle had taken prescription antidepressants and pain medicine for several months. Through professional help, mutual support, love and understanding they had weathered the darkest days of their marriage and went on to know the joys of parenthood with their daughter Kim who was born two years later.

It took a moment longer for Reed to understand the outburst but then he recalled Terry and Michelle's trials and shifted the conversation.

"Has anyone figured out what Marissa was doing in Seattle?"

Michelle got up and leaned over to kiss Terry on the forehead. "I think I'll go out for a short walk and leave you two to talk."

She pulled on a blue windbreaker and stepped out the front door.

Suspects

Terry looked out the window after her and then turned to Reed.

"Sorry about that. It is probably better she is not here. I keep worrying that I'll slip and say something about Kim and Keith spending time with each other. That would worry her sick."

"I understand. Did you find anything else out from McManus?"

101

"A little. Keith and Kim met on Wednesday after school in her car. They talked for a while and he gave something to her but didn't say what it was. Whatever he handed Kim, she reacted by running from the car. Keith chased her part way across the lot but then she stopped and waited for him. They talked for a minute and she returned to her car. The bug under her dashboard couldn't catch their conversation outside, so we don't know what they talked about or what he gave her."

Reed's secret meeting with Terry's daughter Thursday morning and knowledge of the bag of cutting instruments stabbed at him as painful as any knife could, but he steeled himself to hold that information in confidence until he knew more. He shifted the conversation to the investigation in Marissa's hometown.

"So, what have the police found out in Gig Harbor? What did the Archer's have to say?"

"Mrs. Archer is devastated. The last time she saw Marissa was Friday evening. She was still in bed on Saturday morning when her daughter went out. She thought Marissa was just out for the day."

"And Mr. Archer?"

"The last time he saw her was Saturday morning. She told him that she was going out for the day and evening but didn't say where. It was typical for her to stay out late and it wasn't until he checked her room Sunday morning and saw that she hadn't returned home that he began to worry. When the police called on Sunday and told him they may have found his daughter in West Seattle, he suspected she had gone over to see Keith."

Reed remembered what Keith had told Kim about not having talked to Marissa in days. Terry had mentioned the same thing from the original police report.

Reed interrupted, "Didn't you tell me that Keith told the police he hadn't talked with Marissa that weekend. Maybe she didn't go to Seattle to see Keith. She could have been seeing someone else."

"Except he was lying about talking with her. His cell phone records show that he called Marissa's cell Saturday around 8:30 am. The investigators are going to have another talk with him tomorrow."

Now Reed's belief in Keith's innocence was beginning to erode. Keith had lied to both the police and Kim about talking with Marissa on

Saturday. Why would he lie if he was innocent? Maybe he had lied to Kim about the cutting tools too.

Terry finished up, "Other than that, they really don't have anything. There are no leads anywhere other than Keith and there is no hard evidence to connect him to Marissa's death. His talking with her Saturday morning is certainly no crime."

Reed felt sick to his stomach. He was on the verge of revealing his secret to Terry and telling him about the bag but decided to make one more phone call first, as soon as he left Terry's house.

He got up and stretched, trying not to look like he was in a hurry to leave.

"Well, it's only been a week. Sorry I haven't turned up more, but I'll keep digging. I am sure something will turn up soon."

He carried his empty bottle out to the kitchen where he threw it into the trash container under the sink and shouted back towards the living room. "I'd like to stay a little longer, but I need to get home. I promised Angela I would take her out to dinner tonight."

He walked back into the living room and walked over to Terry. "Don't worry brother. I have some ideas that I want to check out. I'll give you a call as soon as I find anything."

Terry stood and the two shook hands. Then Reed walked out to his car.

Invitation

Immediately after getting into the mini, Reed grabbed his cell phone. He spoke with Angela for a minute and then dialed Grace's cell number.

"Hey, this is Grace."

"Grace, this is Reed. How are you doing?"

"I'm okay. I didn't expect to hear from you so quick. Did you find something?"

"Actually, I was just telling my wife Angela about you and how you two are so alike and she would like to meet. She suggested I invite you over for lunch tomorrow. We can talk more about Marissa or just enjoy the lake. The weather tomorrow is supposed to be perfect."

Grace responded, "Wow, that sounds nice. Just let me check with my foster mother. If she is okay with it, then yes, I would like to come and visit. Hang on a moment."

He could hear Grace asking if it was okay for her to visit a friend in Seattle tomorrow. He couldn't make out the response but could detect the concerned tone in a woman's voice. Grace assured her it was someone she trusted, and that she would be safe. Then Grace came back on the line and said she could come over.

Reed said, "Perfect. I'll give you driving directions to our house."

After giving Grace the directions and agreeing to a meeting time, Reed suppressed a smug smile. By having her come to Seattle he could drive around West Seattle and Alki while he and Angela gauged Grace's reactions to the area and some specific locations Reed had picked. Reed was almost certain that Grace had nothing to do with Marissa's death but needed to erase any doubt. If she was directly involved in last Saturday's events or even just protecting Keith, they might be able to sense it.

Expendable

The two men cruised up and down the main street of the Capitol Hill shopping district to scout for a street person that was out on their own. The eclectic collection of cultures, shops, restaurants, and bars made the neighborhood a popular destination for an evening out, and the streets were crowded as usual. It was also a popular neighborhood for young transients to frequent and that is what brought the two men to the district.

The passenger, tall and slim with thick black hair, fidgeted, "Doc, do you really think this is necessary?"

The driver, a short stout man with an additional decade of life on him replied firmly, "Yes Ari, it is. And you know that."

The passenger shook his head, "I'm not so sure. The more I think this through, the more I think we should lay low. There is no to point to what you want to do."

The driver responded, "There is absolutely a point. We can't be sure of how the investigation into Marissa's death is going and if it may lead to us. We need to create misdirection and make sure they don't find a trail. What I do at the clinic is too important to be stopped."

"What about Marissa? I don't want her name to be tarnished."

"You already thought she was tarnished. That is why you said she was a good candidate. Remember, it was you that came to me for my services."

"But this is different. What we are doing tonight is different. This isn't an attempt to cure anyone. It is nothing more than premeditated..." He didn't finish his sentence.

The driver did not respond and continued to scout the sidewalk. At the corner of Broadway and Thomas he spotted a young girl with long blonde hair that fell around her shoulders. She was standing alone and asking passersby for spare change. "There" the driver pointed, "She looks perfect. Probably a heroin addict trying to raise money for her next buy. I bet she even sells herself for it. And with that body and face I would wager she has no problems getting takers. Trust me, other than her customers; nobody is going to miss her."

He drove another half block and instructed his passenger to get out of the car, "Remember the plan. I will park the car and be along shortly."

The passenger walked along Broadway trying to look relaxed and give the appearance of a local out to frequent one of the restaurants. As he passed the girl they had selected, she held her hand out.

"Spare change?"

He stopped and gave her a warm smile. "How about a nice meal instead?"

She smiled back, "Actually, I could really use the change."

He thought that the girl would probably prefer money that she could use for drugs versus a free meal, but he pushed on. "You look hungry. Please, let me help you out. I will buy you a warm meal and then give you some money."

The girl became wary, "And what do you want in return? I am not a prostitute."

He chuckled, "I didn't think you were. And I'm not the kind of guy that goes out looking for prostitutes. I am just trying to help. When I was down on my luck, people helped me out, and now I am trying to pass that on. By the way, my name is," he paused a moment, "John. John Smith. What is yours?"

The girl visibly relaxed and chuckled. "John Smith. That almost sounds made up. My name is Becky. And you know, a nice dinner would be nice."

John Smith said, "Wonderful," and pointed down a side road. "We can go to a great place I know down the street. We'll go this way. It's a shortcut."

Seeing that the way her new acquaintance pointed was a dark street, Becky stiffened. "Umm, on second thought, I don't think so. But thank you for the offer."

He realized his mistake and said. "Oh, the dark street. Sorry. It really is safe. Look, I'll walk ahead of you to the next intersection where it is light and then you can walk up to join me. The restaurant is just around the corner from there."

Becky watched as he walked briskly down the block, first disappearing into the dark and then reemerging in the streetlights at the far end. She relaxed and started walking down the street imagining how good it would feel to have a full stomach. Maybe living on the streets of Seattle for a while would not be so bad. Still, she looked forward to going to her aunt's tomorrow. She imagined having a good night's sleep in a comfortable bed and the safety of her aunt's home. Beginning tomorrow, she would start to put her life back together.

She picked up her pace slightly when she entered the dark stretch of the block and focused on the light a few hundred feet away as she thought about how good her luck had been tonight. She never heard the man that came up behind her and she had no time to react. He swiftly wrapped one arm snuggly around her chest and swung his other up to her face. His hand clamped tightly over her mouth and nose. The small girl was no match for the man, and it did not take long for her to pass out from lack of air.

From the intersection, the first man heard a brief commotion come from the dark stretch of sidewalk and then silence. He ran back to see what had happened and found his partner kneeling on a patch of grass in the shadows, the unconscious girl sprawled out next to him. The man on his knees tossed the car keys over and pointed, "I parked over there. Go get the car and come back, quick. We can't risk anyone finding us."

A flash of remorse passed over the standing man's face as he left to retrieve the car. It took only a few minutes to return to the side street and a minute more to lift the girl into the back seat of the car. He returned to the driver's seat while his companion stayed in back and bound the girl's arms behind her back with duct tape.

The man in back then pulled a syringe from his pocket with one hand and slid Becky's sleeve up with his other to expose her forearm.

"There, that should suffice." He said as he injected her.

Satisfied that she would now stay unconscious from the injection, he returned the syringe to his pocket and picked up a surgical pick that was resting in a cup-holder. He lifted Becky's right eyelid and inserted the tip of the pick between her eyeball and upper eyelid and pushed it in until he met resistance from the membrane behind her eye socket. Then he retrieved a small hammer that also rested in the cup holder and used it to hit the steel pick and punch through the membrane into her brain. The girl jolted awake and jerked her head violently back and forth several times while the doctor held firm on the handle and the probe scrambled the soft tissue in her head.

"Dam, she wasn't under." He cursed.

Becky convulsed several times and then became still. She was still alive but would not be for long. The doctor knew her brain was hemorrhaging, and she would die quickly.

He pulled the ice pick from her head and dropped it on the seat next to the hammer, "There, it is done."

The driver replied, "Okay, we should be there in fifteen minutes."

The driver kept his eye on the speedometer. The last thing he needed was to be pulled over for speeding with a dead girl in the back seat. He heard some shuffling sounds and asked, "Is everything all right back there?"

He turned to see what was making the sound and saw that his partner had removed the girl's jacket, opened her blouse and was lifting her bra to expose her breasts."

"What the hell are you doing?"

The man replied, "You don't have a problem with me copping a little feel, do you? She doesn't mind, and it would be a shame not to enjoy these a little."

The driver felt a wave of nausea and his head throbbed as lights flashed in his eyes and he tried to take in the doctor's actions.

The man continued, "I enjoy women's bodies. That's no sin. I never told you but in my personal practice, when I have a patient with nice breasts, I sometime take their tops off while they are under anesthesia. I don't think any of them ever figured it out and, if they did, they didn't complain."

The driver felt bile rising from his stomach and chocked back the acid that burned his throat. "Please tell me that you have never done this in the clinic."

The doctor answered, "Okay. I have never done this in the clinic."

The driver didn't believe him and began to question his relationship with the doctor and the work at the clinic. What else had the man done?

Nothing else was said until the car parked along Alki Beach at the far west end of the park just before residential homes occupied the property next to the shoreline. It was now after eleven o'clock and the street was deserted. The homes appeared to be dark and both men were comfortable they would not be seen. Just in case they were spotted, they propped Becky's body between them and walked toward the beach hoping it would appear to be three friends just taking a late walk together. The doctor had removed the tape and they wrapped her arms around them to give the appearance that she was hugging them as they walked. They only had to stroll a short distance to the seawall and a concrete stairway that led down into the shadows at the base of the breakwater.

At the bottom of the stairs they laid the girl's body onto the wet gravel and sand. The tide was going out and there was about ten feet of beach between the wall and the waterline.

The man called Ari spoke, "Did she have a cell phone?"

The doctor replied, "Yes. I removed the battery and SIM card and we will toss it."

"What about identification? The longer it takes to identify her, the better."

"She didn't have a purse and I didn't find anything in her pockets other than a ten-dollar bill and a couple of ones."

Ari said, "I'm not surprised. Probably doesn't even have a driver's license. Okay, I'll carry her into the surf. She should drift along the shore for a few hours and then wash back up by morning somewhere else along the beach."

Ari carried the lifeless body out several yards and set it onto the water's surface before pushing it away into the dark. He returned to the beach and the two men walked back up the seawall stairs and across the grass to their waiting car, noting that no one appeared to be around and confident they had not been seen. The doctor took the wheel and Ari returned to the passenger seat.

The men rode in silence for over twenty minutes before Ari spoke, "Doc, I've known you for over fifteen years and I put all of my trust in you. Not only at the clinic, but by supporting your private practice, and I've always considered you a friend in addition to a business associate." Then Ari's voice raised an octave, "But, by God, if I ever have any reason to think that you touched Marissa like you did that girl tonight, I swear I will kill you. That is a promise."

Ari was trembling as he finished. The doctor stared straight ahead and didn't reply.

Night Watch

Grips had been watching the freighter traffic out on the Puget Sound through his binoculars when he observed a large white SUV park directly across from his house by the waterside park. Three people got out and staggered down to the breakwater. Normally it would not have caught his attention being a Friday evening and all. Lots of people stop at the park to watch the boats and lights across Puget Sound and many of those have had a bit too much to drink. Tonight though, the rain had kept most everyone indoors and the park had been empty. That is, until the SUV stopped. Grips watched three people make their way from the vehicle to the seawall and then down the steps to the shoreline. It looked like one of them must have been extremely drunk because the other two were on each side holding the middle person up.

After the three disappeared out of sight, Grips took a long draw on his pipe and held the sweet smoke in his lungs for a moment. As he let it out, he chuckled a bit remembering a few of the times he had been falling down drunk and stumbled around the beach in the rain, even passing out on the sand a few times only to wake up the next morning with some dog licking his face. Oh, to be young again. He took another long puff and put the binoculars back up to his eyes to spot more ships. Grips had no idea how much time passed before he spotted the beach walkers again.

He thought to himself, "Wasn't there three of them before?"

Grips had been smoking some exceptionally strong weed and had also just polished off a bottle of Sailor Jerry. His old injuries had been exceptionally painful today and he had self-medicated on the heavy side. He thought, 'Hell, probably just my head fucking with me again.'

Then he remembered talking with Terry the other day. Something about a dead girl being found at the boat launch and watching for any suspicious activities. He focused his binoculars on the white SUV just as it pulled away and jotted down the license number before falling into a deep sleep in his recliner.

Chapter 8

Vibes

Reed woke-up early Saturday morning and buried his head deep into his pillow. He wasn't ready to crawl out from under the heavy covers to face the cool morning air and the cold hardwood floor that would greet his bare feet. Without opening his eyes, he slowly slid across the king size bed to Angela's side in search of her satin clad warmth to cuddle into. After crossing three pillows and what seemed like too much space, Reed came to the other side of the bed where he was greeted by Rainier purring in his face.

"Rainier, you are definitely no substitute for Angela."

Rainier just purred back while Baker jumped up on the bed to make a threesome.

Reed stared at Baker, "Did your mistress send you to wake me?"

He pushed the covers down and got out of bed to pull on a pair of sweatpants. Then he grabbed a tee shirt from a corner post of the bed and pulled it over his head. After searching in vain for his slippers he padded down the stairs in bare feet and followed the invisible scent of breakfast that now mixed with the smell of fresh brewed coffee.

"Hey love. You look awesome this morning." He walked up to Angela and gave her a big full kiss on the lips.

"Well, aren't we romantic today?" She licked her lips.

"Just in a good mood." He gave her another squeeze and a kiss on the cheek and then pulled a stool up to the counter. "Are you ready to meet Grace?"

"Of course. I look forward to it. She sounds interesting."

Angela pulled on an oven mitt and removed a warm plate of bacon from the oven. After placing it on the counter she reached over the stove and picked up a medium black skillet that held four eggs, easy over, bubbling in bacon drippings. She deftly slipped two of the golden eggs onto each of their plates.

"This should give you energy for the day."

Sitting down on a stool next to Reed she asked, "Do you think we'll find out anything today?"

Reed poured them each a full cup of coffee. "I'm not sure, but there are discrepancies in everyone's stories, and I would like to start sorting them out. I hope Grace can help clear some things up, not only with her answers, but with her reactions to driving around West Seattle. I want you to watch her and try to pick up on her vibes."

"Do you think she was involved?"

"I don't think so. She seems to be a nice girl and I guess I am hoping that she is not involved, but she still may know more than she is telling. That is what we want to find out today."

Beachcombing

Ruth and Morris had lived their entire fifty-year married life in a little house two blocks off Beach Drive not far from the lighthouse. Since Morris retired from the steel mill ten years before, the husband and wife made it a regular routine to rise early every morning and walk to the shoreline where they would beach comb and search for treasures that had either washed up with the tide or had been dropped in the sand by the beachgoers the day before.

Morris liked to walk the stretch from the bath house to the beach volleyball courts while he scanned the sand with his metal detector. He knew there was more treasure further along but, as the years had passed, he found it more difficult to walk long distances on the sand. The beach ball courts were just the right distance. Today he was wearing his regular uniform of khaki trousers, white tennis shoes, dark blue windbreaker and yellow baseball cap topped with the earphones for his metal detector.

Ruth preferred to head in the opposite direction towards the rocks and tidal pools where she could watch the sea anemones and crabs that were exposed during the low tides. She also occasionally found

112

something interesting in the flotsam and jetsam that would wash in on the tides, though the days of finding Japanese glass fishing floats were long gone.

Today, Morris decided to spend time scanning the gravely beach in front of the bathhouse before moving towards the sandy beach. He made his way along the base of the breakwater and swept the long metal arm of his detector back and forth in a wide arc as he listened for the tone that would tell him something metallic was buried in the gravel. He didn't know how long he spent working the first area, but he decided that there was nothing to be found along the seawall and made a turn towards the sandy beach. Just as he swept the arm in his new direction, the alarm tone sounded. 'Finally,' he thought, 'maybe this area won't be a bust after all.'

Morris laid the detector arm on the beach and lowered himself onto his right knee. It made a cracking sound as he knelt, and he reminded himself to start taking that stuff Ruth bought for his joints again. He could never remember the name of it, but Ruth would tell him to take it and it seemed to work, until he would forget to take it. Then his joints would act up and that reminded him to start taking the pills again. After he lowered himself onto both knees, Morris pulled on a pair of leather gloves and scraped at the gravel to uncover whatever the detector had found.

About two inches down, he found an object. He lifted it out and turned it about as he looked to see if it was worth anything. It was a cell phone and Morris shrugged. Cell phones were just about the most common thing he would find on the beach and while one might think they would be worth money, most of the time the elements had got to them and they were worthless. Still, sometimes they were okay and had some value. Morris looked closer. This phone had obviously been buried here for a long time. It was an old model flip phone and had been ravaged by the saltwater. He placed it in his collection bag to dispose of later and stood back up to resume scanning the beach.

It was only a couple of minutes after starting off toward the volleyball courts that Morris heard another alarming sound, but this was not from the detector. It was Ruth's voice, and she was screaming loud enough that he could hear it though the earphones. He turned around and saw her running across the shoreline toward him. She was shouting about finding something and he removed his headphones to hear better. "What love? Did you find something valuable?"

"No," she yelled. "A young girl. I found the body of a young girl."

She ran up to Morris and grabbed his hand, "Oh Morris. It is terrible. I was walking on the rocks in front of the lighthouse and there she was. The prettiest little thing. Just lying there sprawled across the rocks. Oh Morris." She started sobbing onto his shoulder.

Morris had a challenging time taking in just what his wife was saying, "Ruth, are you saying you found a dead body?"

"Yes. Aren't you listening? I called 911 and then went up to the lighthouse station and told the man there. We need to go back now. The police will want to talk with me."

Morris just stared at her.

"Don't just stand there. Pick up your gear and come to the lighthouse."

She turned and ran back the way she came leaving Morris, still in a bit of a daze, to pick up his detector and follow.

Lighthouse

Terry was apprehensive about his shift this morning. It was almost one week since Marissa's body was found and there were still no solid leads in the case. At a little after six, he pulled into the boat launch ramp parking area and sat in the patrol car for a few minutes not too far from the top of the ramp. The weather this morning was clear and calm, and several fishermen were launching their boats as he watched. After a few minutes he decided to leave the beach area and cruise up to his favorite coffee house about ten minutes away.

When Terry arrived at Velvet Green, the owner was unlocking the front door and greeted him. "Good morning. Are things a little quieter than last week?"

Terry replied, "Thank goodness yes. I don't think I am ready for another day like that."

The owner knew that Terry came to his shop to get a break and not to talk about work, so he dropped the subject, "You having your regular?"

Terry nodded yes and put his money on the counter. The owner poured a mug of dark coffee and added a shot of espresso. "There you go. That will keep you going until the end of your shift."

Terry thanked him and picked up a free copy of the neighborhood newspaper from a stack on the counter. As he sat in a booth and sipped at his coffee, he read the local sports. The West Seattle high school basketball team was on a winning streak. He was glad to get his mind off the tragedy and hoped the winning team was doing the same for the community.

Terry had been in the shop for about twenty minutes when his radio came alive. It was a call for all available units to go to the Alki Point lighthouse. There was a report of a body found on the shore. Terry thanked the shop owner and rushed to his car. He turned on his lights but did not activate the siren as he turned onto the main street and accelerated back down to the beach.

It took only a few minutes for Terry to reach the lighthouse, but two other police cars were already there, and officers were cordoning off the entrance to the grounds with police tape. Terry spotted Jack Ross and walked over, "You got here fast."

Jack replied, "I was a block away when the call came in. It's the investigators you should be impressed with. They were here within minutes of my arriving. They must have been staking out the beach area."

Terry could see two plainclothes men talking with an older lady on the lighthouse lawn not too far from the shore. Another man, dressed in blue sweats, stood with them but did not say anything.

Terry asked Jack if the two found the body. Jack answered, "Just the lady. She was out on an early morning beachcombing walk and found a young girl lying on the rocks in front of the lighthouse. She called 911 and then went up to one of the Coast Guard houses and notified the resident, the man in the blue sweats. He is the Coast Guard District Commander."

Terry thanked Jack for the update and excused himself to walk over to the shoreline. When he reached the edge of the well-groomed lighthouse grounds, he could see clearly down onto the rocks where the body lay. His heart raced as he looked at the young woman dressed only in blue jeans and open white blouse, lying on her back in a shallow tidal pool. Her body was mostly submerged in the pool, only her face, bra and toes breaking the surface. Her blond hair floated away from her face in all directions like a halo around her head.

Unlike the girl from last week, this victim was dressed in designer clothes. He recognized them from the brands his daughter always asked for. He also noticed that she had French manicured nails, another trend he had learned about from his daughter. He turned away and choked back the tears. He thought about calling Reed and then decided against it. What was the point? There was nothing to be gained by Reed seeing another dead body right now. He would call him later after his shift was over.

Celtic Cross

On the Grey Kraken, the ringing of the doorbell a little after noon alerted Reed that Grace had arrived. He looked out his office window and saw that Grace looked brighter and more approachable than when they first met. Not the girl in hooded sweatshirt, now she wore a long bright patterned peasant skirt and tee shirt.

"Hi, you must be Grace! I'm Angela." Angela had been cleaning the front deck so that she could be outside when Grace arrived and be the first to greet her. She jumped from the deck that faced out to the lake and onto the dock to walk back to Grace who was standing at the front door further back along the side of the Grey Kraken. "Welcome to the Grey Kraken. Reed told me a little about you and I was anxious to meet."

Grace smiled, "Thanks for inviting me and for trying to help find out what happened to Marissa."

Angela smiled back. "No problem. Reed likes solving mysteries. Follow me. We can sit on the front deck and enjoy the view."

Grace followed Angela along the dock and onto the deck just as Reed walked out through the glass doors. He smiled at Grace, "Good morning and thanks for coming over. Would you like a cup of coffee? I can even make you a latte if you like."

Grace nodded and said it sounded perfect and Reed went back inside to the kitchen. From where he was standing at the espresso machine, he could just hear Grace and Angela talking. He couldn't make out the words but, from the tone of their voices, could tell that they were enjoying talking with each other. When he returned with Grace's latte, the two were sitting comfortably in deck chairs and talking about art and how they both enjoyed making their own jewelry.

As they talked, the sunlight caught and reflected off a pendant that hung around Grace's neck. Angela noticed the Celtic cross and commented, "That's a beautiful pendant. Did you make it?"

Grace fingered the cross, "Marissa made it and gave it to me. She knew I like crosses and gave it to me as a friendship token. I don't have any chains for it, so I keep it on this leather strap."

Angela smiled, "You know, I think I might have a spare chain that it would look good on. Would you like to try it on and see?"

Grace's face lit up. "Really, that would be great!"

Angela went upstairs to the bedroom and Reed pulled another deck chair over and sat down. "Thanks again for meeting with me yesterday. You didn't need to do that and could have just walked away after hearing those girls talking to me about Marissa and Keith."

"No." she answered, "I couldn't have. I loved Marissa and I know better than anyone that Keith wouldn't hurt her. I couldn't let those two get away with spreading rumors and ruining his reputation or hers."

Grace sipped her latte and looked at Reed, "I am so thankful you want to help, and I will do anything to help find out what really happened. I am counting on you."

Reed remembered the conversation with Terry when his brother had also said he was counting on him. He felt his stomach turn and couldn't find the words to assure Grace.

Just then, Angela returned and sat back down in her deck chair. She held her open hand out to Grace. "I actually have two chains that would look nice with that cross. Why don't you pick your favorite and you can keep it? Consider it a gift from a new friend."

Grace leaned over and gave Angela a big hug. You would never have guessed that they just met. Angela returned the hug with just as much emotion.

Reed excused himself and went back inside to let the two be alone. It was clear they had bonded, and the time would give Angela an opportunity to read the girl. He returned to his computer and would give them thirty minutes. Then he would go back down and suggest a drive to West Seattle.

Grace

On the deck, Grace and Angela talked with ease. Angela told Grace about their chain of boutiques and how they enjoyed living on the water next to the thriving downtown area. After a short time, she asked Grace to tell a little about herself. Grace was comfortable and opened up to Angela. Angela sensed that Grace needed someone to talk to and had found someone she could trust, and maybe lean on, in Angela.

Grace told that she had been an only child and, in retrospect, thought that she was probably spoiled by her doting parents. Her father was a machinist at the Bremerton shipyards and her mother a stay-at-home mom. They were a close family and she had what she would characterize as a happy childhood. She had never been very outgoing, preferring to read over playing soccer or other youth sports, and her parents had never pushed her.

For summer vacation after her eight-grade year, her parents planned a vacation in California with trips to Disneyland and the beaches. On the drive down, they would take the Washington and Oregon coast roads to see the ocean beaches. During the second day of driving along the twisting coastline, an oncoming truck crossed the center line and clipped the family car. The accident didn't look that bad. The truck had shown only slight damage and the car had spun and come to a rest with the front end tucked under the trailer of another semi-truck parked on the side of the road.

Grace was only shaken up and her parents were conscious and, she thought, okay. Unfortunately, the crash had mangled the front end of the vehicle in a way that trapped the two adults and they were both bleeding from injuries to their legs. None of the bystanders were able to pry them loose or access their injuries to stop their bleeding. By the time emergency crews arrived with the jaws of life, both of her parents had lost too much blood to save and she became an orphan at thirteen.

Grace had no living relatives to take her in, so Washington State placed her with foster parents in Gig Harbor, twenty miles south of the home she had grown up in. Her parents' home was sold and the proceeds, along with those from the sale of the remaining assets, were placed into a trust for Grace.

As Grace related the story, Angela was impressed by the girl's composure, though she felt it was more from numbness than serenity.

Grace went on to say how good her foster parents were and that she appreciated how lucky she was to have them. But, she added, they would never replace her real parents and how now, without Marissa to lean on, she felt lost. Her composure broke and she started crying. Angela walked over and kneeled to hold her. She gently rocked the girl back and forth and sent soothing thoughts to calm her.

Reed returned to the deck door and saw the two. He knew that Angela needed the hug from Grace just as much as the girl needed hers and he left them alone for a few more minutes. When Angela stood back up, he cleared his throat.

"Ahem, I don't mean to interrupt, but I was thinking we might want to go out for a drive to the beach. The weather couldn't be any better."

Angela and Grace wiped their tears and Angela responded, "I think that's a good idea."

She turned to Grace, "What do you think? Are you up for a drive?"

Grace answered, "Sure. Would we be able to go to where Marissa was found?"

Angela looked over at Reed and gave a subtle nod. It was exactly the response he had hoped for from the young girl and he answered, "No problem. West Seattle and the beach will be perfect today. We can stop at the boat launch and get out if you like."

Grace thanked him and Reed suggested they finish their coffees and go to the car. A few minutes later, the three were walking up the dock to Angela's Porsche Cayenne.

Slip-up

Angela sat in the back seat with Grace and, throughout the drive to West Seattle, the two talked about everything from high school to boys. Angela knew that Reed wanted to gauge Grace's reactions to the area and was careful not to point out where they were at any time. If she had been involved in Marissa's death, she may show some subtle reaction to a landmark that could be tied to the death.

"That's Keith's school. He showed it to us one time when we both came over." She looked intently at the buildings and campus as they continued past.

Then her voice lowered, and she asked, almost hesitantly, "Can we go to the boat launch?"

Reed answered, "That's where we're going now. We'll be there in a few minutes."

After another mile, Reed turned onto a side street and drove down two blocks before turning right again and cruising past the address Terry had given him for Keith's house. Grace and Angela had returned to their conversation and showed no interest in the street or houses. Reed had not told Angela where the home was to prevent her from unconsciously sending Grace any cues. He looked in the rearview mirror and saw that neither woman looked toward Keith's house nor showed any interest outside the car as he drove by. He was curious if Grace had been to the boy's house but, based on her lack of reaction, he guessed she had not.

He returned to the main arterial that wound down to the waterfront and came out a short distance from the boat launch ramp. It seemed that Grace was not familiar with the area. They drove to the boat ramp parking lot and pulled into an open spot. The area was crowded with fishermen and pleasure boaters taking advantage of the nice weather. The three left the car and walked down to the floating docks in silence.

Grace asked, "Where was she?"

Reed pointed out to the water. "Out there to the right, by the end of that dock."

Grace walked out to the end of the dock and knelt. She began crying and carefully removed the chain from her neck and slid the cross from it. After reattaching the chain around her neck, she tossed the cross out into the bay. "I love you Marissa. Good-bye."

Back up in the parking lot Angela took Reed's hand as they both watched the lone girl kneeling at the end of the dock. "She didn't do it."

Reed answered. "I know."

"And if Keith had something to do with it, she doesn't know."

"I know that too."

"But what you don't know is that, while all three were good friends, and while everyone thought Keith and Marissa were a couple, it is actually Marissa and Grace that were in love."

Reed smiled, "I guessed that too. That's why I hurt even more for Grace and swear I will find Marissa's killer."

When Grace came back up the ramp Angela walked over and put her arm around her and the two walked back to the car, heads down, no words spoken.

Reed gave them a few minutes before returning to the vehicle to continue their drive. After leaving the boat launch parking lot, the route took them along Alki Avenue where they passed bikers and joggers plying the wide blacktop path that paralleled the roadway and separated it from the beach. Some of the more adventuresome were in shorts, but a fresh breeze off the water kept most of the beachgoers in regular clothing and light jackets.

Where the beach broadened from a thin band to a wide expanse of several hundred feet, adults picnicked while young children ran and held tightly to strings that tethered kites darting captive overhead in the spring breeze.

The sight of people playing and sound of children laughing forced a crack into the somber mood in the car and Reed spoke, "I think we should pick up some fish and chips and have lunch by the water."

The women agreed, and he pulled into the parking lot of a local fish and chips shop. After getting their order to go, the three walked across the street and across the white sand to an old washed up log where they could sit and eat. Reed unwrapped the three cardboard trays and set the fish and chips precariously on the log's curved top. Immediately, two seagulls spotted the food and started crying out to their brethren. Within minutes the surface of the water in front of the log was dotted with birds bobbing up and down on the rollers, waiting for cast-offs of fish and fries.

Nobody talked as they ate their lunch. All three were lost in thought, contemplating the events of the previous weekend.

Suddenly Angela spoke her thoughts out loud, sounding exasperated as she blurted, "I would give anything to know exactly what happened last Saturday afternoon."

As soon as the words left her lips, she knew what she had done. She clenched her fists and squeezed her eyes shut hoping above all else that Grace had not picked up on the slip. Reed tried not to react as he heard his wife accidentally reveal the time of Marissa's death.

Grace's reaction was immediate, and Angela was mentally kicking herself for making such a big mistake.

"I thought she died Sunday morning. Why did you say Saturday afternoon?"

121

Reed knew he couldn't lie convincingly, and he was now certain that Grace had nothing to do with Marissa's death, so he decided to tell her what the coroner had determined about the time of death, but nothing more.

Reed locked his eyes on the girl's, "Grace, you have got to promise to keep what I am about to tell you to yourself. I will be in serious trouble if anyone finds out that I told you. And so will you if you tell anyone."

Angela leaned forward and buried her head in her knees. Both Reed and Grace could barely make out her repeating into her leg, "Shit, shit, shit."

Grace ignored Angela and assured Reed that she would keep whatever he had to say to herself.

Then Reed told her, "The coroner determined that Marissa died some time Saturday afternoon. She was taken to the ramp later, after she died."

Grace jerked back and almost lost her seating on the log. "Well, your coroner is wrong. I saw Marissa Saturday morning and she had a dentist appointment early that afternoon. She was going to have her wisdom teeth removed or something. There is no way she was over here during the day."

It was Reed's turn to be shocked. "What? Are you sure about that?"

Grace answered, "Absolutely. Marissa and I had coffee at Crème Cafe until about nine o'clock. Then she went home to get a ride to the dentist. She said she couldn't drive herself because they would be using anesthesia and it wouldn't be safe to drive home. I volunteered to drive her, but she said that her dad had to take her. Something to do with filling out insurance forms."

As Reed listened, he thought, 'Could the coroner be off by several hours?' He would have to check that with Terry. Then he wondered about the police report that Keith had called Marissa Saturday morning.

"Were you with Marissa at 8:30?"

"Yes, I just told you. We were at Crème Cafe."

"Did Keith call her while you were there?"

"Yes. They hadn't talked in a few days and he was worried about her. He wanted to come over, but she told him she was busy."

That explained the phone call records. But why had Keith lied to the police and Kim? Reed grabbed a handful of chips and threw them out onto the water causing the scattered birds to fly up and then converge back on the surface in a tight cluster where the chips floated, fighting each over for the bobbing pieces.

"Have you talked with Keith this week?"

"No, I knew he would show up at the memorial service and planned on talking with him there. That is until Steven chased him off."

"He told the police that he hadn't talked with Marissa that weekend. Why do you think he would lie?"

Grace became defensive. "He probably freaked. I would too. He wasn't supposed to be seeing Marissa. She lived over an hour away. And she was found dead over here. He knew people would think he had something to do with it."

"Maybe. But lying to the police doesn't help his case. Now he looks even more suspicious."

Grace looked more upset and Angela sensed it was time to move on. "Come on Grace, we've got sightseeing to do."

Reed trusted Angela's instincts and dropped the conversation.

Crumpets

They all went back to the car and drove to the downtown waterfront where Reed left Angela and Grace to walk along the piers and visit on their own while he went to wander around the Pike Place Market. They agreed to meet in an hour for tea at a crumpet shop adjacent to the market.

After climbing the steps from the waterfront to the top level of the market, Reed found it packed with people and the fish stalls were doing a brisk business. He stopped to join the throng of tourists watching the fish mongers tossing fish orders to each other. A good-sized fresh salmon flew from the hands of a young man standing in front of the counter, across the shop and into the waiting hands of another who deftly wrapped it in white paper for the waiting customer. The process was repeated as each customer pointed out their selection from the variety of fish piled high on mounds of ice, their selection then grabbed, tossed, and wrapped.

Reed walked around the counter away from the fish and selected two Dungeness crabs from dozens that were arranged on the shaved ice and bought them along with enough steamer clams to provide him and

Angela a nice seafood dinner later that evening. After finding another stall where he bought a loaf of sourdough bread, he walked up the block to the crumpet shop.

Inside the shop, Angela and Grace were already seated and enjoying their tea and crumpets. Reed went to the counter and ordered a pot of English Breakfast Tea and two hot crumpets with butter and raspberry jam. While he waited for his order he looked over at Angela and Grace. It appeared their moods had lightened, and they seemed to enjoy each other's company. This did not overly surprise Reed. Angela loved teenagers and could always see through their posturing and bravado to their true hearts. She seemed to bring out the good spirit in everyone she met and touched. She and Grace were laughing about something when Reed sat down at the table.

"You two seem to be having a good time."

"Mr. Carver, your wife is awesome. I love her. We have been talking about all sorts of stuff."

Angela smiled at Reed. "Grace and I have similar tastes in art. She wants to come back into town and go to the Seattle Art Museum some time, so I've offered to take her next Saturday."

Reed nodded his approval as he took a bite of his hot crumpet. The girls laughed as melted butter and raspberry jam ran down his chin.

Angela looked at Grace and shook her head. "It is probably obvious that I love him for his brains. They almost make up for the other stuff."

Reed wiped his chin and tried to speak with his mouth full but couldn't make sense, so he just chewed, swallowed, and stuffed another bite in.

By the time they finished it was late-afternoon and time to get back to the houseboat so that Grace could get on the road before dark. At the house, Reed asked Grace if she would look at something for him before she left, and she said no problem. Then he retrieved the bag from Keith and asked Grace to look inside.

"You said you and Marissa both cut on yourselves. Could these have been Marissa's?"

Grace's eyes welled up. "Yes. She gave them to Keith and promised to stop cutting. I was with them when she did it. We were at Crème Café. How did you get them?"

Reed explained how the bag had made it to him and thanked Grace for her help. Then they walked out onto the dock where Grace gave Reed a hug and then turned to Angela and hugged her. "Thank you for everything."

She started to unlatch the chain around her neck. "I suppose I should give this back since I don't have the cross now."

Angela reached out and took Grace's arms. "Keep the chain. Maybe you can find another cross to place on it to remember Marissa by."

The two hugged again and Grace walked to her car followed by Reed, Angela, and a friendly neighbor dog that wagged his tail and bumped at her ankles looking for attention. After patting him on the head, she climbed into her car and backed out of the parking space, careful to avoid the dog.

As she pulled away Reed and Angela waved before walking back down to the Grey Kraken where Reed returned to his computer to do more research. Reed was now almost certain that neither Grace nor Keith had anything to do with Marissa's death. It was a long shot, but maybe Steven was responsible. It sounded like he had made a threat to kill Marissa and, despite Grace's doubt that he could do such a thing, Reed couldn't rule the possibility out. He decided to do a little digging into Steven.

Public Records

Reed searched public records and hacked his way into school records to learn more about Steven Smith. It appeared that the boy was an exemplary student. In addition, he was a notable athlete. He maintained a 3.8 GPA throughout high school and had been recruited by several colleges to join their varsity football programs. Recently, he accepted an athletic scholarship to the University of Washington and would join the Huskies football team. Sports writers were already forecasting a strong performance from him and saying he could be key in taking the team to the National Championships. From articles in the local press you would think that he had almost single-handedly led the Gig Harbor high school to the state football finals during his junior and senior years.

In all that he could dig up, Reed couldn't find anything negative on Steven. In fact, he thought, a young man with this much going for him would be crazy to risk everything in a jealous rage over a break-up. Then again, love could make people do crazy things and Reed wasn't ready to rule Steven out quite yet. The alternative was worse. If Marissa's friends had no part in her death, then it was possible that she was murdered by a stranger. He decided to put the case aside for the day and go downstairs for dinner.

Lies

As Grace drove home, she thought about how she had enjoyed her day with Angela and Reed. She liked her foster parents, but it was refreshing to talk with other adults. Then she thought about the boat launch ramp. Now that she had seen the spot where Marissa's body was found she could imagine her friend's black Focus sitting underwater with her lifeless body inside only a short distance from where she had knelt on the dock that afternoon and bid her good-bye.

She thought about the slip-up by Angela when they were at Alki Point. If Marissa died sometime Saturday, her father may have been the last to see her when he brought her home from the dentist. Grace had never liked talking to Mr. Archer but decided she would ask him where Marissa went after the dentist appointment. If he told her, then she could tell Reed and he could investigate it. She remembered Mr. Archer standing with Steven at the memorial service and the tone in his voice when she walked by. She wondered if he might be covering for Steven.

That evening, Angela and Reed discussed the day as they prepared their seafood dinner. Both agreed that Grace was not involved in Marissa's death but still wondered about Keith. It bothered Reed that Keith lied to both the police and Kim about talking with Marissa on Saturday, but then again Grace could be right, he might have just panicked and lied so people wouldn't automatically suspect him.

What disturbed Reed the most now was what Grace said about Marissa seeing a dentist on Saturday. Neither of Marissa's parents had mentioned a dentist appointment to the police and taking your daughter to the dentist is not something you would typically forget. But then again, why would you cover it up? Was it possible that Marissa had lied to Grace when she said she was going to the dentist and had gone to Seattle to see Keith instead? That would explain why she declined Grace's offer to give her a ride. But if she was sneaking off to see Keith, she would have had no reason to lie to her best friend about it.

Plus, Grace heard Marissa tell Keith she was busy. Maybe she snuck over to Seattle to see someone other than Keith. If that was the case, whoever she came to see was most likely responsible for her death.

Angela didn't have any further insight into who might have killed Marissa, but held a strong conviction that Grace was not involved.

Coincidences

Terry arrived home from his shift to find both Michelle and Kim waiting in the living room. He looked at them and simply said, "I can't handle this. Last week was bad enough. But today" His voice faded off, then, "I am going to get changed."

Neither Kim nor Michelle said anything. They had seen on the television that another girl's body was found in the water in West Seattle, this time at the Alki Point lighthouse. They wanted to know the details but knew better than to press Terry after last week's incident.

A few minutes later, Terry came out from the bedroom, "It was another young girl. Based on her clothing and make-up I would guess she is from an affluent family. It looks like she partied a little too hard last night and fell into the water and drowned." He paused, "You know, if there is one part of my job I hate, this is it."

Michelle spoke, "Sorry honey. Just relax and try to take your mind off it. Did you call Reed?

"Not yet. There is no point bothering him until we get an autopsy report from the medical examiner."

She got up, "I made a late lunch. Let's eat and then you can take a quick nap."

Terry said that sounded good and the three shared a quiet lunch of tuna salad sandwiches. The television was on in the living room and they could hear a local newsman talking about the latest tragedy at Alki. After lunch, Terry retired to the bedroom where he dropped into a deep sleep

At a little after five o'clock Michelle woke Terry to tell him Reed was on the phone. She handed him the phone and he answered, "I suppose you are calling about today and wondering why I didn't call you first."

Reed answered with a puzzled tone, "How did you know I was with Grace today?"

Now Terry was puzzled, "What? You were with Grace today? No. I thought you were calling about the body found at Alki Point this morning."

Reed wasn't sure he heard right, "Did you say another body was found…. this morning? Jesus, we were down at the beach this afternoon. I didn't have my radio on today and didn't know anything about it. Come to think of it, I did notice a few more police cars patrolling the beach than normal." He paused, "Why didn't you call me?"

Terry sounded tired, "I didn't think there was any point. It was another young girl. It looks like she may have partied too much and fell into the water and drowned. No bruises or anything that I could see. Her blouse was undone, but not torn, so it was probably consensual. We'll know more when we get the medical examiner's report."

He paused, "She was on the rocks in front of the lighthouse. It was not a sight I want to see again, and you are better for not having been there."

Reed responded, "Do you think it is related to last week?"

Terry answered, "Different kind of girl. Different location. Probably a coincidence. One thing I can tell you though. If the two girl's deaths are connected, Keith was not involved in Marissa's death. Kim invited him over to our house after school yesterday and he ended up spending the entire evening. After we got through the initial awkwardness, we had a good visit. He really isn't a bad kid. Just a little different. Kind of like you bro."

He chuckled and Reed responded, "You laugh, but now maybe you see how people, including you, made assumptions about me when we were young."

Terry answered, "Okay, I get it. But back to the Alki Point body, I just hope someone reports her missing or some friends fess up to being out with her and admit they partied too hard and lost her along the beach. An accidental drowning would be tragic but, I think, better than the alternative. I don't want to think about the possibility of a serial killer on the loose here."

Reed spoke in a sobering tone, "You may not want to think about it, but it might be time we did. Let me know when you get more information on the autopsy report."

He paused, "The real reason I am calling is that Angela and I spent the day with Grace and learned some new details about Marissa's last day alive. They are interesting, but I don't know if they mean anything. You sound tired. Maybe we should just talk tomorrow."

Terry answered, "No. I am waking up now. What did she say?"

Reed proceeded to relay what Grace said about being with Marissa Saturday morning until 9:00 and that Marissa said she was leaving to go to the dentist. He didn't tell Terry that Angela had slipped up in front of Grace and revealed the time of Marissa's death.

He added that Grace overheard Keith's phone conversation with Marissa at 8:30 and heard Marissa tell Keith that she couldn't meet him later that day. Terry took notes on a small pad as he listened. It certainly was new information but only seemed to raise more questions.

When Reed was done, he asked, "Is it possible that the coroner could be off on the time of death?"

Terry responded, "Not likely. She died Saturday afternoon. Either Mr. Archer is lying, or Marissa was lying about her plans that day."

He told Reed he would pass the information on to McManus and thanked him for his help.

Julie

It was early afternoon when Robert McManus received initial findings from the medical examiner. A thorough search of the girl's clothing found no identification, but deep in one of her pockets was a soggy piece of paper with a name and phone number on it. Fortunately, the writing was in crayon and the water had not disturbed it. Robert was given the number and name to follow-up on.

A needle mark was found on the girl's arm and the frontal lobe of her brain had been penetrated and lacerated in a manner similar to the Archer girl, but the brain damage was more significant and indicated the attack was violent. That was all the examiner had at this time. Initial blood tests would be completed shortly.

Robert wasted no time in calling the number on the note and the phone picked up almost immediately, "Hello, this is Julie."

Robert introduced himself and had barely completed saying that he was an investigator with the Seattle Police when the person on the other end shouted, "My god, its Becky, isn't it?"

Robert answered, "I am calling because we found your phone number in the pocket of a deceased woman earlier today. May I come to your house to talk?"

The girl started crying, "Of course."

She gave Robert her parent's address and he said he would be over shortly. A half hour later he arrived at the house and met with Julie in the living room while her parents joined them and listened. Robert showed her a photograph of the deceased girl's face and Julie started crying. She told the investigator it was the girl she knew as Becky. She recounted how she had picked up the young hitchhiker in Ellensburg a little over a week ago. Robert started to admonish Julie for helping a run-away minor, but she interrupted him and told about Becky's father and that he had raped his only daughter on her sixteenth birthday, the day before she left for Seattle. Robert felt his blood pressure skyrocket and he struggled to keep his voice calm. He had no problem keeping his cool with drug dealers and gang bangers, but sexual assault by a family member sent him over the edge.

He asked if Julie knew where Becky was from and she answered that she was pretty sure that Becky had said Coeur d'Alene. Robert asked Julie if she had any more information that might help. Julie told him that Becky had called Friday and said that she planned take the bus to Portland on Saturday to stay with an aunt. She asked if she could come to Julie's house to shower and clean up before going and added that she planned to panhandle Friday evening on Broadway Street in the Capitol Hill neighborhood. They agreed to meet at one of the Pioneer Square coffee shops Saturday morning. Julie had gone there and waited for several hours, but Becky never showed up. She had been worried about her all day.

Robert finished taking his notes and thanked Julie for her help. He would contact the Coeur d'Alene police department and see if they had any missing person reports for a girl matching Becky's description.

Chapter 9

Confrontation

Grace knew that Marissa's parents attended early church service on Sunday, and she was waiting on their front porch when they returned just before ten. She greeted Mrs. Archer and then asked Mr. Archer if she could speak with him for a few minutes.

He told his wife to go on inside and, when she had shut the door, turned on Grace. "What exactly do you want young lady?"

"I just want to know where Marissa was last Saturday afternoon."

Mr. Archer became agitated. "How would I know? She just took off, as usual. I'm surprised she wasn't with you."

Grace responded, "She was until around nine in the morning. She told me that she had to leave to go to the dentist with you."

Mr. Archer's eyes narrowed, and his voice lowered as he gave a slow and measured response. "I don't know what you're up to little girl, but you better watch what you are saying and get your facts straight. She didn't have any dentist appointment on Saturday, and I didn't see her after she left the house that morning. If she wasn't with you, she was already in Seattle with Keith. And this time she spent the night and he killed her. Now, quit wasting my time. If it weren't for friends like you and Keith, Marissa would probably still be alive."

With that Mr. Archer turned and walked into his house.

Grace stood on the porch in stunned silence. Why would Marissa lie about going to the dentist? She slowly turned and walked down the cement steps to her parked car where she sat for several minutes before calling Reed.

Reed picked up on the second ring, "Grace, I'm surprised to hear from you. Do you miss us already?" he chuckled.

She answered, "Actually, I was wondering if maybe I could come by again tomorrow after school for a quick visit. I'd like to talk with you about Marissa some more and visit with Angela if she is free."

Grace didn't really have anything new to tell Reed and Angela, but the conversation with Mr. Archer made her uncomfortable and she was suspicious that he was covering something up. She felt she needed to share her feelings with Reed.

Reed answered, "Of course you can come over. What time are you thinking?"

"I get out at 3:30, so I can be there a little after five."

Reed said, "Perfect, you can join us for dinner. We'll see you tomorrow."

Angela was in the room with Reed during the call and heard his dinner invitation to Grace. She commented, "Grace is coming back already? Is everything alright?"

Reed answered, "I'm not sure. She didn't say anything specific, but her voice sounded different."

"She is still processing her best friend's death and I am sure some days are worse than others."

"You're probably right. Funny thing is, I hardly know the girl and I am already worrying about her like she was a relative."

"I know. Me too." Angela paused, "You know, we have a Celtic cross at the shop that would suit her perfectly. I think I'll pick it up tomorrow before she comes over. It won't replace the one Marissa gave her but maybe it will help her feel better."

"You're a good person. Just one more reason I love you so much." Reed gave Angela a big hug.

Favors

Mr. Archer was uncomfortable with the conversation he just had with Grace. He stood at the door and thought back to his conversations with the investigators. They never mentioned anything about Saturday. What was Grace up to?

"What did Grace want?" It was his wife.

"She was curious if the police had found anything yet. That's all."

Then he added, "I need to go into work to check on something. I shouldn't be long."

Without changing out of the suit he had worn to church he turned and went out the door to his car and pulled his phone from his pocket.

The phone rang several times before a groggy voice answered, "Hello? Who is this?"

"Steven, this is Mr. Archer. Sorry to get you up. Could you meet me in a little bit? I would like to talk with you about Marissa."

Steven perked up, "Did the police find something?"

Mr. Archer answered, "No. But I need to talk with you. Can you meet me down at Skansi Brothers Park in half an hour?"

Steven agreed, and Mr. Archer drove around Gig Harbor backstreets to kill time before they met.

When Steven arrived at the public park, he saw Mr. Archer standing by a rail overlooking the marina.

"Good morning sir."

Mr. Archer turned around, "Good morning and thanks for coming down. I need to share some information with you and ask a favor."

"Sure Mr. Archer, whatever you need."

Mr. Archer told Steven about Grace's visit earlier and his concern about her questions. He said he still believed that Keith was responsible for Marissa's death and didn't want Grace's confusing story about Marissa's whereabouts on Saturday to lead the police off on a wild goose chase.

Steven was relieved at Mr. Archer's continued conviction of Keith's guilt. He couldn't wait to see Keith jailed for Marissa's death.

Mr. Archer placed his hand on Steven's shoulder, "Here is what I am asking. Could you keep an eye on Grace and see what she is up to? I am not sure I totally trust her. Maybe she was even involved. Can you do that?"

Steven answered, "No problem. I'm on it."

Mr. Archer thanked Steven and left to go back home.

Steven got back into his dad's grey Audi and swore that he would not let Grace screw things up.

Coeur d'Alene

First thing Sunday morning, Robert called an investigator he knew with the Coeur d'Alene police department to see if they had a missing person report for a girl that matched the description of the victim now known as Becky. He and Fred Keelson had worked a case together some years back when a man from Seattle robbed a liquor store in Coeur d'Alene and shot the storekeeper. Since then they had stayed in touch and occasionally visited when in each other's town. After explaining the situation, he emailed a photograph of the girl to Fred and the investigator immediately recognized her from a local missing person report filed the previous Monday. The girl's name was Becky Rose. She was the daughter of a local insurance agent John Rose and his wife Carol. Fred said he would contact the Roses and ask them to make a positive identification, but Robert asked if he could wait instead for Robert to drive over and join the investigator to meet the couple in person. He recounted Julie's story of the father's sexual assault on Becky on her birthday night and said that he wanted to question the father on his own. The investigator understood and agreed to his request.

After hanging up, Robert went straight to his car and began the six-hour drive to Idaho. Along the way he tried to piece together any similarities that would make Marissa and Becky targets for a serial killer. The only parallels he could think of were that both were from out-of-town and both were outcasts in their own way, one dressed unconventionally and one on the streets panhandling. Perhaps someone was targeting girls they thought were vagrants and wouldn't be missed.

And then there were the needle marks. His gut told him that Becky would test positive for Fentanyl just like Marissa. Maybe both were involved in drug deals gone badly. But that made no sense either. No dealer sells drugs and then kills their customers. That is just bad for business.

Robert was still puzzling over the murders when he arrived in Coeur d'Alene and exited the freeway to make his way to the police department headquarters only a few blocks away. When he turned into the parking lot, he spotted Fred just getting out of his own car in front of the facility. Robert honked and Fred waved him over to the empty spot next to his car. Robert pulled in and got out to greet his friend. After the two exchanged pleasantries, Robert mentioned that he hadn't stopped to eat on the way over and asked if they had time to go for a bite before going to the Rose house. Fred said it wasn't a problem and invited Robert to ride with him in his squad car to a local diner.

When they reached the diner and adjacent truck fueling station, Robert noted the overflowing parking lot of tractor-trailer rigs. It was common knowledge that truckers knew the best places for a good home-style meal, and this was clearly a popular stop.

Inside, Robert looked over the menu and it didn't disappoint him. The selection ran from meatloaf and mashed potatoes to grilled liver topped with bacon to homemade chicken pot pie. Robert settled on the meatloaf with a tall coffee. Fred selected a peanut butter milkshake from the extensive list of handmade malts and shakes

As Robert ate, the men discussed a game plan for their meeting with Becky's parents. Robert had an idea for handling Mr. Rose and Fred agreed to go along with it. It was a bit unconventional but, if what Robert had heard about Becky's father was true, it was justified. It was a little after five when they arrived at the house and they could see through the screen door that the couple was settling in for an evening of television.

Fred rang the doorbell. He had been to the house a few days prior when John Rose had called to say his daughter was missing and Mr. Rose recognized the investigator at the door.

Mr. Rose walked over and opened the door, "Investigator Keelson, have you found Becky?"

Fred introduced Robert and said that they had some information they wanted to discuss.

Carol Rose joined her husband at the door wringing her hands. "Please, tell me you found our daughter safe."

Fred asked them to take a seat in the living room and the couple returned to their recliners facing the television that Mr. Rose now turned off. Robert and Fred took their places on a couch that sat under the living room window and, when everyone was seated, Fred looked at Mrs. Rose and said, "Your daughter may have been found in Seattle. That is why Robert is here."

Robert waited a moment and then spoke, "I am sorry to say the girl we found is deceased. I have a photograph of her. I know this is difficult but, could you please look and tell us if this is Becky?"

He stood and walked over to the Roses and handed the photo to John. The man only nodded before handing it to his wife. Mrs. Rose broke down in tears and Mr. Rose asked, "How did she die?"

Robert answered, "She was found in the water on a shoreline in Seattle. We don't have a full medical examiner's report yet, so I don't know the cause of death, but we will know more soon."

The investigators gave the couple a few minutes to absorb the news and then Robert spoke, "The initial examination of your daughter indicates that she may have been assaulted."

He paused to let them take it in and then continued, "May I ask a couple of questions? Your answers could help us determine her activities in Seattle and lead to whoever is responsible."

Mrs. Rose spoke through her tears, "Our baby was killed? Who would do such a thing?"

Mr. Rose held the picture again, hands trembling, "What do you want to know? I don't know what we could tell you that would help?"

Robert asked, "First, do you have ideas why she would run away to Seattle?"

Mrs. Rose blurted, "She would never run away. Someone kidnapped her."

Robert asked again, this time directing the question at Mr. Rose, "Sir, do you have ideas at all why she might have run away?"

He looked at the investigator and then down at the floor, "No. Not one. Like Carol said, she must have been abducted."

Robert remained standing and continued, "To your knowledge, did Becky ever use drugs?"

Becky's mother yelled, "What are you trying to do? Our daughter is dead. Why are you trying to tarnish her reputation?"

Robert kept his voice steady, "We need to eliminate as many variables as we can. Trust me. The more I know about Becky, the more likely it is to find who is responsible."

Carol looked hard at Robert, "You better find who is responsible. Our Becky was the sweetest girl that ever lived. I want whoever is responsible for this to be caught and I want them to pay with their life."

She looked at Mr. Rose, "Say something John. Tell them to do their job and find the person responsible. They need to pay."

He looked at his wife, "Yes love. The person responsible will pay."

She began crying again and Robert asked if he could speak with Mr. Rose outside for a moment.

The two men went out front while Fred stayed behind to comfort Mrs. Rose.

As soon as they were out the door Robert asked Mr. Rose again, "Now that we are alone, I will ask you again, do you know of any reason Becky would have run away last Monday."

Becky's father looked at the ground and answered, "I already told you, she was taken by someone."

Robert moved closer to Mr. Rose and pulled himself up to his full height. He let the silence drag on for a minute and then he recounted to Mr. Rose what Julie had told him about picking up the young girl who was running from a father that had raped her the previous evening. Mr. Rose went pale and said nothing as Robert talked.

Robert continued and said that the medical examiners preliminary report showed trauma to his daughter's vaginal area consistent with a recent forcible entry.

Mr. Rose looked up, tears beginning to well up in his eyes, and choked out, "I have nothing more to say."

Robert responded by asking him to join the investigators down at the station where they could talk further in private and reminded Mr. Rose that he had just promised his wife that the person responsible for this would pay.

He closed the conversation by saying, "You, Mr. Rose, are the one ultimately responsible for Becky's death. How will you live with that?"

Inside the house, Fred knew what the conversation outside concerned and that they would be taking Mr. Rose to the station. He continued to comfort Mrs. Rose and waited for Robert to signal him that they were ready to go.

Outside, Mr. Rose was considering refusing to go to the station. Then he looked up at the towering investigator and felt Robert's eyes burn down into his soul. Robert knew the truth and Mr. Rose knew the investigator would get it out of him. He changed his mind and told Robert he just needed to get his wallet out of his car before they left.

Robert said that was fine and watched Mr. Rose walk across the yard to the home's detached garage. Satisfied Mr. Rose had entered the garage and not run away, the investigator returned to the house to tell Mrs.

Rose that he and Fred would be taking Mr. Rose down to the station to get some more background information.

Fred had barely risen from the sofa to join Robert when they heard an explosion from the garage. Robert raced out the door and ran for the garage, Fred only a few steps behind. When they reached the side door Robert told Fred to go around and watch the main garage door in case Mr. Rose was making a run for it. Then he slowly pushed the side door open and stepped inside.

What he saw took his breath. The far side garage wall looked like a Jackson Pollock painting of sprayed blood and brain matter. On the floor lay a headless Mr. Rose, still holding a double barrel shotgun in his hands. Fred came back around to the side door and stepped into the garage where he immediately threw up his entire milkshake onto the floor. Then the Coeur d'Alene investigator went back out to call the station and stop Mrs. Rose before she could reach the garage and witness the carnage that had been her husband only a few minutes before.

Robert looked at the body and thought to himself, 'Well Mr. Rose, that was not exactly the reaction I expected from you but, just between you and me, I have no regrets. You got what you deserve."

Chapter 10

New Information

Another storm was bearing down on the region, its roaring wind and slashing rain whipping Lake Union into a frenzied dance of waves and whitecaps. It was mid-morning and Reed was still in sweats sitting in the living room and watching the waves. He enjoyed listening to the rushing sound of the gale winds as they blew into the side of the houseboat and rocked it back and forth. If the moorings held, it would be a good day.

In the years he and Angela had lived on the Grey Kraken they had weathered numerous storms and, though the siding and roofing occasional required minor repairs, no major damage had ever occurred to the houseboat. Sometimes, if they had guests over during a big blow, their friends would get a bit queasy in the swaying house, but Reed and Angela always found the rocking motion to be soothing.

Angela was spending the day out meeting with the managers of each of their boutiques and Reed was thinking how nice it was to have a quiet day alone with Baker, Rainier and his thoughts. He was finishing a mental exercise to clear his mind before working on the Marissa Archer case when the phone rang. It was Robert McManus.

Reed listened as Robert explained that his investigation into Marissa's death had not gone anywhere and now, he had a second murder to deal with. He had just completed reading the autopsy report on the girl found by the lighthouse and he wanted to meet with Reed to share some information. He asked if they could meet that morning and Reed invited him to come down to the Grey Kraken.

Fifteen minutes later, the doorbell rang, and Reed let the wet investigator in the door. They went to the kitchen and Reed poured two cups of coffee.

"Let me guess. The two girls and their deaths are connected."

Robert smiled, "Well, you are partially correct. The girls may not be connected but the manners of their deaths are. And those connections make this whole thing more serious than I imagined. We may have a serial killer on our hands and if the killer starts a pattern of killing each week, it is critical we find him or her before next weekend."

Robert spent the next few minutes recounting the story of Becky and how she came to Seattle the prior Monday. There was no reason to believe that there was any connection between Becky and Marissa other than they may have been out on the streets of Seattle when they were abducted and killed.

"So how are the murders connected?" Reed asked.

"Both girls had a single needle mark in one forearm. Both had opiates in their blood stream. And both had the frontal lobe of their brain ripped up by an object inserted next to the eye."

Reed was taken by surprise, "Holy cow. Are you saying that we may not only have a serial killer, but we may have one that sedates girls with opiates and then kills them by scrambling their brain?"

Robert responded, "That, or whoever killed Marissa either on purpose or by accident decided to murder Becky to throw us off the track."

Gamble

Reed thought for a moment and then decided to take a big gamble, "I have some something to show you and some new information that I believe absolves Keith of any implication in Marissa's death. And that should also rule him out from Becky's."

He left and returned with a crumpled paper bag and emptied its contents onto the table.

Robert took it in and asked, "What is this?"

Reed prepared Robert by retelling what Grace had said about Marissa's habit of self-cutting and how she had made a commitment to stop. He explained that the contents of the bag had been Marissa's and that she had discarded them as proof of her commitment.

Robert looked at Reed, "So how did they end up with you?

Reed needed to step carefully now, "Well, it seems that she gave the bag of blades to Keith to prove to him that she had stopped cutting."

He waited for Robert's reaction but there was none, so he continued and ran the next part into a fast run-on sentence, "Then, Keith gave the bag to Kim and she gave it to me and I have been keeping it so that you wouldn't jump to conclusions." He took a breath.

Robert silently counted to ten, but it didn't help, and he exploded, "You what? You withheld evidence in a murder case that you knew would implicate a suspect? I can have you arrested right now. What the hell are you thinking?"

Reed leaned back, "Robert, listen."

He lifted the pick with a napkin, "I showed this to Marissa's friend Grace and asked if she or Marissa had ever used something like it to cut on themselves. She said it was a dissection needle and Marissa had taken it from science class at school and used it to cut herself on the arm."

Reed passed the pick to Robert, "I checked, and this type of pick is used in school science classes."

Robert eyed the pick and Reed continued, "I know what you are thinking. I have a pick that could be the murder weapon so why am I protecting Keith?"

Robert answered, "Damn right I do. Why wouldn't it be?"

Reed smiled to himself, "Because, Marissa's injury required a sweeping movement of the probe that entered her head in order to sever her brain tissue."

He took the probe back from Robert and held the metal point in his left hand. Then he rocked the handle back and forth with his right. The thin, needle-like probe easily flexed between his hands.

"This tool is too flexible. It wouldn't have been stiff enough to tear through brain tissue and would have bent under the stress. We are looking for something stiff, like an ice pick."

Robert shifted from a friendly posture into full-on investigator mode and pulled himself up into his most intimating posture.

Reed continued to speak quickly, "Plus, there is more. We sort of let it out to Grace that Marissa had died on Saturday."

Robert exploded again, "You what? My God, you could be fucking up the whole investigation. As of right now, you are banned from any further involvement."

Reed pleaded, "Robert, just let me finish."

Robert stood still and stared at Reed.

"Grace was with Marissa Saturday morning. She confirmed that Marissa and Keith talked on the phone while she was with her. Keith invited her over, but she told him she had a dentist appointment and couldn't make it. I don't think she was with him that day."

He held his breath for Robert's reaction.

Robert tried to calm his voice, "I think we need to talk some more at the station. Now. And I also want to talk with Kim, and Keith, and Grace. Hell, Reed, what else haven't you told me."

Reed apologized and said that was everything. Then he said, "Robert, I know you are pissed off, but I don't think these kids are the bad guys. They have been trying to help. Don't send your crew out to round them up. I will bring Kim down. You can have Terry pick up Keith at school. And I will give you Grace's phone number and you can call her. If you want, you can ask her to come over after you hear what she has to say.

Follow-up

Robert was not totally comfortable with Reed's approach but agreed. Reed gave him Grace's phone number and Robert left, taking the bag and contents with him.

In his car Robert called the number. The phone connected and rolled into Grace's voice mail and he left her a brief message asking her to call him. Only fifteen minutes later Robert was pleasantly surprised when the high school girl returned his call during a break between classes. After he explained who he was and the reason for his call Grace said that he must have talked to Reed and she hoped that she could help.

Over the next few minutes, Grace confirmed that Marissa had talked with Keith Saturday morning and that she heard her say she couldn't meet him that day. Grace also told him that she thought Marissa had left to go to the dentist when she left the coffee house. Robert asked if she was aware of Marissa's cutting and Grace confirmed what Reed had said. Robert thanked her for her time and let her go so she could make it to her next class. He decided he had enough from the girl for now and did not ask her to make the drive over.

After writing Grace's input on a memo pad, he picked up the phone and dialed the next number. It picked up on the second ring.

"Mr. Archer, this is Investigator McManus with the Seattle Police Department, do you have a moment?"

"Sure. What can I help you with?"

"I don't seem to have in my notes anything about Marissa having a dentist appointment last Saturday, but one of her friends said that she may have been going to one. Do you know anything about that?"

"No. Who told you that?"

"One of her classmates. Her name is Grace. Do you know her?"

"Grace? Sure, I know her. She hung around with Marissa a little, but they weren't that close. And as far as a dentist appointment, I have no idea what she is talking about. If Marissa had an appointment, I would certainly know about it, and she did not have one on Saturday. If you don't believe me, you can call her dentist. It's Dr. Jacobson and his office is in downtown Gig Harbor."

Robert responded. "I'll take his number, but I don't think calling him will be necessary. I can't imagine why a girl would sneak to a dentist behind her parent's backs."

Ryan gave Robert the number and the investigator thanked him, "Thanks for your help Mr. Archer. We are doing our best to track down whoever is responsible for your daughter's death and will let you know as soon as we have anything. Goodbye for now."

Robert finished his notes and then replayed the conversation in his head. Something about the tone of the conversation nagged at him. Mr. Archer had not answered the call from the investigator as he would have expected. It almost seemed as if he had expected the call. His first question was how he could help. Typically, the relative of a deceased person first asks if the police have found something important or even solved the case.

Robert thought it over a few minutes and dialed the number of the Archer family dentist, Dr. Thomas Jacobsen. Dr. Jacobsen was very cordial and confirmed what Mr. Archer had already said. Marissa was one of his patients but did not have an appointment on Saturday. The doctor finished by saying said that he knew the family well and grieved for their loss. He wished the investigator luck on finding her killer.

After her conversation with Robert McManus, Grace thought of one more piece of information she had not shared with Reed or Robert. It hadn't seemed pertinent before and she had kept it to herself to protect Marissa but now she felt Reed needed to know. Before returning to class she called Reed

He answered, "Hello Grace. Did Robert call you?"

She answered yes and told Reed about the call. Then she asked if she could still come over after school that afternoon and told him that she had some more information that she hadn't shared with anyone. Reed asked what it was, but Grace said she would rather talk in person. He would have preferred to know what she had to share before going into the police station but knew better than to push and told her that he looked forward to seeing her later. He had to go into the police station but would be back home in plenty of time.

No More Secrets

Reed finished the brief phone conversation with Grace and turned himself to the task at hand. He dialed Kim's number and when she answered said. "Hey Kaykay, this is Uncle Reed. I need to see you right now. It's important."

His call took Kim by surprise, "You want me to skip school? What's going on?"

"I just need to talk with you. Don't worry about skipping. We'll clear it with the school later. I'm at Velvet Green. Just come over here as soon as possible. Okay?"

Kim said she would be right over and hung up, confused about what could be so important that Reed would take her out of class. She went directly out to her car and started for the coffee house.

Inside the shop, Reed ordered a double espresso from the girl behind the counter and then took a stool by the window to look out and watch for Kim. Within a few minutes her bright yellow car pulled in next to the Mini and she quickly got out and came into the shop.

Reed walked over and gave her a hug. "Hey Kaykay. Thanks for coming. Let's go sit in the corner over there for a minute."

They took a table in a far back corner of the shop even though it was completely empty except for the counter girl and even she was out of earshot in the kitchen.

"So, Uncle Reed. What's so important that you need to pull me out of school? Did you find something?"

"Well, not exactly. I shared the paper bag with Robert McManus this morning and explained that I thought it only showed that Marissa had mental issues, nothing to implicate Keith in her death."

"And?"

"Well, he sort-of went off-the-handle about us hiding evidence and now he wants all of us down at the station."

Kim looked at Reed, "We're in deep shit, aren't we?"

Reed answered, "Maybe. But, right now we need to meet with McManus and explain ourselves. I told him I would come in with you. He is also calling your father and having him pick up Keith."

Kim looked worried and Reed tried to comfort her, "Don't worry Kaykay. It will be fine."

He tried to hide the fact that he was also worried that they probably stepped over the line and could be in big trouble.

"Okay, let's go to the station and get this over with."

They got up from the table and Reed said goodbye to the barista as they left and got into his car. It was only a fifteen-minute drive to the station, but the drive seemed much longer. He had seen McManus come down hard on others and did not look forward to being on the receiving end of the investigator's interrogation style.

When Reed and Kim arrived at the station, Investigator McManus seemed to have cooled off a bit. He shook Reed's hand and said hello to Kim as he led them to a small conference room. Robert knew Kim from his occasional visits to the Carver house when he and her father would take their bikes out for the day.

From what he knew of Kim, she was an honest girl on the straight and narrow. He had no reason to distrust her. He had also known Reed for years and had utilized his skills and input several times to successfully solve cases. Reed had always shown good judgment and had never crossed the lines of legal conduct.

Now, it appeared that these two had kept a secret that could be critical to a case. He was upset at their deception but, then again, he had used Kim for the surveillance of Keith without letting her know. That surveillance was ultimately Robert's responsibility and not knowing that the boy had passed evidence to Kim was partially the department's fault. They should have had better eyes on the two. Robert had his own judgment to question as well as that of Kim and Reed.

When they reached the conference room Kim and Reed took seats side by side at the empty table. Robert remained standing on the opposite side and placed the paper bag on the table. He removed his jacket and hung it over the back of the chair in front of him. Then he loosened his tie and look at Reed. "Why did you keep this secret? You are supposed to be helping us."

He looked at Kim, "And you, young lady? Why are you protecting someone that may be a killer? You could be putting yourself in danger."

Kim just looked down at the table and Reed explained his logic, running through the same points he had made at his house earlier.

Robert continued to look angry, "I still don't see why you didn't turn it in."

"Because I knew it would have thrown too much focus on Keith and I didn't think he was the one responsible for Marissa's death."

Robert was not placated. "That is for the police to figure out. I have always appreciated your help but this time you have gone too far. Do you really think we are that easily misled and likely to screw up a case?"

Reed instantly felt regret at what he had done. The investigator was right. It was one thing to dig up facts that could help an investigation, but it was quite another to start acting like a maverick investigator, trying to solve a case by withholding important information. He had clearly overstepped the bounds and may have lost the trust and respect of a good investigator in the process.

"I'm sorry. You're right. I was wrong to keep this from you."

Robert stood up and left the room. A red blinking light by the ceiling caught Reed's attention. He looked up and then over at Kim, "Smile for the camera."

Terry did not want to make a scene when he picked up Keith at the high school, so he asked the principal to have the boy brought to the front office by one of the school's counselors with as little fanfare as possible.

When Keith saw Terry in his police uniform, he looked confused, "Hello Mr. Carver. Do you need to see me?"

Terry answered, "Yes. I need you to come with me."

Keith asked what it was about, and Terry said they needed to go to the station where an investigator would be meeting with him.

Twenty minutes later, Terry parked his cruiser on the street and escorted Keith into the building where Robert McManus was in the lobby waiting for them, his jacket back on and tie straightened. He thanked Terry for bringing Keith down and told him he would call him later. Then the investigator led the boy to an elevator, and they rode in silence up several levels before the doors opened and Robert directed Keith to a conference room. Robert opened the conference room door and asked Keith to take a seat at the empty table in the center of the room. Then he told the boy to remain there while he attended to some other business.

Reed and Kim still sat in the next room over, waiting for the return of McManus. The investigator opened the door to their room and said "Keith is next door. I'd like to talk with him for a few minutes and then I'll come back. Would anyone like a coffee or water while you wait?"

The two said they were fine, and Robert picked up the bag and blades and left, closing the door behind him.

Reentering the room next door, he laid the bag and contents on the table and for the next half hour questioned Keith about his relationship with Marissa, Marissa's cutting habit, the bag of blades, the last time he saw Marissa, the phone call he made to Marissa Saturday morning, his relationship with Grace, and the last time he talked to Grace. Then he threw in a question out of left field. Had Keith ever met a girl named Becky Rose?

Keith's head was spinning from the rapid-fire questioning. Many of the investigator's questions had been asked before, but the questions about Grace and some girl named Becky were new. Keith answered as best he could, and the investigator's reaction was neutral. Keith couldn't tell whether the investigator had believed him or not.

When Robert was satisfied, he asked the boy to join him in the room next door. When they entered, Keith saw Kim sitting at the table with another man. Based on Kim's descriptions of her Uncle Reed, he guessed that must be him. Robert told him to take a seat with the others and addressed the group, "Okay, I will start out by saying that I don't think anyone here had anything to do with the deaths of Marissa and Becky. First, the circumstances of the first incident were too convenient. Keith is an intelligent young man and no intelligent person dumps a body just down the hill from where they live. Second, we know Keith was not involved in the latest death because he was at Terry's home at the time of the girl's death. Third, we are certain both deaths were caused by the same person or people so that rules Keith out of the first incident. And finally, with all the testimony and evidence that you have been hiding up to this point, I am convinced that these deaths were caused by someone outside of this group."

Keith and Kim looked relieved and Reed looked satisfied.

"But, and this is a huge but, if you are hiding any more evidence and I find out, there will be consequences. Does each of you understand?"

They all nodded.

"That is not good enough. I want each of you to look me in the eyes and say you are not hiding anything."

One by one, each of them said there was no more to share.

With that, the investigator told them they could go, but to not to share anything of what was shared today with anyone outside of the police department.

Reed said he would take Keith and Kim back to their school and nodded to the two teenagers to leave the room. Reed held back a moment as the teenagers left the room and then looked at Robert. "We are back to square one, aren't we?"

McManus shrugged, "We never left it."

Reed risked the next question, "I know you are angry with me and I understand, but I would still like to help if you will let me."

Robert did not smile or show any signs of forgiving Reed for his actions. He waited a full minute before responding. "You can help on one condition. No more secrets. Okay?"

Reed felt a wave of relief. "You have my word. Thanks Robert. I really want to help get to the bottom of this before anyone else is hurt."

Robert simply turned and started to walk down the hallway. After a few steps, he turned back. "We'll take the bug out of Kim's car. There is no need to put Terry's family through anymore."

He turned again and walked away.

Reed drove Kim and Keith back to Velvet Green where Kim's car was still parked. Before getting out Kim said, "Thanks for your help uncle Reed. I knew Keith didn't have anything to do with this."

She looked over at Keith.

Reed said, "I didn't either, but we needed to work it through a bit more. Fortunately, the combination of the death of Becky Friday night in a fashion like Marissa's, and the surveillance showing that Keith was at your house until after the time of Becky's death, ruled him out. McManus was just playing hardnosed today because he was pissed that we withheld things from him."

Kim visibly stiffened. "Did you say Keith has been under surveillance?"

"Uh, yeah, I did." Reed realized that he may have just let the last secret out of the bag.

"Does my dad know about this? Were they watching me too when Keith and I were together?"

"Uh, yes, I am afraid so."

He was about to explain when Kim shouted, "You have all been spying on us and didn't tell me!"

He tried again. "Actually, the police were spying on Keith. And it was also for your protection when you were with him. Listen."

She got out of Reed's car, slammed the door and walked back to hers, driving off without a glance in Reed's direction.

Keith was still in the back seat. "If it's okay with you Mr. Carver, I think I will just get out and walk back to school on my own."

He got out and walked away.

Reed picked up his phone and dialed Terry. "Hey brother. I think you need to spend some more time with your daughter tonight. No more secrets. She knows about the surveillance and is not happy. Robert has decided to stop it and remove the bug, but you and your daughter need to reconnect. Okay? Good. Take care. I'll give you a call tomorrow."

Stalker

Grace completed her last class of the day and walked to her school locker to put her books inside. She wouldn't be doing any homework tonight so there was no point lugging a pile of school stuff home.

Outside, she ran through the rain to her car and could see Steven standing under a tree by the student parking lot. He was talking and laughing with some of his friends, but she could tell his eyes were on her. Fortunately, he was nowhere near her car so she wouldn't have to confront him.

Within moments of getting into her car and starting the engine, all the windows steamed up from the moisture on Grace's wet clothing. She set the heater fan on high and flipped on the rear defrost switch. Soon two round circles began clearing on the front windshield while a horizontal pattern of clear stripes grew on the back glass.

After waiting a few minutes for the windows to clear, Grace put her car into gear and headed for her usual gas station before the drive to Seattle.

Filling the tank on a day like this was miserable. Even though cars and customers were supposed to be protected under the large awning that spanned the filling area, the March wind blew in and swirled around the pumps carrying with it a chilling rain that made its way past her collar and down their back.

On top of that, the awning drain at the station was backed up and waterfalls of rainwater streamed off the cover's high edges and snaked back and forth across the cars underneath. Grace got out and rushed to open the car's gas cover, insert the filler nozzle, pull the lever, and return to the protection of her car to wait while the tank filled. As she sat in her dry refuge, she could see that the driver at the pump behind her was doing the same. No one in his right mind would stand outside in this mess.

When Grace heard the nozzle click off, she got out and hastily returned it to the pump, replaced her gas cap and ran inside to pay. Coming back out she saw that the vehicle behind hers was already idling and the driver appeared ready to leave. They must have paid by credit card and were just waiting for her to pull out.

She hated it when people in the gas lanes were too lazy to back up and pull around. They made it seem like it was her responsibility to rush just so they could drive straight out. If she knew the driver, she would tell them to chill, but she didn't recognize the grey Audi and the driver had a baseball cap pulled low, so she couldn't make out their face.

After getting into her car, she looked in the rear-view mirror and raised a middle finger at the Audi just for good measure knowing full well that it's driver could not possibly see through her wet and fogged rear window.

Sure enough, they were just waiting for her to drive out. As she pulled away, the Audi also pulled out right on her tail and then fell back as she accelerated onto the highway toward Tacoma.

"Man, people need to slow down a little. They are just the type to cause an accident."

Grace put on some music and settled in for the drive. The rain didn't let up and the limited visibility made Grace increasingly uncomfortable driving. She moved into the right lane to slow down and a stream of cars immediately passed on the left, coating her windshield with a greasy spray that streaked on the glass and only made driving more difficult.

She noticed in her rear-view mirror that one car had also moved over and stayed behind her when all others had passed. After several miles it was still there, its headlights remaining a constant distance back no matter what her speed. Probably an older driver also spooked by the poor driving conditions. She remembered riding with her grandmother on days like this and how embarrassing it was when traffic would stack up behind the grey-haired woman and her plodding Buick.

After a few more miles of squinting through a smeared windshield and repeatedly hitting the washer fluid button, Grace decided it might be better to move back into the faster lanes and do the passing versus sitting in the line of slower cars and navigating through their rooster tails. As she pulled over to the left, she was surprised to see the car behind her also moved over. Now she looked hard in the mirror and recognized it as the grey Audi from the gas station.

She shook her head and spoke out loud to her empty car, "Incredible. Maybe he did see me flip him off. Crap, that's all I need. Some road rage nut following me."

As she left the Tacoma area the same car continued to trail her about a quarter mile back. Knowing that she was probably being paranoid she spoke again, "Hell, even a pissed driver wouldn't follow me for this long." She decided to test her fears and took the next freeway exit into a roadside rest area.

As she approached the rest stop parking area, Grace slowed and looked in her rearview mirror. All clear, no grey car. She continued to drive through the lot, past the public facilities and onto the freeway entrance ramp at the other end where she accelerated back into traffic. She glanced into her rearview mirror again and now saw the grey Audi exiting the rest area and following onto the entrance ramp behind her.

"It was just my fucking finger! Let it go!" she yelled as she stepped on the gas. Only thirty minutes till she was with the Carvers and would be safe. Then it occurred to her that it might not be just some irate driver following her. She had never seen the driver at the gas station get out and use the pump. And there was no way he could have seen her hand gesture. The car windows were just too fogged up.

My God, could the person that killed Marissa be targeting her too? Then she remembered Steven's threatening tone as he questioned her today and when he confronted her in front of the Funeral home. What if it was Steven following her? What if he was the killer?

"My God, that maniac is after me."

Grace grabbed her cell phone off the seat and dialed Reed. He picked up and she talked rapidly, "Hello Mr. Carver, this is Grace. I think someone has been following me since I left school. I think it might be Steven and I'm scared."

"Relax Grace. I'm sure you're just being paranoid."

She responded "No, I'm not. The same grey Audi has been behind me since I stopped for gas in Gig Harbor. I didn't recognize the car and couldn't see the driver, but I tried to lose him at the rest stop north of Tacoma and he still followed me."

"Okay Grace. You are almost here. Just call when you are about five minutes away. I will be out on the street and watch for a car tailing you when you get here. If a grey Audi comes down the street, I will stop them and find out who they are. Okay?"

Hearing Reed's voice calmed her, and she wished she were already at the Grey Kraken. "Okay, I will see you in a bit. But just in case I don't make it I need to tell you something."

Reed interrupted, "Seriously Grace, calm down. Nobody is following you. I will see you soon."

She insisted on telling him more details about Marissa's personal life and then said she couldn't wait to get to his place. After she shared the information, she hung up and decided to speed up and change lanes, weaving through the building traffic as she approached Seattle. The Audi stayed a short distance behind her the entire way.

By the time the freeway entered downtown Seattle, Grace was determined to lose whoever was following her once and for all. The Audi now trailed by only a couple of car lengths and she'd had enough of this game. If it were Steven, she would not give him the pleasure of finding out where she was going. She came up with a plan and switched on her left turn signal and moved into the second lane of the freeway. The Audi followed as expected. Then, she signaled a left lane change again but instead quickly accelerated to get in front of a car to her right and veered hard right for the exit, knowing her pursuer could not follow.

The Call

Reed and Angela were relaxing in the living room enjoying the warmth of the fireplace as they watched the whitecaps out on the lake. Reed was tired from his afternoon at the station. Thankfully, everything had gone well, and he was back in Robert's good graces. Grace would be here soon, and he was anxious to discuss the new information she had shared. It might just be the key to not only Marissa's murder, but also Becky's. He wondered if she really was being tailed. If she was, he hoped that it was a police tail. Maybe Robert was concerned about or for her.

At a little after five Angela asked if it wasn't about time for Grace to arrive. She had no sooner finished her sentence when Reed's phone rang. Reed was in the kitchen, so Angela picked up the phone and looked at the display. It showed Grace, so she answered the call. "Hello Grace. Are you almost here?"

Reed came into the room, "Is it time for me to go up and find who is driving the mystery car?"

Angela waved him off and spoke into the phone, "This is Angela Carver. Who is this?"

She listened for a minute and then said, "Yes, she is a friend. She was on her way over to our house to visit."

Another pause, then, "Yes. She lives with her foster parents. Yes. I can call and notify them. Thank you."

Angela collapsed onto the couch. Reed sat down and looked at Angela's face, now streaming with tears. "What is it? What happened?"

Angela replied without looking up. "That was a State Patrol officer. He had Grace's phone and dialed her last phone contact." She wiped her face, "Grace's car lost control and hit a freeway exit abutment. They are taking her to Swedish Hospital right now. The officer said she is in bad shape and it doesn't look good. We need to call her foster parents and then go to up to Swedish."

Outside, the wind subsided and the sound of a torrential downpour beating on the deck merged with Angela's low cries as she buried her head into Reed's chest.

Chapter 11

Department Meeting

Tuesday morning Reed called Robert and told him about Grace's accident Monday evening. He recounted what witnesses told the State Patrol and that Grace claimed she was being tailed from Gig Harbor and thought it might be Steven.

Then, he told Robert that Grace had called with more information that could be a key to both murders. Apparently, Marissa had been addicted to Opioids, specifically Fentanyl, for several months and used the drug regularly. As far as Grace knew, she was the only person that knew of Marissa's habit other than whoever was selling the drugs to her. Not even Keith was aware of her drug use.

Grace didn't say anything earlier because she didn't want to tarnish Marissa's reputation and didn't see a link to her death, but now she had wondered if the incident could be drug related.

Reed told Robert that he was a little out of his league in understanding the drug culture and asked if Robert could point him in the right direction to start a new line of investigation. Robert said he would email some materials he had on street drugs in Seattle immediately after his morning staff meeting.

At the Tuesday morning department meeting, Robert shared the latest information from Reed and asked an assistant to call the Washington State Patrol and get the accident report from Grace's crash the prior evening. Perhaps it was not an accident and she had been forced into the barrier. While the assistant went for the report, the team of investigators reviewed several other ongoing cases. Fifteen minutes later, the assistant returned with a printout of the accident report.

Robert scanned the document and slid it onto the table. "According to witnesses, Grace's car was in a middle lane driving normally when she put on her left turn signal and then sped up and made a hard-right turn in front of another car just before the Lakeview Boulevard exit. She lost control on the wet surface and slid sideways into the barrier."

Another investigator looked at the report, "Well, it doesn't sound like she was forced into the barrier but, based on what Reed told you, she may have been trying to lose another car when she lost control. Maybe it is time to have a talk with Steven. He might have been Marissa's drug supplier and wanted to silence Grace in case she knew anything."

Everyone agreed. They would not notify the school or local police. Steven was a hero in the local community, and they didn't want anyone to warn him that an investigator was coming to see him. Hopefully, they would find him at school and get some more answers before the day was out.

Principal's Office

A little before eleven, Investigator Scott Thomas checked in at the Gig Harbor high school front office. A middle-aged receptionist with a nametag that read 'Mrs. Wilson, Volunteer Receptionist' smiled and greeted him, "Good morning. Can I help you?"

The investigator showed his identification and said he wished to speak with the principal. Mrs. Wilson's face turned serious and she lowered her voice, "Is this about Marissa? Did you find who killed her?"

Scott Thomas kept a straight face and said he really couldn't talk about the case but that he needed to see the principal as soon as possible. Mrs. Wilson was visibly unhappy that the investigator would not share any information and showed it by abruptly spinning away and marching off toward an office marked Principal in gold letters over the door. A moment later she emerged and waved the investigator over to the office. "Principal Peterson will see you in his office."

Scott walked around the desk and over to the office where the principal met him at the door, "Come in and have a seat. Mrs. Wilson said you are with the Seattle Police. I assume this has something to do with Marissa?"

Scott answered, "It does. In fact, I am here to talk with Steven."

The principal made it clear that he was irritated about the intrusion and asked, "What's so important that you need to come into my school during class hours? Why can't you wait until this evening and talk at Steven's home or somewhere else?"

Investigator Thomas deflected the questions and simply thanked the school administrator for his assistance. "I know this is inconvenient, but it really is necessary. I suggest we meet him as he leaves class just to make sure I don't miss him. Wouldn't want to have made the drive for nothing."

Scott looked at the clock and smiled as he stood up.

"I suggest we walk to his class now. Can you direct me to it?"

Principal Peterson stood up, now looking even more irritated, and walked out to the receptionist. "Mrs. Wilson, can you look up Steven Smith's current classroom?"

The receptionist tapped some keys on her computer and responded, "He is in English class in room 108."

The principal thanked Mrs. Wilson and started out to the hallway without a word to the investigator. Room 108 was only two doors away from the reception area and the two men were there within a minute, just as the hall buzzer signaled the end of the class period. Students poured out of their classes, barely noticing the plain clothed investigator that stood next to the principal by the hallway wall. Several said greetings to the principal as they passed.

The flow of students from the classroom directly across from the two men had slowed to a trickle before three large boys exited, engaged in a debate about the final four playoffs and which University had the best basketball team.

As the three turned and walked away down the hall, Principal Peterson and Investigator Thomas followed. The principal spoke up. "Steven, would you join us for a minute in my office?"

The other two boys chided. "Ooh, Steven. Now you're in trouble." Both slapped him on the back and walked away, continuing their debate.

Without introducing the investigator, the principal led Steven to his office and, once there, asked him to take a seat.

Then he turned to the investigator. "You can use my office to talk with Steven. When you are done, I would like to know what this is about." He turned and walked away.

Investigator Thomas closed the door and took a seat in the principal's chair.

"Hello Steven. You look smart, so you've probably already guessed that I am an investigator with the Seattle Police Department. Here is my card."

He slid a business card across the desk. "I would just like to ask you a couple of questions about yesterday. Okay?"

Steven shuffled his feet and looked anxious

The investigator continued. "It's no big deal. I would just like to know where you were yesterday afternoon. That's all."

The boy asked, "Why? This isn't about Grace is it? I heard about the car accident. I didn't have anything to do with that."

Investigator Thomas continued in a relaxed manner. "Of course not, why would you?" He took a pad out of his pocket. "I would just like to know where you were after school yesterday. Say, from right after school until around six."

The pitch in Steven's voice became higher. "I was here with my buddies. We work out in the weight room after school every day. If you don't believe me, you can ask them. Hell, ask the principal. He knows I am always down there."

The investigator leaned forward. "Steven, were you harassing Grace yesterday?"

"Who told you that?" Steven began clenching and unclenching his fists.

"Were you following her and making threats?"

"I didn't threaten her. I just told her to be careful about who she talked to and what she was saying. Hey, I'm just trying to help you guys."

Scott leaned back into the principal's chair. "Oh? And exactly how is that?"

Steven's voice calmed a bit but quivered as he spoke. "Marissa's father says he is certain Keith was responsible for his daughter's death, but he doesn't have the proof. He thinks Grace might be trying to protect Keith by misleading the police and he asked me to keep an eye on her."

"Why would Grace protect the boy that killed her friend?"

Steve answered, "I don't know. Those three are different. Who knows what they think?"

"When did Mr. Archer ask you to keep an eye on Grace?"

Steven thought for only a moment. "It was the day before yesterday. Sunday. He called and said he needed to talk right away and asked me to meet him down at Skansi Brothers Park. When we met, he said that Grace told him a story about where Marissa was on the Saturday before she died. He said the story was crazy and he wanted me to watch Grace and stop her from spreading false rumors."

He paused and then continued without looking the investigator in the eyes. "I talked to her during the day yesterday but, like I said, I was here after school. I didn't follow her to Seattle."

After writing a few more notes, the detective stood up, "Well, I won't keep you any longer. Just one last question, what do you know about opiate use by students at the school?"

Steven was clearly taken off-guard by the question and looked confused, "Opiate use. You mean like Heroin?"

Scott nodded, "Yes, heroin or any other types."

Steven just shrugged, "I don't know. I guess there are some druggies at school, but I don't know anyone personally. Why?"

Investigator Thomas answered, "Just curious."

He opened the office door and beckoned the principal back into the room.

Thank you both for your time." He looked at the principal, "By the way, were you here after school yesterday?"

"Are you joking? I never get out of this place before six. Why?"

"Did you happen to go by the weight room and see Keith? He says he was in there working out."

He thought for a moment. "I can't say I actually saw him in there yesterday, but he always works out after school."

He looked at Steven proudly, "Staying in shape and looking forward to college football. Right big guy?"

Steven smiled. "Right principal. Can I go now?"

Principal Peterson looked at the investigator who nodded okay. After Steven walked away the principal asked, "So now can you tell me what this is about?"

The investigator tucked his note pad back into his pocket. "We just needed a little more information. That's all. I think I found what I needed. Thanks."

Back out in his car, Investigator Scott Thomas called Robert and passed on his findings. When he finished, the two agreed that Scott should make a visit to Ryan Archer and ask about his meeting with Steven.

Steven was shaken up by the talk with the Seattle investigator. He never meant for Grace to get hurt. And why did the investigator ask about drugs? Everything was falling apart. After school he called Mr. Archer and asked to meet at the park again.

Cover-up

Ryan Archer was the only person in the park when Steven arrived. Marissa's father stood at a railing and watched a large pleasure cruiser make its way through the harbor to its home moorings. Steven walked up to the rail and watched for a few moments before breaking the silence. "Thanks for seeing me on short notice Mr. Archer."

Marissa's father looked hard at Steven, "Tell me this is not about the car accident that Grace was in. I saw it on the news last night. They showed the car wrapped around a cement barrier. It is a miracle she lived. You weren't involved, were you?"

Steven looked down over the rail as he spoke. He couldn't look into Mr. Archer's eyes. "I was following her like you wanted. But I was nowhere near her when she crashed. She just swerved and slid into the barrier."

Ryan turned. "Jesus, Marissa dying was bad enough, and now this? I may not like Grace, but I never wanted her hurt."

Steven ran his hand through his hair and walked a few steps along the path. "The police questioned me at school today. I told them I was not in Seattle last night. I said I was working out."

Ryan looked at him, "So why are you telling me this? What do you want from me?"

Steven looked surprised, "I need you to cover for me. If the police talk to you, say you saw me here in town, maybe at the supermarket."

Ryan turned and started to walk away then stopped and looked back, "Okay. I will cover for you. Just don't tell anyone what you were up to. No one, okay?"

Steven nodded, and Mr. Archer left the park.

Fentanyl

Reed spent Tuesday afternoon on his computer reading Robert's summary on opioid abuse and going to the internet links he sent. Both victims of attacks on Alki had traces of Fentanyl in their blood. Regardless of the cause of death being brain trauma, the fact that Marissa used Fentanyl recreationally opened the possibility that this was drug related and that the girls may have been killed in drug deals gone bad. Becky had seemed innocent enough, but it was possible that she had a secret habit just like Marissa.

His research into drug use opened a whole new world to Reed. It was not that he was totally ignorant of the drugs, but his personal exposure had been restricted to his own use of weed when he was younger and the experiences of some friends that had experimented with cocaine. He decided to restrict his study to Fentanyl since it was involved in both deaths and it was the drug Marissa had used recreationally.

What he found was overwhelming. The drug Fentanyl was a synthetic opioid used for pain management and its use was widespread for everything from sedation for oral surgery and colonoscopies to pain management for chronic pain due to cancer or other conditions. The drug could be administered intravenously for medical procedures or in trans-dermal patch or lollipop form for pain management. It was even available in nasal spray form.

The fast action and effectiveness of Fentanyl made it popular, but it also had its dangers. Accidental deaths from Fentanyl overdoses could be called an epidemic and the drug and its dangers had recently made the headlines when it was implicated in the death of an international celebrity.

Reed found that it was not uncommon for people dealing with chronic pain to get addicted to their prescription opioid pain medications and, when their primary care doctor limited their prescriptions, shop multiple doctors to continue getting their drugs.

In addition to these legitimate users of the drugs, there were the countless recreational users. Fentanyl in lollipop form was popular on the streets. So were the patches. Fentanyl was even being mixed with Heroin to give it an extra kick. Intravenous use of the drug occurred but was less common due to the difficulty in getting a proper dose and higher danger of overdosing.

Reed gathered all the information he could on the use of Fentanyl and then moved to the chain of sourcing. This drug was not like cocaine that was being trafficked in from Latin America or meth that was manufactured illegally in local labs. This was a prescription drug that made its way from the pharmaceutical manufacturers to the street through either unknowing or unscrupulous professionals in the medical profession.

Reed wanted to track down the sources of the Fentanyl that was getting on the streets of Seattle. His new hypothesis was that Marissa lied about going to a dentist on Saturday and instead drove to Seattle to score the drug. She may have tried injecting Fentanyl with the help of her source and overdosed. The source then panicked when she stopped breathing and killed her to cover up the overdose, hoping the macabre scene at Alki would misdirect the police.

Reed called Robert and asked if there was any way to track opioid overdoses in the King and Pierce county areas over the past two years. He wanted to look for a pattern that might lead to sources for the drugs. Robert said he could get the information compiled and would email it over later in the day.

After the call, Reed decided it was time for a break and a trip up to Swedish hospital to look in on Grace. He knew she was still in a coma but felt the need to be there. Her foster parents, Sarah and Roy Landsberg, had driven over Monday evening after Angela gave them the news about Grace and had slept at the hospital overnight. Angela went up to the hospital first thing in the morning to keep Grace company and planned to offer Sarah and Roy the use of the Grey Kraken as a temporary home if they wanted to stay in Seattle for the next few days.

Hospital
At the hospital, Reed found Sarah, Roy, and Angela in Grace's room, sitting to either side of her. Sarah and Angela held her hands. She was in

intensive care and the room was quiet except for the occasional beep from the monitors that tracked her vital signs.

Grace did not look good. Her face was bruised, and it seemed tubes and wires ran from her body from head to toe. Reed disliked hospitals and avoided them at all costs, even when he hurt himself around the house. He would rather duct tape a cut closed than go in for stitches. For him, a hospital only represented death. Both of his parents had died in this very hospital. He knew it was not the fault of the hospital, but it depressed him none the less.

He pulled a chair from the wall and sat next to Angela. Sarah and Roy both thanked him for visiting and the offer to stay at their place for a few days. Sarah said she accepted the offer and then apologized for the imposition. Both Reed and Angela assured her it was no imposition and that she could stay as long as she wished. Roy needed to return to work in Gig Harbor but would try to come back over in a few days. The four then spent the next few hours visiting.

It didn't take long for Reed to decide that the state had done a good job when they placed Grace with this couple. They were easy going and he could tell that they provided an accepting environment for Grace.

Sarah was in her fifties but looked younger with spirited eyes that practically conveyed her thoughts without her speaking. She was a florist by trade and had an artistic flair to her. When she spoke, it was with a soft voice that enveloped him with a sense of calm. She wore a flowered peasant blouse and floor length black skirt and Reed noticed when the skirt rose above her ankles that she had a tattoo of a raven on the top of her right foot.

Roy worked as an electrician with a local contractor in Gig Harbor. At first glance Reed gauged him to be a conservative sort, and an odd match for Sarah. When Roy pushed the sleeves of his shirt up to reveal full-sleeve tattoos of tribal art on both arms, Reed knew he and Roy would get along well. And when both discovered the other also drove a Mini, you would think they were longtime friends.

When the couples talked about Grace, they both talked with an understanding of the girl and what she had been through. It was clear that Sarah and her husband cared about Grace and tried to support her. Sarah also talked about Grace's friend Marissa and how she too was a free spirit and how unfortunate her death was. She had felt sorry for

Marissa. It seemed that her father had never tried to understand his daughter and had made life difficult for her.

Reed enjoyed listening to Sarah and Roy and learning more about Grace and Marissa, but he needed to return to the Kraken and resume his research into opioids. He excused himself and said he would see them later. Angela said that she and Sarah would be home by five for dinner unless something changed with Grace's condition.

Epidemic

When Reed returned home, he opened his emails and found Robert's report on opioids overdoses in the surrounding area over the past two years. Reed had no idea how big the problem was, and the number of documented overdoses shocked him. He took the data from the spreadsheet and plotted it onto a map and a pattern began to appear. The highest density of overdoses was in the metropolitan areas of Seattle and Tacoma. Outside of that, the overdose incidences appeared to be randomly scattered around the region. He continued to plot the overdoses including both those that resulted in death and those that were treated and saved. The patterns became clearer with more cases filling in the metropolitan areas and spilling into the neighboring communities such as Gig Harbor.

Now Reed was even more convinced that he was going down the right path. He called Investigator Thomas and asked if anything he found in his interview with Steven indicated that the boy might be involved in drugs. The investigator responded that the boy was genuinely surprised when asked about drugs and that he didn't think Steven was involved in dealing them nor had any knowledge of those who were.

Reed felt he had hit a wall. If there was a dealer in or near Gig Harbor that sold the Fentanyl to Marissa, how could he find him? He called Robert and asked for ideas. Robert suggested that Reed might want to talk with a local freelance investigative reporter that he knew. Her name was Elizabeth Moo and she had been working on a piece about opioid abuse in the region for the past several months. She might have information Reed had not turned up. Robert gave Reed the reporter's contact information and Reed immediately called Ms. Moo. He found Elizabeth easy to talk with and more than willing to share her research with someone else that was studying the drug abuse epidemic. When they finished their conversation, Reed thanked her and promised to share anything more that he found through the course of his investigation.

Elizabeth did not have a significant amount of information beyond what Reed already knew, but something she mentioned confirmed one of his suspicions. Ms. Moo said that some of those she spoke with on the Seattle streets told her that they thought some of the Fentanyl in the area came from a doctor. No one knew his identity, but they did not think he was from Seattle.

A Bigger Net

Reed decided to cast a bigger net for more information and look for a specific coincidence that could lead him right to the dealer. He called Robert and asked for copies of the police interviews with potential witnesses near the launch ramp on the morning Marissa was found. He also asked for any interviews that police conducted in the Capitol Hill business district regarding Becky's abduction. Finally, he asked for any camera footage the police had obtained from the Capitol Hill area the evening of Becky's abduction. He knew there were a few cash machines and parking lot security cameras. If any of these sources led to an out-of-town doctor, he might have his dealer.

Robert emailed all the information and files Reed asked for and then wished him luck. He knew what Reed was attempting was like finding a needle in a haystack when you don't even know what the needle looks like. Reed knew that combing through the files would be a daunting task, but he reminded himself it was simply a matter of looking for patterns or matches.

He began with the statements from witnesses at both crime locations and found no similarities between the two, other than no one had seen anything suspicious. A Capitol Hill shop owner saw a girl matching Becky's description panhandling outside his business, but he did not see anyone with her or know when she left.

After reading through all the witness statements, Reed moved on to the Capitol Hill surveillance footage and struck out again. None of the feeds from parking lot cams or cash machines showed a young woman that looked like Becky.

He was beginning to think it was a lost cause when he opened a file titled, Alki Car Plates. Two officers had recorded the license numbers of parked cars in a wide area surrounding the boat launch ramp on the morning of Marissa's discovery in the event the perpetrator had abandoned their vehicle. The department had already checked out the vehicles and their owners and didn't find anything out of the ordinary. The registered owners either lived nearby or were visiting the area.

Reed read through the plate information again knowing that the investigators had not been looking for the same information he was now searching for. He thought, 'Wouldn't it be interesting if one of those cars turned out to be from Marissa's hometown or nearby Tacoma?'

After hours of checking all the license plate numbers recorded by the officers, he was astonished to find that one was registered to a Dr. Jacobsen in Gig Harbor. Reed thought to himself, 'Now wouldn't that be a frigging coincidence.'

He retrieved Robert's case notes hoping the investigator had followed up on Grace's information about Marissa saying she was going to her dentist on the Saturday of her death. He paged through the notes and couldn't believe his luck. Mr. Archer had provided the name and contact information for their family dentist, and it matched the car registration for a Dr. Thomas Jacobson.

His pulse quickened as he thought about a potential scenario. Marissa may have met with Dr. Jacobson that Saturday, not for a legitimate dentist appointment, but to buy Fentanyl. He read the police follow-up on the plate. It only said that the owner stated he was in Seattle on business that day and had taken the ferry into town to enjoy the view and avoid downtown parking.

Reed thought it would be a mighty big coincidence for the doctor and one of his patients to both be in the Alki area that morning. But he couldn't figure out how or why the doctor would be tied to Idaho girl's death? There was nothing to link the doctor to the two girls.

He dug more and went back through the camera footage of the Capitol Hill area. His first time through, he had not bothered to go through the traffic camera videos thinking that the odds of the perpetrators speeding and tripping a police camera were slim to none.

No one in their right mind would have risked doing anything that would draw attention to them. But now he was desperate and needed to find something in the police data. He would leave no stone unturned. He settled in and began scrolling through the videos of cars triggering the traffic cams in the Capitol Hill area from eight o'clock until eleven and couldn't believe how much footage there was and how many cars had earned tickets by triggering the speed cameras.

After spending what seemed like an endless period staring at his computer monitor and trying to spot something suspicious, Reed had almost given up on the traffic cam videos when he spotted something in one that made him say out loud, "You have got to be shitting me. You son-of a-bitch. I have you."

He was looking at video from a police traffic camera that began at the time stamp 10:07. There, driving through the intersection away from the camera was a car that had triggered the speed camera for not slowing for a flashing pedestrian crossing sign. But it was not the ticketed car that triggered his reaction. Another vehicle just happened to get captured in the video as it passed through the intersection in the opposite direction. It was a white Escalade and its plate matched the one from the boat launch area. It was Dr. Jacobson's. Reed looked up at the ceiling and said, "Well, I guess there is karma."

It was almost five o'clock and Angela and Sarah would be returning from the hospital soon. Reed was satisfied with his discovery and progress on the case and pushed away from his desk. As difficult as it would be, he would not mention his latest discovery to the ladies. They were probably exhausted from keeping watch on Grace all day and they would just want a quiet dinner and relaxing evening.

As promised, Angela and Sarah returned home shortly after five. Reed was beginning to prepare dinner as they came in and he asked, "How is Grace doing?"

Angela said she was stable, and her injuries were no longer life threatening. She had several broken bones and a concussion. The biggest issue was the coma. There was no telling how long it would be before she woke up. It could be a long time, or she come could out of it tomorrow.

Reed poured three tall glasses of Cabernet and told the women to go out to the living room and enjoy the view while he finished with the beef stroganoff. A short time later, the three gathered around the kitchen table and enjoyed Reed's creation while they talked about Grace's accident and potential suspects.

Reed was surprised that Sarah and Angela wanted to talk about the accident instead of wanting to escape the subject, but they were anxious to hear if he had turned up anything. Even though they were curious, he didn't tell them what he had found. Not only did he not have any firm proof that Dr. Jacobsen was involved with Marissa and Becky's deaths, he certainly had no proof that he had anything to do with Grace's accident. He needed to do more combing before he would share anything.

Chapter 12

Forgotten Clue

Wednesday morning, Grips decided it was time to do some housekeeping and clean up his living room. After all, even an old bachelor druggy can only put up with so many empty beer cans and liquor bottles on the floor in addition to ashtrays overflowing with cigarette butts and roaches. It took him nearly an hour to pick up the litter and fill eight paper bags that he put out in the recycle bin.

Next, he pulled out the vacuum cleaner and started cleaning the carpet, working from one side of the room and sliding furniture around as he made his way across. When he moved the recliner to one side, he noticed a piece of paper with something scribbled on it.

Grips picked up the note and read it, "Damn, you stupid old fart. You completely forgot."

He picked up his phone and called Terry.

Terry answered, "Hello. This is Terry."

Grips said, "Hey young man. How's it hangin?"

Terry thought to himself that talking with Grips was always an experience, but he played along, "Straight and long. How about you?"

Grips laughed, "Crooked and short. Old age you know."

He laughed again and then took on a serious tone, "Hey, you remember asking me to watch for anything unusual around the beach?"

Terry answered, "Yes. Have you seen something?"

Grips hesitated and then said, "Well, you might say I got some good news and I got some bad news. You see, I did spot something unusual going on across from my house. It was late at night and I am certain I saw three people get out of a white SUV and go down to the water. Only two of them came back up from the beach. Here is the good news. I wrote down the license number of the SUV."

Terry's ears perked up, "Grips, when did this happen?"

Grips answered, "Well, that is the bad news. You see, I kind of forgot about it until I found the note with the license number today. It was last Friday night. Sorry I fucked up. Probably too late for you now."

Terry practically shouted, "Grips, I owe you a beer. You didn't fuck up at all. Are you sure you weren't too stoned to get the license number, right?"

Grips sounded hurt, "Hey, I may have been stoned, and a little drunk, but that has never hindered my powers of observation. That license number is spot on. And I will be waiting for that beer."

Terry took down the license number thanked Grips and then called Robert and Reed with the latest information.

Trap

Reed had been almost certain that he'd identified the man that was supplying Fentanyl to the local teenagers and now the information from Terry was further confirmation that the same vehicle had been in the vicinity of both Marissa and Becky's crime scenes. Dr. Jacobsen's dental practice was near a cluster of opioids overdoses in the Tacoma area and he was Marissa's dentist. As a dentist, he could have Fentanyl as an anesthetic for oral surgeries and he would have benefited quite nicely from a side business of dealing illegal prescription drugs.

The piece of the puzzle that had not made sense before now fit perfectly. Reed had always been bothered by Grace's comment about Marissa having a dentist appointment the day she was killed and both her father and dentist denying it, but now it all made sense if the dentist was also her supplier. Of course, Dr. Jacobsen would deny seeing her, and Marissa would not have told her father about seeing the doctor for obvious reasons.

She probably slipped up when she mentioned seeing the doctor to Grace and then fabricated the story about a dentist appointment to hide from her best friend the fact that she had not broken her drug habit. Reed guessed that the doctor typically dealt the Fentanyl away from his office, preferring the streets of Tacoma and Seattle where his identity was not known. In fact, it was likely Marissa never scored her drugs at his office. More likely she would buy them from him on the street. That Saturday she was probably desperate for a fix and knew Dr. Jacobsen would be working Seattle and made the trip to the city to find him.

Reed decided he needed to talk with Dr. Jacobsen to learn more. Perhaps he could lay a trap to expose his drug business. It was a long shot, but there was an outside chance that the doctor was also illegally prescribing pain killers for patients if they were willing to pay. Reed would call and make an appointment for a routine checkup as a new patient. Then, during the time with the doctor, he would mention that he suffers from chronic back pain and ask the doctor if he could prescribe something strong for him as a favor. If Reed could get the doctor to give him the prescription for Fentanyl or other opioids, he might have enough for the police to investigate further.

Once he convinced himself it was a good idea, Reed made a call to Dr. Jacobsen. He was surprised at how easy it was to get an appointment. The doctor said he had just had a cancellation and could see Reed at noon the next day. Reed was proud of his plan and couldn't wait to tell Angela about it. Plus, he was overdue for a routine dental exam anyway. He looked at Baker and Rainer, both sitting on the couch staring at him and asked out loud, "What could go wrong?"

He looked at the clock and couldn't believe that it was already four in the afternoon. He had been so deep into his research that the day had simply disappeared. Angela was up at the hospital and he called her to say he would be there shortly.

Slainte

A short time later, Reed parked his car on the side street near the hospital and began the walk to the front entrance. With each step, the hospital's depressing effect on him increased. He thought, 'Death. That is all this place has ever meant to me. If Grace dies in this god-forsaken building I swear I will never set foot in it again unless it is feet first with no breath left in me.'

He walked into the lobby and made his way to the IC unit. Before he reached the door to Grace's room, Angela came out and greeted him. She took his hand and he could feel her shaking. Oh god, Grace must have died. He looked at the floor and felt tears pooling in his eyes.

Angela put her other hand under his chin and lifted it. She had a smile on her face that practically went from ear-to-ear, "Hey baby, why the tears. She came out of the coma. It just happened. The doctors are in with her now."

Reed couldn't believe his ears. He hugged Angela and shed more tears, this time of joy. Then they walked into the room where two doctors were talking with Grace.

Reed walked over to Sarah and hugged her.

Sarah returned the hug and said, "It was Angela. She did it. She placed a small Celtic cross in Grace's hand and moments later, Grace's eyes opened."

Angela blushed, "I don't really think I am responsible for Grace coming out of her coma, but it is wonderful nonetheless."

Sarah took her hands, "Don't underestimate the power of a strong spirit. Thank you for being here for us today."

One of the doctors asked if he and his assistant could have a few minutes with Grace on their own while they examined her. Reed, Angela, and Sarah retired to the lobby where Reed pulled out a silver flask. "I brought a little Laphroaig Scotch to help me cope with this place but now I say we should have it to celebrate."

He unscrewed the top and handed the flask to Sarah. She raised it and said, "Slainte", before taking a long draw and handing it to Angela.

Angela made a toast, "To Grace," and tilted the flask to her mouth before handing it back to Reed who added, "To strong spirits."

He bowed to both women and then kissed the flask, "In all forms." Then he winked and took a long slow sip of the Scotch.

When the doctors were finished with Grace, Reed and the ladies returned to her room and visited briefly. She was extremely tired and still trying to get her bearings on where she was and what had happened to her. The last thing she remembered was that she was driving to see Reed and Angela and that she might have thought someone was following her, but she wasn't sure. It was still all a bit foggy. Reed told her to relax and not worry about it. Then they all wished her a good night and Sarah said she would be back first thing in the morning.

Back at the houseboat, Angela tossed together a quick Caesar Salad with shrimp and divided it into three bowls. Dinner was quiet, with each alone in their own thoughts and mixed feelings of fear and cautious optimism. When they were finished eating, Sarah asked if it was okay if she turned in early. It had been a long and eventful day and she was exhausted. She thanked Reed and Angela again for their support and hospitality before she walked upstairs to the bedroom.

Reed went to the kitchen and poured two shots of Scotch before returning to the living room and handing one to Angela, "One more toast to Grace's recovery and possibly cracking the case."

They clinked their glasses and Angela asked, "And possibly cracking the case? Did you find something new?"

Reed smiled, "I think I may have just found the linchpin to all of this, and I think I may be able to expose him tomorrow."

He proceeded to tell Angela what he found in the police files and how it all led to Dr. Jacobson. Then he shared his plan for meeting with the dentist the next day.

Angela did not share his enthusiasm and suggested he just share what he had learned with Investigator McManus and let the police follow up, but Reed said he needed to follow it through and that he had more chance of getting what he wanted from Dr. Jacobson than a formal police interview would.

Chapter 13

Concerned

Angela didn't sleep well Wednesday night. She couldn't help but be concerned about Reed's plan to confront a potential drug dealer. What if Reed was right and Dr. Jacobsen was supplying drugs illegally to teenagers and patients and what if the doctor turned violent and hurt Reed.

After Reed had shared his plan with her the prior evening, she decided that she would conduct her own background check on Dr. Jacobson. She was probably worrying for nothing, but she wanted to be certain. She got up early Thursday morning and set her laptop on the kitchen table where she wouldn't disturb Reed sleeping on the living room couch and could fuel herself with cups of coffee as she searched for anything on the doctor that might raise a red flag.

It was not difficult to find information on Dr. Thomas Jacobsen, but nothing jumped out as being suspicious or out of the ordinary. He graduated from the University of Washington School of Dentistry in 1976 and set up a practice in Gig Harbor. She found an article from a February 1977 issue of the local newspaper announcing the grand opening of his office. It was accompanied by a photograph of Dr. Thomas Jacobsen standing in front of the medical building alongside his father, Dr. Alfred Jacobsen.

The article recounted that Dr. Alfred Jacobsen, a psychiatrist, had opened his own small two-room practice attached to his house in 1967. Now that his son, Thomas, had graduated from dental school, father and son were joining to create the Jacobsen Medical and Dental Clinic, co-locating their businesses in a new building in town. Angela found it a bit odd to co-locate a dental and psychiatric practice but guessed that it was expedient for the family. She searched records to find any cases of malpractice suits filed against Thomas and came up empty.

The rising sun was just illuminating the top of the Space Needle when Sarah came downstairs and saw Angela sitting at the kitchen table, staring intently at her laptop screen. Angela didn't notice Grace's foster mother enter and jumped when Sarah said, "Good morning. My, you are up and working early."

Angela closed the screen and looked up, her eyes tired from staring non-stop at the monitor for the past two hours, "I couldn't sleep. But now I need a break and another cup of coffee. Would you like a cup?"

Sarah answered, "That would be lovely, unless you might happen to have some tea on the shelves."

Angela smiled, "You are in luck. We have several loose teas for you to choose from."

She opened an upper cabinet and looked in, "Would you like English Breakfast, Earl Grey, or Darjeeling?"

Sarah looked appreciative and answered, "A nice pot of English Breakfast would do me fine."

Angela retrieved a royal blue tea pot from the shelf and clicked on the kettle to boil some water. Reed heard the voices in the kitchen and got up off the couch to join the women. "Good morning ladies. How is everyone this fine morning?"

Sarah answered, "I will be just brilliant after my tea."

Angela looked up from pouring hot water into the tea pot, "I'm feeling a little better than I was earlier. I still think your scheme to trick the doctor is hair brained and, even though I hope you catch the person or people responsible for everything that has happened, I hope the doctor is not responsible and you are not putting yourself in danger."

Reed walked over and gave her a hug, "Don't worry. I have it all worked out. He won't know what I am up to and I will be in and out just like that."

Angela set the blue teapot with steeping tea on a tray and retrieved a teacup from the cupboard. "I hope so."

Sarah hadn't heard about Reed's plan and asked what Angela was concerned about. Reed sat down next to her at the table and took her hand, "I think I have a good idea who is behind the deaths of Marissa and Becky and maybe even Grace's accident and I have a plan to find out more this afternoon. Angela is just worried that I might do something stupid, but it is all perfectly safe. Nobody needs to worry. This afternoon we may be a step closer to solving everything."

Angela set a tray of croissants, butter, and jelly on the table and joined the other two.

"Okay, I will stop worrying and look on the bright side. Whether you find that the doctor is dealing drugs or not, you will get an overdue dental check-up and come home with shiny clean teeth."

Reed smiled, "Exactly."

While the three ate their croissants, Sarah told Reed and Angela more about Grace's childhood and her parents before they were lost in the car accident. It was obvious that Grace had grown up in a close family and that the loss of her parents had been extremely hard on her. It was also clear that Sarah and her husband were a positive presence in Grace's life. Together, they would survive this tragedy and be the stronger for it.

Danger

A little after nine, Reed stood up and said that he needed to get ready for his dental appointment. He could give Sarah a ride up to the hospital on his way if she liked. Sarah agreed to the offer and excused herself from the table to get ready for the day. Angela said she would join Sarah at the hospital after she made a stop at one of their shops.

It didn't take long for Reed and Sarah to get ready and leave the Grey Kraken and Angela found herself again worrying about Reed and the doctor. She opened her laptop and tried to think of anything she might have missed. If Reed was right and Dr. Jacobson was dealing illegal drugs, what would be his motive? He had a successful practice and made a good living. Why would he risk everything just to make a little more? It didn't make sense. She decided to put off going to the shop and do a little more research, this time broadening her focus and including Dr. Thomas Jacobson's partner, his father, Dr. Alfred Jacobson. The elder Jacobson had passed away but maybe there was something in his practice or history that would yield more clues about Thomas.

Angela's search found that, prior to setting up his own practice; Dr. Alfred Jacobsen had been on the staff of Western State Hospital, a psychiatric hospital in the town of Steilacoom just outside of Tacoma. He had garnered some local fame as one of the doctors that tended to the actress Francis Farmer during her stays at the mental institution. He was also known as an advocate of Dr. Walter Freeman's frontal lobotomy procedure as an expeditious method of treating a wide range of mental disorders. He had assisted Dr. Freeman on several occasions in addition to performing the operation on his own.

Dr. Jacobsen was also a strong proponent of other popular procedures of the time including insulin shock therapy, ice baths, and electro-shock. While many of the procedures continued to be practiced in later years, the introduction of anti-psychotic and anti-depressant drugs in the fifties, combined with the public distaste with Freeman's icepick lobotomy, eventually brought an end to the era of widespread prefrontal lobotomies. Dr. Jacobsen left the hospital and opened his own private practice in Gig Harbor in 1960.

A sense of nausea overwhelmed Angela. Reed had shared with her that both Marissa and Becky had died of brain hemorrhages caused by a pick-like object being jammed through their eye sockets and into their brains, scrambling the frontal lobes. Dr. Alfred Jacobsen had performed lobotomies, a procedure that involved inserting a probe through a patient's eye socket and into the brain to sever frontal lobe brain tissue, possibly in the very office that adjoined his son's dental office. Maybe growing up with a father that scrambled brains for a living twisted his son's brain and now Dr. Thomas Jacobson was killing young girls with his father's lobotomy tools.

Angela decided Reed was in over his head and tried to call him before he reached Gig Harbor, but he wasn't answering his phone. She called Robert McManus and shared Reed's plan to trap the doctor for dealing drugs. Then she shared the information on Dr. Jacobson's father performing lobotomies.

Robert agreed that the coincidences were just too great, and that Reed could be in danger if the doctor suspected him. It was now noon and Reed was probably already in the dentist's chair. Robert called the Gig Harbor police and told them the situation and to get to the doctor's office ASAP. He also told them to make sure they had Narcan with them. Then he left to race to Gig Harbor hoping Reed would be okay.

Doctor's Office

Reed checked in to Dr. Jacobsen's office at 11:45 so that he could fill out some paperwork. The doctor seemed very pleasant and Reed could not imagine that he was involved in anything illegal, let alone the murders of two young girls. After filling out the forms, Dr. Jacobsen led him into his examination room. It was well lit and outfitted with all the latest equipment. Soft music played in the background and Reed relaxed.

The doctor asked Reed to open his mouth so he could take an initial look at his teeth and take some x-rays. He asked Reed who had recommended him. Reed hated when doctors asked questions when their hands are in your mouth but was glad for the obstruction. It gave him time to think about a response. When the doctor removed his fingers, Reed named an acquaintance he had in Gig Harbor.

The doctor responded, "Funny. I don't recognize that name as one of my patients. I must just have a good reputation in the community. Hey, I can't complain about that."

He laughed and asked Reed to hold a square of film in his mouth while he took an x-ray. He repeated the process until he was done and took the film to be developed in the next room. Reed thought things were going well. He would talk a bit more about general things before he began to complain about his chronic back pain.

When Dr. Jacobsen returned, he said, "You are lucky you came in. You have a cracked tooth that needs to be repaired as soon as possible. I can do it right now and it will be a simple procedure. If I was you, I wouldn't let it go. It could break and lead to an infected tooth."

Reed said, "A cracked tooth? Wouldn't I feel that?"

The doctor smiled, "Oh no. Not necessarily. The crack is small and not impacting your nerves yet, but it could go at any time. I really recommend we just take care of it quickly right now."

Reed figured why not and told the doctor to go ahead.

"Good. Let's get started." He reached around and picked up a hypodermic needle and saw Reed's eyes widen. "No worries, just a little Novocain to numb the area. You will just feel a small prick."

He inserted the needle into the gums and depressed the plunger. Reed had previously had Novocain, but this was unlike anything he experienced before. His head felt a rush better than any weed he had ever smoked, and an intense feeling of calm came over him.

The doctor said, "Like that, do we?"

Reed could see and hear the doctor but felt disconnected.

Sweet Dreams

Dr. Jacobsen sat down on the stool next to the reclined chair Reed sat in and spoke, "So, now we meet. Ari told me that the police had a private citizen helping with Marissa's case. He was able to get the name through some contacts he has in the department. I would guess that you are here because you have put the pieces together. I really didn't think anyone would, but then I should have known you could. It's quite funny. When I heard your name, I thought it was familiar and after some digging, I found that you and I met before, a long time ago. It's ironic that you should be the one to bring my practice to an end."

Reed tried to parse his words and give a response, but it seemed easier to just sit and listen. Dr. Jacobsen continued, "I've done a lot of good in the clinic over the years. My father and I cured dozens of patients that would not have functioned properly in society if not for our procedures. Instead of hunting me down, you should be thanking me."

He paused and lifted an ice pick from the tray, "Marissa's death was an accident. She was a regular dental patient of mine and Ari recommended her for the procedure. The lobotomy went as planned and then she crashed. I immediately knew what had happened. An artery in her brain had been nicked and she was dying of a brain hemorrhage. There was nothing I could do. She is only the second patient I have ever lost."

Reed wanted to get up and run but realized the doctor had strapped his arms to the chair without his noticing.

"Then there was the street girl. Her death was unfortunate but necessary. I had to protect the clinic and she was a perfect candidate. She was panhandling on the street, probably homeless and selling her body to score drugs. Nobody would miss her, and her death would throw everyone off the track. They would think there was a serial killer on the loose in Seattle. I know what you're thinking. I'm a monster. But you are wrong."

Reed managed to mouth the words, "How do you justify selling drugs?"

The doctor laughed, "Selling drugs? Whatever made you think that I was selling drugs? Just because the girls had Fentanyl in their systems? That was for sedation. I told you, I am a good person. I don't sell drugs."

The doctor took on a somber tone, "But, none of that is important now. You are here because you suspect me. And I am guessing that you have told others about your suspicion, so now I must abandon my practice here and at the clinic and disappear, all of which makes me extremely angry. You put an end to something good."

He eyed the ice pick and looked at Reed, "Don't worry. I won't use this on you. I am not a cold-blooded killer and certainly would not kill you. But enough talk. You need to sleep for a little while, so I can get away from here before your police friends show up."

He retrieved a syringe and poked it into Reed's arm carefully metering the dose, "Sweet dreams."

As he depressed the plunger, the front door of the clinic burst open and someone shouted, "Police!!"

Dr. Jacobsen jerked and pushed the syringe plunger to its stop. "Damn."

He pulled the needle out of Reed's arm and threw it at the floor as he ran out the back door to the rear parking area where he jumped into his white Escalade and sped away.

A policeman ran into the exam room to find Reed losing consciousness and going into respiratory depression. He unstrapped his arms and laid Reed on the floor. Then he pulled out a nasal injector containing Narcan, an opioids antidote. He pressed the injector up to Reed's left nostril and pressed the plunger. He repeated the procedure in Reed's right nostril and began performing CPR hoping the Narcan would take effect quickly. If Reed did not respond to the first dose within five minutes, he would administer another.

The Narcan did its job and temporarily neutralized the overdose of Fentanyl before the medics arrived. It would wear off in about thirty-minutes and, if the overdose was great enough, Reed would slip back into unconsciousness and respiratory depression and would require another dose. But, if the overdose was not significant, Reed would remain conscious and recover from the sedation just as a patient would after being anesthetized for a procedure such as a colonoscopy. He might be woozy for a bit, but none for the worse.

The paramedics arrived and checked him over, they determined that Reed had survived his near brush with death with no additional complications or concerns and would be able to return home without any need to go to the hospital. Dr. Jacobson had injected enough Fentanyl to stop Reed's breathing initially, but not a significant dose that would lead to a relapse after the Narcan wore off. By the time Robert McManus arrived, Reed seemed almost his normal self, talking to the paramedics and attempting to laugh off the incident.

While Reed was being attended to, another local police unit was dispatched to Dr. Jacobson's residence to apprehend him but when they arrived, they only found the Escalade parked in the driveway. Inside the home, the closets were empty. It appeared the doctor had switched to another vehicle and made a run for it.

One of the officers called in to check for the license plate number and description of any other car registered to Dr. Thomas Jacobsen. They would put out an all-points bulletin for his capture and arrest. While the one officer waited in his car for the information, the other took a cursory look through the SUV.

"Now this is interesting." He held a shiny object up for his partner to see. It was a stainless-steel surgical pick and there appeared to be some sort of matter on it including dried blood. "I found this in the crack between the seat and seat back.

The other policeman walked over and looked, "I'll get a bag. Who knows, it might be evidence."

The policeman also spotted a small stainless hammer on the seat but didn't think it could be anything important. After all, it was not like you could do much harm to anyone with a miniature hammer. Neither of the officers knew the details of the recent deaths and would have looked at the instruments in a different light had they known how the tools had been used. They returned to their car and waited for a CSI team that was being sent over. While they waited, they heard back on the car registrations. Washington State records showed only one vehicle registered to Dr. Thomas Jacobsen and it was the Escalade. It appeared he had a second car that was not registered in the state. It would be harder to track him down now.

After the medics left, Robert asked Reed what he could remember of his encounter with the doctor. Reed could only recall flashes of Dr.

Jacobsen's conversation. Something about his performing lobotomies to help people with mental disorders. And that he denied selling drugs illegally.

Reed finished, "He said 'Sweet Dreams' before I lost consciousness." He couldn't remember anything else.

Codes

Other investigators arrived and combed the clinic for evidence. They found several vials of Fentanyl as expected. In addition to the surgical instruments that they would expect to find in a dentist's office, they found a collection of sterilized surgical picks and small stainless hammers.

Reed and McManus concluded that Dr. Thomas Jacobson had been performing transorbital lobotomies, the same procedure the senior Dr. Jacobson had applied in his psychiatric practice right up to his death.

One of the investigators found an appointment calendar in a desk drawer and thumbed through it to see if it indicated an appointment with Marissa on the day of her death. To everyone's amazement, there was an entry for Marissa logged in the book for that Saturday.

2:15PM Marissa Archer – OF, SP

Reed's appointment was also logged in the book – OF, DP

Dr. Jacobson apparently kept detailed records. The inside front cover of the appointment book had a legend for the shorthand appointments.

OF – Dental Office, CL – Clinic, SP – Surgical Procedure, DP – Dental Procedure, MT - Meeting

McManus found the first two interesting. If OF was the dental office they were currently in, then where was the clinic. He took the book and looked through the pages for clues. On the second Wednesday of every month, an entire morning would be booked out for CL. It appeared the doctor worked a regular schedule at a clinic in addition to his personal office.

Another pattern was a regular appointment with a patient only identified by the initials R.E. Every Thursday at 8:00a.m., Dr. Jacobson had a one-hour MT, or meeting, with R.E. Hearing the initials RE, Reed remembered that Dr. Jacobson had mentioned that someone named Ari had recommended Marissa for her lobotomy. Was this the person he was referring to?

Home

Robert set the appointment book down and asked one of the assisting investigators to drive Reed's car home for him. Reed was still groggy from the drugging and Robert would take him home. On the way, Robert asked Reed if any more of his memory had come back, but Reed was not able to retrieve any more of the conversation. All he could say was that it was a miracle he decided to focus on Jacobsen as a suspect, thinking he was closing in on a drug dealer that had killed the two girls. It was just bad luck for Jacobson that his practice was in an area of overdoses and that Marissa had told Grace that she was seeing her dentist the Saturday she died. Reed was completely wrong about her going to get drugs, but it had still led him to her killer. He wasn't sure if he should be proud for solving the case or embarrassed for being so wrong about the drugs.

Robert called ahead to Reed's house and told Angela he was bringing Reed home. He only shared a portion of what had happened at the dentist office, purposely leaving out the part about the Fentanyl overdose. There was no need to worry Angela, and Reed was recovering nicely. By the time he and Reed arrived at the Grey Kraken, Reed was his old joking self, aside from having a blank period in the middle of his afternoon. Reed and Angela asked Robert to stay for a drink, but he declined. He now had the task of driving back to Gig Harbor to inform the Archer's of their daughter's killer. He didn't look forward to the meeting. How would they feel about their own dentist killing their daughter?

After Robert left, Reed retired to the living room and lay down on the couch. His adrenalin was dropping, and he began to absorb the full gravity of his situation only a few hours earlier and how close he had come to death. During the ride back from Gig Harbor, Robert told him that it was Angela that had put the pieces together and sounded the alert. He was alive because of her.

Angela and Sarah sat together on the love seat facing Reed, both showing looks of concern. Baker and Rainier sat perched on a windowsill and stared at Reed. Only the sound of water lapping at the sides of the houseboat broke the dead silence until Angela spoke.

"Do you want to tell me what really happened over there? I know Robert did not tell me the whole story. Nobody has said anything about Dr. Jacobson, and you are more than a tich out of it my love. Tell me you didn't let him sedate you and then run away while you were sleeping."

Reed choked. If only it were that simple. "Well, not exactly. Just don't get all worked up when I tell you. I am here, and everything is good. Okay?'

Now she looked even more concerned. "Okay. You can start any time."

Reed proceeded to tell what he recalled in addition to the details that were filled in by the officers that found him. At first, Angela's green eyes flashed with anger, "You stupid man. I knew it was a bad idea."

Then she ran across to him and hugged him as she cried onto his shoulder. "You silly fool, I love you so much. Don't you ever do that again. From now on, you just do your brainy crime solving thing here at home and leave the field work to Robert and the others." She hugged him tighter and rocked back and forth.

He rubbed her back, "Okay, okay. I'm fine. The Narcan worked its magic, I am okay, and we helped solve the murders. What can be better than that?"

"You not almost getting yourself killed." Angela cried.

After several minutes of hugging and more silence, Sarah said, "May I suggest we go out for dinner, my treat."

Angela sat up, "That sounds like a great idea. I'm not really up for cooking." She looked at Reed. "Do you have the energy to go out?"

Reed was slightly drowsy but knew it was more from thinking about his brush with death than the Fentanyl and that it would be good for him to get out. He wanted to get his mind off Dr. Jacobson and what he had done. He said he had plenty of energy and agreed with Sarah's suggestion. After that, they would go up to the hospital and see how Grace was progressing.

The Call

Robert called the Archer's and said he would be there in two hours and had the probable identity of their daughter's killer. Mr. Archer asked if it was Keith and Robert said he would tell them in person once he was there.

When he arrived, Marissa's father answered the door and let him in. He seemed agitated as he led the investigator to the living room where Mrs. Archer was sitting on the couch, holding a handkerchief.

Robert wasn't quite sure how to begin so he started with Keith, "First, I can tell you that your daughter's killer was not Keith."

Marissa's mother looked relieved and Robert guessed that she did not hold the same negative feelings for the boy that her husband did.

The he said, "I expect this will be hard to hear but it was your dentist, Dr. Thomas Jacobsen."

Ryan's face went white and he immediately reacted, "What makes you think that? You must be wrong."

Robert continued, "Because he admitted it, right before trying to kill a private investigator. He is on the run right now."

Mr. Archer's upper lip became wet with sweat and he asked, "What exactly did he say?"

Robert understood the father's reaction. It is difficult hearing the identity of the person that killed your loved one, especially when it is a family acquaintance.

"Nothing else. We probably won't know any more until we catch Dr. Jacobson. But at least we now know who is responsible for the death of your daughter. I won't keep you anymore. You need some time alone. Please give me a call if you think of any motive why the doctor would have done this to Marissa. Thank you. I will see my way out."

He got up and said again that he was sorry for their loss and that he would do everything in his power to catch Dr. Jacobsen.

Chapter 14

Ari

Angela and Reed turned in early Thursday night after returning from the hospital. Reed fell asleep as soon as his head hit the pillow. The next morning over breakfast, they talked with Sarah about the past weeks and all that had happened.

One family mourning the loss of their daughter to a man that was trying to improve society by practicing neurosurgery on those deemed different.

Another destroyed by a father that committed incest, an act that led to a chain of events ending in his daughter's murder and his own suicide.

And Grace's close call with death because of the misled intentions of Marissa's ex-boyfriend.

It was a lot to process in such a brief time.

All three of them said how they felt sorry for the Archers and what the family had gone through. Reed opened his laptop to read about the family again. He had researched them before when he was investigating their daughter's death but now, he just wanted to read about them in an unsuspecting light to better know the family he was feeling sorrow for.

He pulled up an old newspaper article that talked about the new superintendent of the Corrections Facility in Gig Harbor, Ryan Evan Archer, and read it out loud to Angela and Sarah. The piece recounted Mr. Archer's history at the corrections center and how he had begun his tenure at the facility as assistant superintendent and later was recommended for the position of superintendent by the outgoing superintendent.

The article had run in the local paper and looked like it was one of those 'Get to know your neighbors' columns that community papers run and are mostly fluff, but the new superintendent had used it to take a public stand on the popularity of powerful prescription drugs for everything from attention deficiency to depression to autism spectrum disorders. He believed society had become too dependent on prescription drugs and took a strong position against their wide use.

Mr. Archer stated that his time as assistant superintendent had given him the opportunity to see what prescription drugs were doing to society and how he felt they were exacerbating instead of mitigating the problems we face today.

In his facility, he wanted to promote alternative methods of treating mental disorders. Instead of relying on medicating the residents, they would use intense counseling and exercises to modify behavior.

Reed finished reading and closed the laptop. He looked up at Angela and could see something was going on in his wife's mind. "Okay, I can see you are thinking. What is going on in there?"

She looked at him, "When you told me about your visit with Dr. Jacobsen, didn't you say that he said Marissa was recommended for the procedure by someone named Ari?"

Reed said, "Yes. And there were the initials R.E. in his appointment log. Robert thinks they might be one in the same. We just don't know who it is."

She wrote on a piece of paper Ryan Evan Archer and underlined the letters R E. "There is your Ari. Mr. R.E. Archer doesn't believe in medications. He says so in the article."

Reed was stunned. He grabbed the phone and called Robert. Could it be that Ryan Evan Archer had hired Dr. Jacobson to perform a lobotomy on his own daughter? The idea of someone doing that to their child sounded absurd, but he had to tell Robert what Angela had just suggested.

When Reed told Robert about his theory, the investigator was at first skeptical and slowly came around to thinking it just might be plausible. That would explain why he was so sensitive about Grace's statement that Marissa had visited Dr. Jacobson that morning. And why he was having Steven tail Grace. It would even explain his fervent public stand that Keith was responsible for Marissa's death. Robert called in one of his fellow investigators.

Confession

"May I help you?" The corrections facility security guard asked the two men as they approached the desk.

"We're here to see the superintendent." They showed their identification.

"Is he expecting you?"

"No, but he'll see us. Just call and let him know we are here."

The guard called the superintendent and told him about the two visitors. Then she set the phone down and addressed the visitors, "The superintendent said he will be available in a few minutes. You can wait over there."

After hanging up the phone Ryan Archer sat in silence in his office. He realized that perspiration was beginning to soak the armpits of his shirt and his hands were shaking. He couldn't put this off and got up to go meet his visitors.

Ryan met Robert McManus in the lobby and Robert introduced the other investigator before they all walked back to Ryan's office.

Ryan started out, "I am sorry, I don't have any more information on Dr. Jacobsen or any reason he would have for killing my daughter. Have you found something?"

Robert waited and let the silence fill the room, "I don't think he killed your daughter on purpose. I think he was trying to help her and there was a tragic accident. And I think you know that."

He paused again and watched the sweat now running off Mr. Archer's forehead.

"I don't know what you are talking about."

"We have his appointment log. It is very detailed and has turned out to be quite enlightening. For instance, Dr. Jacobson spent one Wednesday of each month at a clinic. We checked and found out he works here every month at the times noted in his calendar."

Ryan looked worried but said, "Yes. He works at the facility clinic and provides his dental services on a monthly basis."

Robert continued, "He also had a weekly appointment on Thursdays at 8:00 with someone with the initials R.E. We checked with your assistant and learned that you had a standing meeting with Dr. Jacobsen every Thursday at 8:00."

Ryan started to wonder if the investigators had anything or were just fishing. "Yes. We would talk business once a week in case I needed him to come in before his next scheduled clinic day."

"Your assistant also told us that Dr. Jacobson called you Ari for your first initials instead of calling you by Ryan. That is why his calendar showed R.E. for his meetings with you."

Mr. Archer became more agitated, "Where are you going with this and what does any of it have to do with Marissa's death?"

Robert had been looking forward to this part. "Before Dr. Jacobsen escaped, he shared something that didn't make sense until we had the other pieces. The good doctor said that Ari had recommended Marissa for the lobotomy he gave her."

Another pause and then, "You are Ari. You are on record as opposing prescription medications to deal with mental illnesses and you employed a doctor that continued to practice a surgical procedure some would refer to as an ice pick lobotomy."

He paused again, "I think we will be able to prove you not only employed Dr. Jacobsen to perform the procedures at the clinic in your correctional facility, you also gave him permission to operate on your daughter."

Suddenly, without warning, Marissa's father broke, and his head fell forward onto his crossed arms. He began sobbing. "It was an accident. I loved Marissa and I was doing what I thought was best for her, but it all went wrong, and I have suffered every day since."

Robert was puzzled, "You've suffered? Really?"

He stopped himself from going into a rant and calmed his voice. "There is something I don't understand. There is nothing illegal about psycho surgery or even transorbital lobotomies, though now days they have been abandoned in favor of more advanced surgical techniques. The point is, the doctor was performing a legal medical procedure and his patient died. It was a tragic accident, but an accident just the same. If he had reported it, there would have been an investigation and he would have lost his license at most. Why the elaborate scheme to cover it up? And why kill another innocent girl?"

Robert didn't think Ryan would confess to both deaths and was surprised with Mr. Archer's response.

"Because we wanted to hide what we were doing at the correctional facility clinic. If a connection had been made, we would have both been arrested. We were performing psychosurgery on unruly inmates without their knowledge or permission by them, their families, or the state."

"And that is why you killed, Becky?"

Ryan rocked back and forth in his chair and wrapped his arms across his chest. "I am so sorry. That was his idea. He said we had to do something to lead the police away from us. He killed her. I just drove the car and helped put her body in the water."

Robert stopped Ryan, "I think we need to stop right here. Before you say anything else, I need to read you your rights and you may want to call your attorney."

He walked over to the superintendent and helped him up from his chair. "Sorry, but I have to cuff you for the ride to Seattle."

Robert read the superintendent his rights then walked him out to Robert's SUV and placed Ryan Archer into the back seat.

Robert called headquarters and reported that he was bringing in Mr. Archer in connection to the deaths of Marissa Archer and Becky Rose.

Regrets

In Robert's car, the drive passed in silence, each man lost in his own thoughts. Robert wondered where Dr. Jacobsen had run to and how they would catch him. And Ryan remembered. He remembered how much he loved his daughter and how he wanted to cure her of her mood swings and depression. And he remembered the Saturday that she died.

He had told his daughter that she had a dentist appointment with Dr. Jacobsen that Saturday afternoon to have minor oral surgery. He and Dr. Jacobsen had planned the day several weeks in advance.

During a dental visit two weeks prior, the doctor told Marissa that he needed to take care of two infected teeth. To prepare her for the possible side effects of the planned surgery, he also told her that she might experience a headache afterwards and might even have slight bruising around the eyes.

In fact, the doctor would be performing a transorbital lobotomy. To some it would seem a radical action to take, but to Ryan it had made absolute sense. He had met Dr. Thomas Jacobsen over thirty years before and learned of the surgical procedures his father, Alfred Jacobsen, was performing in the office adjoining his dental practice. As Alfred aged and became less confident at performing the procedures, he taught his son how to perform lobotomies and the Jacobson clinic continued to offer their psycho surgery services in semi-secret.

Shortly after Ryan became superintendent of the correctional facility, he contacted the younger doctor and asked if he would be interested in providing both his dental and surgical services at the correctional facility onsite medical clinic. Dr. Jacobsen accepted the offer, and they set up a monthly schedule when Dr. Jacobson would visit the facility clinic and provide his services.

As often as not, Dr. Jacobsen performed only routine dental services but, occasionally, he would be called on to perform a lobotomy. None of the brain surgery patients were informed that they had been given the procedure. Any after affects were explained away as being a result of the dental procedures.

Ryan was certain they had improved the lives of those that had received the procedure and held the strong conviction that psycho surgery was preferable to medications.

Further, having witnessed dozens of successful procedures over the years Ryan, had become immune to their bizarre nature. When his daughter showed increasing signs of emotional instability, he started thinking about the procedure for her. His wife had been in therapy for years and Ryan blamed the antidepressants she took for robbing him of the spontaneous and energetic women he had married. He felt that he was losing control of his daughter and saw the psychosurgery as a potential lifeline to save her without turning to medication.

After several discussions between Thomas and Ryan, the two agreed that it was in Marissa's best interest to receive a transorbital lobotomy. She had recently progressed from mood swings to self-mutilation. Ryan also suspected that she was getting into illegal drugs and feared that taking no action would either lead to her death by suicide or overdose, or that he could even eventually see her in his institutional center as another inmate.

He continued to remember back to the day she died. The Saturday of her surgery, Marissa had been in one of her better moods. Driving to the dentist she talked about her upcoming graduation and how she was looking forward to the summer. At the dentist office Thomas again explained that the tooth extraction might leave her with a slight headache and a little bruising. Marissa had said no problem; she would just relax at home and curl up with a book for the rest of the weekend.

Then Ryan remembered looking at his daughter sitting in the dentist chair as Thomas sedated her with a dose of Fentanyl. She looked so small and helpless and really didn't look that much different from all the other teenagers he saw, dressing wildly and just acting crazy in general. But he had convinced himself she was different and that the action he was taking was justified.

As Marissa had started drifting off, she had taken his hand and said. "I love you daddy. See you in a bit."

The operation had gone like the multitude of others he had seen Thomas perform. The dentist inserted a long pick up under Marissa's eyelid next to her nose and tapped it into her head. After a few sweeping movements he removed the pick and said, "All done." The two then waited in the outer office while Marissa was recovering from the anesthetic.

Everything after that was a blur in Ryan's memory. Only flashes of Thomas telling him something had gone terribly wrong. Hearing that his daughter had died. Letting the doctor convince him that they had to cover it up or both go to prison. Driving Marissa's car to Seattle in the middle of the night as Dr. Jacobsen followed in his white Escalade carrying her body in the back. And finally, staging her accident at the boat launch ramp in West Seattle to throw suspicion on her boyfriend.

Interrogation

Ryan was shaken out of his dream state as Robert opened the back door of the cruiser and announced, "We're here Mr. Archer. Let's go."

Reed was at the station when Mr. Archer was brought in and Robert invited him to watch their interview through a two-way mirror. What he heard was alarming and sad, all at the same time.

The superintendent gave a detailed confession detailing how and why he gave Dr. Thomas Jacobsen permission to perform a lobotomy on his daughter.

In addition, he confessed that he had been part of a conspiracy at the women's corrections center that, over a span of decades, had secretly performed over forty lobotomies on women that he had felt traditional treatments wouldn't help. One of those surgeries had led to a fatality many years back, but they had covered it up, claiming the dead girl was the victim of a stabbing.

By the time the superintendent and investigators completed their meeting with the doctor, Reed was mentally exhausted from the experience and ready to go home. He called Terry to report what had just taken place. Terry had already heard through the grapevine that Robert and another investigator had gone to the women's correctional facility to question Mr. Archer, but he hadn't heard anything more. Reed filled him in on the details and then the two agreed to get together in a day or two and celebrate.

As soon as he had finished talking with his brother, Reed called Angela and told her they were going out for dinner again that night. He needed to extract himself from the shadow that had cast its darkness across all those who had been there to hear the confessions of a father, now lost in mourning and self-hate.

He wanted to get out and surround himself with people having a good time and laughing and he knew the place to do it. He told Angela, "Dress casual and tell Sarah to do the same. We're going to an Irish Pub tonight. And call a cab. I think I'm going to kill off a lot of Guinness."

Chapter 15

Homecoming

Grace was well enough to leave the hospital on Saturday and Reed, Angela, Sarah and Roy waited Saturday morning on the Grey Kraken for the call telling them they could come up to the hospital for her discharge.

While they waited, Reed decided to poke around the web and read up on lobotomies out of curiosity. He was amazed at how little he knew about the history of psycho surgery and mental health treatment in general. His only prior exposure to that world had been watching the movie, One Flew Over the Cuckoo's Nest and he was pretty sure that was not an accurate accounting.

His reading was interrupted with a call from the hospital. They could pick up Grace and bring her to her temporary home on the Kraken. He gave the thumbs-up sign to Angela and Sarah and they applauded in response. All three wasted no time in putting on their coats and leaving for the hospital. Grace's temporary bed had been delivered and set up in their living room earlier in the day and the area was all set and waiting for her. Large vases of fresh flowers from the market adorned the end tables and a large welcome home sign that Angela and Sarah had painted earlier was hung across the lakeside window.

For the first time in his life, Reed didn't have feelings of apprehension as he entered the hospital. This time, the building was a place of celebration and happiness. Sarah told the receptionist that they were there to pick up Grace Boyd and the receptionist said she would be down shortly. A few minutes later, the elevator door opened, and a nurse pushed the wheelchair with Grace over to the waiting trio. Angela and Sarah cried as they hugged Grace. Reed told her she looked great and tried to hold his emotions together as his voice quivered while he told the three that he would go bring the car around.

The rest of the day was a celebration. Robert McManus stopped in to wish Grace well and thank Reed for all his help.

Terry and Michelle visited and got to know the young woman that his brother and sister-in-law were so fond of. Terry congratulated Reed on solving another case and, once again, told him he should join the department.

Keith and Kim dropped in to give their best wishes and both gave Grace a big hug. Then they told the gathering not to make too much of their being together. They weren't necessarily dating, they but had become good friends brought together by crazy circumstances. Terry and Michelle assured the two that they were not concerned.

Things finally quieted down in the evening when all the visitors left. Reed stayed in the living room and visited with Grace and Roy while Angela and Sarah retired to the kitchen to finished preparing a celebratory dinner of roast beef and Yorkshire pudding; Reed's favorite and, it turned out, a favorite of Grace's too.

After dinner, the Landsbergs said it was time for them to make their drive home. Sarah kissed Grace on the forehead and thanked Reed and Angela for their hospitality. They told her it had been their pleasure to host her and they would take good care of Grace.

Chapter 16

Adoption

Two weeks after Grace had moved to the Kraken, doctors gave her approval to return to her foster parents' home. It was a Saturday morning when Angela and Reed made the drive with Grace to Gig Harbor and the three were unusually quiet. Finally, Angela broke the silence.

"Okay, I guess this is as good a time as any to bring up an idea that Reed and I have."

Reed knew what she wanted to talk about with Grace. He and Angela had been doing some other investigating over the past two weeks and had decided to propose something to Grace that, if she agreed, would impact all their lives.

Angela spoke quickly, letting the words fall out of her mouth, "Grace, I know you are happy with your foster parents, but I think it would be nice for you to have real parents. I'm not saying that the Landsbergs are not real, just that it might be nice for you to be adopted into a family. Of course, it would have to be a family you liked. And they would have to like you. And Reed and I really…"

Grace looked a bit confused and wasn't sure if Angela was suggesting what she hoped she was. In an instant, she knew she wanted to be adopted by Reed and Angela more than anything else.

Finally, Grace broke the silence. "I don't know if it is what you are trying to say, and I will terribly embarrassed if it isn't, but are you suggesting that you would like to adopt me?"

Angela looked at Grace, "Yes. That is what we are saying. Would you consider us as parents? We will understand if you don't. I mean, it is a big decision. And you don't have to decide now. You can just think about it."

Grace started crying and stopped Angela from running on, "Yes, yes, of course. I would love to have you as my parents. Can we really do that?"

Now it was Grace that started running on, and Angela interrupted her to explain what she knew.

She told how she had brought up the topic with Sarah the last time they were together, and that Sarah had supported the idea. Sarah said it was her opinion that the Carvers could provide a stable household for Grace and already had a positive relationship with her. With the support of the Landsbergs, the adoption process should go smoothly. Grace could join Reed and Angela as their daughter after the state had completed a home study and given final approval for an adoption.

When Reed, Angela, and Grace arrived at the Landsbergs, Roy and Sarah were already outside and waiting for Grace. It had been a week since they had last seen her. Grace left the car and went over to her foster parents and all three hugged tightly. Then they all went inside where Grace told her foster parents how much she enjoyed her time living on the water in the Grey Kraken. About thirty minutes into her stories she suddenly jumped to the subject of her possible adoption by the Carvers. Sarah had expected the topic to come up at some point, based on her earlier conversations with Angela and Reed. She said that she and Roy had talked it over and would completely support an application by the Carvers to adopt Grace.

The rest of the afternoon was spent in lighthearted conversation. Reed and Roy went out to the garage to talk about their Minis and how each had customized his vehicle to make it unique. Sarah, Angela, and Grace stayed inside and talked about everything from Angela's boutiques and current fashion trends, to Sarah's work with plants and landscaping, to Grace's latest jewelry creations. Angela even suggested that she could carry some of Grace's pieces in her shops.

Reed and Angela returned home after joining the Landsbergs and Grace for dinner. Everyone gave their approval for Reed and Angela to start looking into adoption as soon as the weekend was over. With that,

Reed and Angela each gave Grace a big hug before getting in the car to drive home.

That evening, Reed and Angela turned in early, hoping to get their first good night's rest in several weeks.

In bed, Angela kissed Reed as he swiftly fell into a snoring slumber and whispered, "Good night love. Don't have any weird dreams of lobotomies."

Dreams

It was June 19th, 1978 and Reed had just started school summer vacation. He was anxiously looking forward to a week away from the city in the solitude of the family cabin that sat on the shore of the ocean on the Olympic Peninsula. Seventh grade had not been good to him and the stress of school and life in general had been driving him crazy. It felt like he couldn't control his emotions anymore, one moment feeling like everything was going great in the world and the next simply wanting to jump off a tall building. He just wanted to get away from everything and everyone and have some time alone to collect his thoughts. Reed knew his parents were at their wits end with him and they planned this week especially for him to get away and decompress. Terry was spending the week with one of his friends and his family, so Reed would have the cabin to himself and his parents.

Unfortunately, before they could go to the cabin, they had to make a side trip.

His mother told him that she had scheduled an appointment with a dentist first. Reed was long overdue for a dental exam and the dentist had been recommended by a friend. His office was in Gig Harbor, so it was right on the way to the cabin and would only delay his vacation by an hour or so.

Reed couldn't believe that his mother hadn't given him more notice about a dentist appointment. He could do without one more thing to stress about, but it had been a while since he'd been to a dentist and his teeth had been bothering him. The occasional tooth pain just added to his anxieties, so maybe a quick check-up was worth it.

About an hour into the drive to their cabin, they drove into Gig Harbor and his mother found the office without problem.

Inside, there was a small seating area with a couch and two chairs. A frosted glass door led back to the examination rooms. The door was open and a man in black slacks and white lab coat appeared to be organizing things on a tray attached to the dentist's chair in one of the rooms. When the front door shut, the man looked up and spotted Reed and his mother.

"Hello. You must be Mrs. Carver. And you must be Reed. I am Dr. Jacobson, but you can just call me Thomas."

"Hello doctor. Thank you so much for seeing Reed today. You come highly recommended and this is very convenient, right on the way to our cabin."

The doctor took Reed's mother's hand as they greeted each other. It seemed to Reed that he held it just a little too long, as though they had met before.

Then the doctor turned his attention back to Reed.

"So how are we today? Are you having any problems with your teeth? Any pain or discomfort?" The dentist had a calm voice and friendly face.

Reed answered "I don't think so. Sometimes my teeth ache a little when I eat something hot or cold, but I don't think it is anything big."

"Well, you never know. You could have an infection that we need to treat, so let's take some X-rays and see what we have. Better to be safe than sorry, right?"

Reed nodded.

Reed's mom stayed in the reception room as Dr. Jacobsen led the teenager back through the door and closed it behind them. In the examination room, the chair and attached post with three spider-like arms reminded Reed of some sort of torture device. One of the long black angled appendages supported belts and pulleys that led to a frightening looking drill on the end. Another held a tray and the third supported a spit basin.

Reed sat uncomfortably in the chair as the doctor placed a heavy lead shield on his chest to protect him from the x-rays.

"We'll just take some quick pictures and see what shape your teeth are in."

The doctor took a series of X-rays and left to develop them, saying he would only be a few minutes and had to go next door to develop the film.

After what seemed to Reed to be forever, the doctor came back in with a knowing look on his face.

"Well, I won't say that this is definitely the cause of your tooth aches, but you do have an infection in the root of one of your front teeth. This type of infection can cause pressure and pain up through the sinus. Even if you are not totally aware of it, the infection could be stressing your body and creating some anxiety. It should be taken care of as soon as possible and your mother has agreed that I go ahead and treat it now. Don't worry. It's really not a big thing and you will be asleep while I do it."

Reed didn't look forward to having a tooth worked on but didn't figure he had much choice.

The doctor continued. "So, here is what we are going to do. I will drill a small hole in the tooth and clean out the infection. Then I will seal it back up and you will be good as new. Before I do the procedure, I will put you under with gas, so you don't need to put up with any pain while I am working. Because of the area I am working in there is a slight chance you may have some slight after-effects but if you do, they will go away within a few days"

Reed asked. "Just out of curiosity, exactly what do you mean by slight after affects?"

The dentist smiled. "Nothing to worry about. You may have a minor headache when you leave. And there is a chance of bruising around your eyes for a couple of days. But it will be worth it. After we are done, I am sure you will feel a lot better. Your teeth will be perfect and you won't need to see a dentist for another six months."

Reed said, "Okay, let's do it. Then I can get to the cabin and just lie in the sun and relax for the next few days."

Dr. Thomas rolled a cream-colored stand supporting two gas tanks, some gauges and knobs, and a mask, across the room and next to the chair and then washed his hands in a large white ceramic sink hanging on the wall. Then he returned with a white cloth that he unfolded and placed across Reed's chest.

After pinning the protective sheet to Reed' shirt, he removed the black rubber gas mask and attached hose from its stand and placed it over Reed's mouth and nose. "Now, just breath and let the gas relax you."

Reed stared at the etched floral patterns on the room's single glass window and began feeling relaxed. He started to daydream about the coming week at the cabin. Then he turned his head to the side and looked at the tray with its array of dentist tools only a few inches away. To one side lay a collection of the drill bits and dentist picks. To the other side lay a larger steel probe that reminded him of the ice pick they had at home. And next to that lay a small hammer.

Then he remembered the dentist's promotional flyer from the lobby. It read, For Painless Dentistry, Dr. Thomas Jacobsen.

As his head became foggy, he could hear Dr. Jacobsen say, "Sweet dreams."

"OH MY GOD!"

Reed jerked up into a sitting position and found himself in bed, his t-shirt soaked in sweat. Angela rose onto her elbow and rubbed his back.

"Honey, it's okay. You were having a nightmare. It was just a dream."

Reed shivered and looked back at her, "I'm not so sure."

Epilogue

Today, the thought of cutting into someone's brain to modify their behavior seems macabre. The ice pick method, while conjuring up scenes from a horror movie, was developed to be a less intrusive form of surgery that could be performed by anyone with a medical practice. Because of the simplicity of the operation, there was no requirement that those performing the operation be certified surgeons.

Some sources claim that over a forty-year period, over 40,000 patients underwent psychosurgery in the United States alone, many of these procedures involving prefrontal or transorbital lobotomies. In some cases, patients received second or third lobotomies if the results of the first were not deemed sufficient. Western State Hospital, in Lakewood, Washington, was one of the primary hospitals in the United States to perform the procedure.

More disturbing than the practice itself was the acceptance of it to treat people that were deemed not to fit society's current acceptable norms. It was adopted to address a wide range of behaviors including overeating, smoking, drinking, bad tempers, and rebelliousness. It is reported that the U.S. Government studied lobotomies as a treatment for those with communist leanings, believing that people who were over-emotional were more likely to accept communist propaganda.

The first lobotomies were performed in the mid-1930s by Dr. Egas Moniz, who would later win the Noble Prize for developing the procedure. The first versions of lobotomy involved drilling several holes into each side of a patient's skull near their temples and then inserting a cutting instrument into the brain to sever the connection between the frontal lobe and the balance of the brain. The disruption of signals from the procedure resulted in a reduction of brain activity that caused emotional unbalance and behavioral problems."

In the mid 1940's, Dr. Walter Freeman developed a new technique sometimes referred to as the ice pick lobotomy. Dr. Freeman's procedure involved inserting a sharp pick-like device under the eyelid next to the eyeball and nose, and then punching the pick through the membrane behind the eye and into the brain. Once the pick was plunged into the brain, an arc was made by sweeping it back and forth. This accomplished the goal of severing the frontal lobe connection of the brain. He promoted his trans-orbital lobotomy as an outpatient procedure, and it was widely adopted across the United States and other parts of the world because of its simplicity.

The only side effects patients typically suffered were a headache and some blackening around the eyes. Dr. Freeman traveled extensively promoting his procedure and staging press events where he would perform lobotomies for a room of onlookers. One of the most famous of these events was held at Western State Hospital. At this event, approximately 30 patients were lined up in wheel chairs in front of the press and sedated as, one by one, Dr. Freeman inserted his ice pick through their eye sockets and hammered it into each patient's brain, making a sweeping arc with the handle and then retracting it to move onto the next.

With the wide adoption of antipsychotic drugs in the mid-fifties, lobotomies were all but abandoned in favor of prescription pharmaceutical treatments. The Soviet Union had already banned lobotomies in 1950, followed by Japan and Germany. Dr. Freeman performed his last lobotomy in 1967. Ironically, he was performing a repeat procedure on one of his first patients from 1946 and accidentally severed an artery in her brain resulting in a brain hemorrhage and her death. Dr. Freeman performed no more procedures. By the late seventies, lobotomies were performed rarely if at all, but they were never formally banned in the United States.

Currently, psychosurgery is deemed appropriate only when other methods to address specific brain disorders have failed. Modern surgical procedures are precise and non-destructive and are not used in the same fashion as trans-orbital and pre-frontal lobotomies in their hey-day, when they were used to address any behavior that the general public deemed as being abnormal.

There are still some that promote psychosurgery as preferential to prescription drugs in all cases, believing that surgery addresses psychological issues directly versus compromising the body with chemicals. One can imagine a rogue doctor that would perform black market trans-orbital lobotomies for those that wish to make a loved one fit their personal definition of being normal. Not likely, but it makes you think. Especially as you are drifting away during a dental or minor surgical procedure. Do your loved ones think you are normal?

And what exactly is normal?

Acknowledgements

Thanks to everyone who has supported me through the process of creating Alki Point. Special thanks to Bill Foote, David Schranck, Trudy Schranck, Diane Brush, Tom Chudecke, Erin Hunter, Pam Kehrberg, and Debbie Jardin for their invaluable input, feedback and help in fine-tuning this story. Thanks to my mother who was a writer and who planted the seeds of my love for writing. Special thanks to Dorothea 'Miss Moo' Mootafes, an exceptional journalism teacher at West Seattle High School that truly started me on the writer's journey. And, of course, thanks to my wife Linda, who has supported and encouraged my creative writing throughout the years.

About the Author

Henry Walton is the author of the popular humorous young reader book series, *The Journals of Thaddeaus Shockpocket.* During a career in technology product marketing, Henry directed the creation of several award-winning marketing and advertising campaigns, working in both print and video media. A*lki Point* is Henry's first entry into the Suspense and Mystery genre. Henry and his wife, Linda, grew up in West Seattle and now live in Chanhassen, Minnesota.

ALKI POINT

Made in the USA
San Bernardino, CA
17 June 2020

73684468R00129